NO LONGE
SEATTLE

D0193105

# THE BEATEN TERRITORY

# THE BEATEN TERRITORY

## RANDI SAMUELSON-BROWN

**FIVE STAR**
A part of Gale, a Cengage Company

Farmington Hills, Mich • San Francisco • New York • Waterville, Maine
Meriden, Conn • Mason, Ohio • Chicago

Copyright © 2017 by Randi Samuelson-Brown
Five Star™ Publishing, a part of Gale, a Cengage Company.

**ALL RIGHTS RESERVED.**
This novel is a work of fiction. Names, characters, places, and incidents are either the product of the author's imagination, or, if real, used fictitiously.

No part of this work covered by the copyright herein may be reproduced or distributed in any form or by any means, except as permitted by U.S. copyright law, without the prior written permission of the copyright owner.

The publisher bears no responsibility for the quality of information provided through author or third-party Web sites and does not have any control over, nor assume any responsibility for, information contained in these sites. Providing these sites should not be construed as an endorsement or approval by the publisher of these organizations or of the positions they may take on various issues.

LIBRARY OF CONGRESS CATALOGING-IN-PUBLICATION DATA

Names: Samuelson-Brown, Randi, author.
Title: The beaten territory / Randi Samuelson-Brown.
Description: First edition. | Waterville, Maine : Five Star Publishing, a part of Cengage Learning, Inc., [2017]
Identifiers: LCCN 2017018157 (print) | LCCN 2017029959 (ebook) | ISBN 9781432836993 (ebook) | ISBN 1432836994 (ebook) | ISBN 9781432834067 (ebook) | ISBN 1432834061 (ebook) | ISBN 9781432834050 (hardcover) | ISBN 1432834053 (hardcover)
Subjects: LCSH: Brothels—Fiction. | GSAFD: Western stories.
Classification: LCC PS3619.A4865 (ebook) | LCC PS3619.A4865 B43 2017 (print) | DDC 813/.6—dc23
LC record available at https://lccn.loc.gov/2017018157

First Edition. First Printing: October 2017
Find us on Facebook–https://www.facebook.com/FiveStarCengage
Visit our website–http://www.gale.cengage.com/fivestar/
Contact Five Star™ Publishing at FiveStar@cengage.com

Printed in the United States of America
1 2 3 4 5 6 7 21 20 19 18 17

To courageous women everywhere
who struck out on their own paths through life

# Prologue:
# 1878
# Denver Really Is Murder

It was hard to accuse Denver of being a hospitable place.

The original landscape consisted of cottonwood trees and high grasses forcing a dry, brownish-green slash against the wide, relentless sky. The mountains menaced in the purple distance, good for cold misery and gold or silver on occasion. But when a few miscreants found some flakes of gold in the meandering banks of the Cherry Creek, Denver lurched like an inebriate into being. Those flakes of gold lured the shiftless and unsettled into her territory followed by an eruption of makeshift structures interrupting the prairie grasses. Those structures trampled down anything green and replaced it with the mud of progress. Any vegetation that survived the rush was hard, like the inhabitants of the town—undecided whether their condition was temporary or something more serious.

Nineteen years later the entire town still had a makeshift feel to it, and Market Street was no different. Perhaps it was worse with its bawdy houses and gin mills. It was a good-time town where vice sprung up like the weeds—and with the same tenacity. Denver was like those damn cottonwood seeds. They stuck and grew where they stuck and grew. The air smelled of cattle and dust, dung and desperation, smelters and sawed lumber . . . and the strange fragrance of opportunity for the reckless of heart.

Saner men might argue that was just the taint of opium in the air.

And, like the cottonwood trees, Denver grew and sprawled. Structures spawned. Rickety wooden buildings, permanent red-brick residences, dirt roads, and hovels rubbed along, irritating each other in the process. Rivalries and snobbery grew in the race to cultivate. But the underside was wide-open and obvious. No one could claim there were near enough laundries, schools, or greengrocers. But with plenty of beer, whores, and good times to be had, it was something to write home about. If the reader wasn't squeamish.

Claire slapped the bare rump of the man sleeping next to her a bit harder than intended. Her palm striking flesh sounded like the crack of a bullwhip.

"Ow! What the hell?"

But sometimes that's just how things went.

"Time to go," she said, head throbbing. A wave of nausea hit her. Hard. "Get up, or I'm going to charge you another five dollars."

The fellow grunted, turned over toward her, and rubbed the heels of his palms in his eyes. He had a beard peppered with crumbs, and maybe something worse.

None of which made Claire feel any better, struggling not to throw up in the half-filled piss-pot.

The jake sat up, the dirty sheet covering his privates. "Damned if I'm going to pay you another dollar." He threw aside the sheet, foregoing modesty, and grabbed for his pants. He thrust a foot down one leg and then the other. His shirt fell discarded on the dusty floor, and he pulled that on, decisive. Rough and ready, his wild, dirty hair stuck out in all directions. "You passed out on me. I can do that at home and alone. *For free.*"

She didn't know a damn thing about what he had or hadn't done, but at that moment she couldn't have cared less. "Get out," she said, louder and close to yelling.

He gave her a hard look, but one tinged with sadness. "Your baby ain't going to be born alive if you keep on like that."

He threw a two-bit piece on the bed as he left. Her stomach churned, her head pounded, and her mouth felt dry, dry, dry like cotton. She tried to fall asleep, but couldn't. Her body wouldn't shut down to sleep, nor would it allow her to get up. She was stuck someplace in between. Miserable.

A few unpleasant hours later, Claire pulled on some clothes as best she could. A hot day in the middle of summer, the heat pressed down from the sun beating on the tin roof. Oppressive and uncomfortable, it didn't slow anyone down all that much, but made beer sales soar. Everyone in Colorado was in a rush to strike it rich, and hangovers didn't come for free. And the jake was right about her passing out. But that he could tell she was carrying bothered her some.

Despite all the precautions she knew to use, Nature had prevailed, and Claire found herself knocked up. It sure didn't figure into her plans, scant though they were. There were women who got rid of such things, but her family didn't go in for that. They all adhered to a code based on the faint assumption that they had to draw the line somewhere. But because the inevitable conclusion wasn't what she wanted, she ignored the signs— putting her missed monthlies down to drinking too much and servicing too many men. A combination known to knock a girl off her rhythm more than once.

There was no denying she had started to get thicker about the middle, and her skirts wouldn't fasten all the way up.

It was about one in the afternoon, and she found her sister fussing behind the bar, tallying up something or other. "Hey, Annie, I need to borrow one of your skirts."

Annie didn't skip a beat with what she was doing. "Like hell you do. What's wrong with yours?"

Claire half draped herself along the bar with something approximating a lurid suggestion, then glanced over her shoulder. The pickings were slim at that hour, and it was just as well. "Too small, if you have to know."

Of course, Annie took the older sister stance. "I haven't seen you eating much, but I've sure as hell heard you puking. Beer doesn't count as bread, no matter what anyone says."

"It's not that kind of problem." The last thing she wanted was to get Annie started on the booze.

"Is that a fact?" Annie stopped, pencil in hand, and looked at Claire full-on.

"I'm pretty sure."

Annie's eyes narrowed. "So. That might explain a few things. What part did you forget about, the rinses?"

Claire rolled her eyes. Damn. "It's not like it hasn't happened to you."

"What of it? At least I know May's father was that railroad muff. Whores make bad mothers; it's a known fact. Look at ours; hell, look at me! The day May and Julia got put into the Good Shepherd was a good one, although I didn't know it at the time."

Claire tried to take the high road. "That railroad muff wasn't exactly a fine example of a man. Back in the day, I remember you sneaking around giving the goods for free. Just a bar girl my ass. I could have dropped a word, but I didn't. Why? Because you're my sister in this piss-poor excuse of a family. Anyhow, I was thinking I could pin the baby on Sam Golding. Maybe one of the boys could have a word with him."

Annie snorted. "This 'piss-poor' family knows how to take care of its own, within reason. Sam's an asshole who'd need a lot of convincing. Probably within an inch of his life. You sure you want him around that much? Chances are you'd be hand-ing your money over to him, instead of the other way around."

Claire stretched and patted her belly. She considered her reflection in the mirror behind the bar—still good-looking, no mistaking it. Even with a hangover, even a few months pregnant. "It was just a notion."

"Well. Think again."

Claire eyeballed her sister, big boned and jealous. "Maybe not. Our parents were married."

"Are you *sure* about that? Because I'm not. And who the hell knows where Pa got off to, so what good does it do? You had better tell the Old Terror about your plight."

Claire sighed. "She's not going to like it."

Annie resumed wiping down the bar. "No, she's not. But I'll loan you a skirt. One of my old ones. Now look sharp. A couple of likely jakes just walked in through the door."

Claire headed over to them, all purring and pretty and with intent. Annie trailed behind her. Like she always did, picking up the scraps. The fact that Annie had to take the leftovers made Claire feel better, for the moment at least.

She pressed her breast against one man's arm. "Buy a girl a drink, preferably whiskey?"

Of course, he said yes. Of course, she drank it.

Good-looking or not, after another month passed, it was obvious Claire couldn't go on hooking. Probably about five months pregnant, her condition gave most men the willies. Even the drunk ones. It finally sank into her brain that she needed to start planning.

"I had a watch when I went upstairs," was the accusation shot across the bar on more than one occasion. Annie or the Old Terror was usually on the receiving end. Such complaints were taken seriously and treated with the respect they deserved.

"Well, I remember when you came in, handsome. You already

had a few drinks under your belt. How do you know you lost it here? Have a drink on the house, just to show that there's no hard feelings."

Usually the fellow would settle for that, unless Claire got caught red-handed. Her execution left a lot to be desired, since she was usually too drunk to be subtle.

And The Exchange started getting called crooked by jakes who had lost a thing or two along the line.

Of course her brothers Jim and John, known collectively as 'The Boyos,' were always sniffing about on the fringes, eager to pounce. Left to fend for themselves from their early teens, they kept an acquisitive eye on The Exchange. They sauntered into the establishment with complete disregard for the fact that their presences were unwelcome. They acted like the women didn't have it handled, an assumption that rubbed Annie the wrong way. Especially today, when Jim came barging in through the saloon door and approached her with a gleam in his eye. Typically, like all men, Jim wanted to have a *word*.

"Word is you've got some type of panel house running here. You might want to rein Claire in a bit. Things seem to go missing when she's the one doing the deed," Jim said.

At least he kept his voice down, but Annie didn't exactly like his tone. "Like nothing ever goes missing at your place. I assume you'll have a drink. On the house, of course."

He nodded.

She made sure to pour his measure out of the second best whiskey stocked and felt she was being kind enough, considering the implications.

Shrugging as she handed him the drink, she decided to fake ignorance. "Anything in particular brought you in, apart from hearsay?"

"I don't need to spell it out for you." He leaned against the bar, scanned the clientele before turning his attention back to

Annie. "Something's got to be done. Everyone knows we're related. What goes bad here is blamed on all of us."

Annie cocked her head. "You might want to take that into account with some of the girls you're running."

That was the honest truth, too. While The Exchange wasn't much to brag about—a low, one-story clapboard with partitioned spaces in the back that served as something approximating bedrooms—they knew women. Their girls were as close as things in Denver got to clean. Jim and John didn't know a damn thing on that score and were too squeamish to find out, although they'd already set themselves up in one of the fancier concerns going, located on Larimer Street. Two brick stories where anything could happen. And it usually did.

But Claire remained something special, a top earner by Market Street standards. That counted for something, too.

Finished flashing her temper, Annie drummed her fingers on the wooden surface of the bar.

He fiddled with his glass. "What do you figure the chances of her having a live baby are?"

Annie shrugged. "I've got to say low, at the rate she's carrying on."

"I'm not happy about this," Jim told her, finishing off his drink. "But tell you what. I'll take Claire, and send you one of the girls we've got. After the baby is delivered, she'll be working for us for six months to pay off the considerable inconvenience. And I want a five-dollar finder's fee for the girl I'm supplying. Deal?"

The terms were hard, but sometimes it was worth paying five bucks to shut him up. "We'll take that French woman you have. She's older, but knows what she's about, or so I've heard." She was also Jim's top earner.

"Nothing doing. I'm sending you the slip of a thing that John came across. He's grown tired of her, and she keeps insisting

13

she loves him. Hellfire. She's somewhere around seventeen going on thirty, but you'll need to smooth off the rough edges. Deal?"

Annie shrugged. "If she's pretty or at least passable enough. But if she's not, I get to choose another. She isn't diseased is she?"

Annie could tell by the way Jim flinched that he didn't know. " 'Course not. You owe me one, Annie."

She shook her head. "Not when I've paid you five dollars, I don't."

Jim gave her a look. "Things aren't looking very good here, if you catch my drift."

And so she did. That was exactly why Annie thought she should be more on the business end of things. Pretty women came and went. Brains were more important.

Sometimes.

Claire's stint with the boys hit a pretty sizeable bump about one week in.

"Claire's gone on a bender and is scaring the horses!" Looking panicked, John announced the dilemma to any and all as he ran through the front door of the saloon. He headed straight for Annie, who was seated on some jake's lap. The jake looked a mite uneasy, not to mention uncomfortable.

"Shit, I'm coming. You," she said to the jake, "wait right here."

Annie ran toward The Circus, where she found her sister in her nightgown, raving in the street. Howling and staggering around. Doubled over and clutching at her stomach, she was an unholy picture with hair hanging down in tangled locks. She glared up at Annie.

None too pleased, Annie grabbed her by the arm. "What the hell has gotten into you?"

Claire blathered something to the effect that, "He called me fat, goddammit. I'm still pretty. Someone should love me . . ."

"Oh, for pity's sake. I get called fat and you don't see me flying off the handle."

A passing police officer gave them both the eye. "Move it along. You're not supposed to be on this street."

Annie considered swearing at him, but decided she had enough on her hands dealing with Claire. "She just needs to lie down. I'm trying to get her moving."

"If you can't, I'll toss her in jail or the police box on the corner there. She can scream all she likes then."

Annie managed to get Claire to their mother's house, where she was locked in a room for the remainder of her confinement. And a baby girl was born, a tiny little thing that hadn't enough common sense to die at birth. They called the child Pearl.

Claire regained her figure quick enough, all things considered. Men in Denver outnumbered the women about twenty to one. Fine odds for hookers. And for a while, she stayed away from the drink. But then she found opium. A lot of women did, but it wasn't considered good news. The other hookers at The Circus helped look after Pearl, fawning and cooing over her. Which was a fine thing, considering how Claire was having trouble keeping track of herself, much less the child.

Jim and John sent Claire back to Annie after a mere two months. For free.

There was a more serious reason for her quick return, as Annie soon learned. Her sister had only been back at The Exchange for about a week when she came out into the main room, partially dressed in her undergarments. Hair undone, she looked ragged as she eyed the saloon like she had never seen it before. A jake walked over to her and wrapped her in a sweaty bear-hug before swinging her around like a rag doll. Her feet didn't touch the floor.

That was it, as far as Annie was concerned. "Claire's done for the night, so set her back on down."

"She likes this, don't you, honey?" The jake looked mean, and Claire's eyes weren't focusing right.

Annie gave the man her best last-ditch saucy look. "Better someone who can function, if you want a good time."

"Mind your own business. This one is nice and little." He gave Annie a pointed look.

"She's not going upstairs with you, or anyone else." Annie wasn't joking around, and she was getting tired of references to her size.

The jake started dragging Claire toward the stairs.

"I said she's done for the night!" Annie's voice was clear, loud, and drew attention from the men at the bar.

Claire gave her a helpless, limp look, so Annie hauled off and punched the jake in the jaw.

The man let go of Claire and staggered back a couple of steps. Annie grabbed her and set her to the side, which cost Annie a couple of seconds. When she turned around, the jake smacked her across the face—hard. At that point some of the bystanders got involved and tossed the man out into the street accompanied by jeers.

Annie's nose was streaming blood. "That's it! Back you go to Mother's."

Her hands were streaked with blood, and her nose was swelling. The barman handed her a towel, none too clean. Annie hauled Claire and the blood-soaked towel back to her mother's house. Her mother was fairly drunk, so Annie left them thrown in together, not caring if either or both were dead by morning. Smarting, she had to return to work, seeing as how there were a lot of men and The Exchange had suddenly become short-staffed.

It was a hell of a way to run a business.

Annie resumed hooking when she returned to the saloon, but had to decrease her price by a dollar a screw, on account of the bruising.

And things only got worse from there.

# CHAPTER 1
## EARLY FALL 1889
## PAST HISTORY AND A
## QUESTIONABLE FUTURE

Annie would have liked to say that she and her daughters flounced into Denver, but it was more like they tumbled into town. Like that damn tumbleweed, all dusty and bruised from the stagecoach crammed too full. The driver insinuated it had something to do with the size of Annie Ryan and her daughters. Annie decided to interpret that as a compliment—something to do with the quality and quantity of their luggage and possessions.

But the man's attitude still bothered her, no matter what interpretation she slapped upon it. It's not like she didn't have feelings, and no woman wanted to be called fat.

The driver let two more scrawny fellows board, and they were promptly shoved and folded into the corners. The girls apparently scared them some. If the girls didn't, Annie sure as hell did. At any rate, they didn't have much to say on the journey from Central City to Denver, but all travelers were relieved when they reached town—elbows sticking out of windows, bodies contorted, birds squawking and all of them covered with dust. It was not the defining impression Annie had hoped for.

Denver had changed in the time Annie had been away, some of its rough and ready replaced by a thin veneer of polish. She eyed Market Street, and felt the familiar allure of money rushing through her veins. The underside would be the same. It just looked a bit better. That was all.

Advertising their return might be a bit premature, but it was important to get established quickly and decisively. Denver was her town, and Market Street had always been her family's territory. These new people—well, they were just upstarts. Still, she needed to claim her position and assert that she meant business straight from the beginning. The drunken shouting and the general push of masculinity made her feel lively and itching to get started. The density of saloons and brothels drove that point home into a properly functioning mercenary heart.

And Annie would have had it no other way.

But ambition and desire could not mask the inconvenient fact that she had no place to set up shop. That actuality held her back a bit. Just for the moment.

Market Street had never been for the timid unless they planned on getting rolled.

Annie marched into the nearest saloon and took its measure with a practiced eye. Rough floors, almost finished walls and a liberal distribution of sawdust and spit were punctuated by listing tables and a battered chair here and there. There were no decorations to speak of other than booze bottles and men.

Plenty of pricks, and no girls to use them on—at least as far as she could see.

It could use a woman's touch. Hell, it was practically crying out for one. Of the physical variety.

"Running any girls out of the back?" she asked the barman, by way of starting a conversation.

The brute eyed her up and down, then spat out a glob of tobacco and phlegm. "Mebbe," he replied.

"If that's as good as you can come up with, I have my answer," Annie shot back.

The man continued to stare at her, considering the implication. "Well, it's not like women ain't allowed in here. Talk to the boss. He's sittin' over there."

She followed his gaze over to a man seated at a battered table

The Beaten Territory

with a bottle of whiskey as company.

Annie plastered a smile on her broad face, and half sashayed over. Her teeth were still good. "Well, this place looks like it's a good earner, but you could be doing more. And lucky for you, I have experience in the *trade*."

The man rose halfway. "And which trade are you referring to? My name's Caldwell Hollingsworth," he said, and gestured for Annie to sit. "And you are?"

Annie sat her bulk down. "Annie Ryan, just returned to town. Right now I'm running two girls in addition to myself. But I know where I can get more."

His blue eyes went a mite wide and his eyebrows shot up. "You don't exactly look the part." He had the good grace to flush, but it was too late to take anything back.

Annie's smile didn't falter, but her jaw set firm. "Now, didn't your mother teach you any manners? My girls are eighteen and twenty, and there's one that's sixteen who might be coming along any day now. How does that strike you?"

"That part strikes me fine, but I'm not sure about the rest of it. Who said I wanted women using this as a hunting ground? What the hell, let me at least buy you a drink. What will you have?"

"Whiskey," Annie replied, nodding at the bottle.

"A woman after my own heart," Hollingsworth said, and signaled for another glass.

Two very full glasses of whiskey later, Annie and Hollingsworth were nearing a general understanding, Annie having persuaded him that she knew what she was talking about. In no uncertain terms.

It was just the details that needed shoring up.

"So what is it, exactly, that brings you back to Denver?" Hollingsworth still needed some convincing.

Annie sighed, implying he could never understand the fickleness of the human heart, and how she was a victim of its vagaries.

She actually thought it fairly obvious. Any change of location had to do with a problem, and the problem was usually men.

"I was keeping company with a no-account asshole that started cutting the whiskey." She shook her head at the memory like it was hard to believe.

That asshole was known more commonly as Leonard Healy—a little guy that only reached Annie's cheek. She had fallen into the habit of tacking a few adjectives onto his name in her mind and on her tongue. Just so everyone knew exactly where she stood on the matter.

Hollingsworth poured her another drink. "You had a falling out over that? Hell, most of the whiskey in Denver is probably cut. But not here, of course."

Annie cast back to Leonard's lovely brown eyes, dirty collars, and how he wore the world lightly upon his shoulders. A little too lightly. "We would have gotten married, except as how I was banned from the Church. But we set up business together. I ponied up the girls, he plunked down the whiskey. And for the next couple of years, things more or less paid out."

She recalled her plump fingers reaching for his scrawny neck. Pressing against his windpipe as he spluttered. She had only choked him because she loved him. Damn it.

"I'm boring you with this," she purred, jutting her ample bosom forward.

"No. I wouldn't say that, exactly." Hollingsworth watched her changing expressions, apparently wondering just how much trouble she was likely to cause.

Annie smiled, and felt flattered. It was nice to know that someone assumed she could still cause plenty of trouble if the spirit moved her. Not to mention she kind of liked the size of him.

"You see, even though we were doing fine, we weren't doing fine enough for that muff. At first I noticed the whiskey supply lasted a bit longer, but we always ordered the exact same amount. Then the jakes started complaining of headaches, and turned drunk on next to nothing. That really didn't add up, not to mention it was bad for business. Something was off."

She sighed with drama, and cast a quick glance toward Hollingsworth. He continued to listen to her—another good sign.

"And what do you think happened next? One afternoon early like, I went into the tent and caught him red-handed. He was mixing turpentine and water into the whiskey to make it go further.

" 'Damn, Leonard,' I said, 'that's going to kill somebody.' He told me no one had died yet. And that I wasn't giving him enough money, which was all just so much bullshit."

"And that was that," Hollingsworth mused.

From the way he said it, Annie believed he didn't baptize his drinks. Which was a step in the right direction. Theoretically speaking. It was the age-old question of money versus pride and reputation, which could be played either way. As long as one kept everything in proportion.

But then she remembered the worst part of all.

"Well, it should have been." Getting riled up and indignant at the memory, Annie forgot to make sure her tale unfurled in a beneficial way. "When it came right down to it, I might have been able to tolerate the doctored booze. It was that two-bit Chink dope fiend he kept on the side—Ah Sin, or whatever the hell her name was. That really nettled me fierce." Annie patted her heaving bosom to make sure it was still there, the comparison fresh in her mind. Then she remembered this conversation was a prelude to a business venture, not a fight. Her time in the mountains was affecting her, and she needed to sharpen up. Uncertain how to fix the impression she was casting, she tossed her head to shake it off.

The gesture reminded her to flirt. She patted back her brown hair, laughed for no discernable reason and raised her glass. "Here's to the blood suckers of the world—may they all get what they deserve."

Hollingsworth looked a little bit wild-eyed, but raised his glass in return.

Annie put it down to her fabulous display of wiles, and thought how nice it was to sit across a table from a man with manners. As a reward, she showed him a plump bit of leg.

# CHAPTER 2
## HISTORY LESSONS

Annie knew all about bad blood, but it didn't slow her down much.

And her view of family was as peculiar as circumstances allowed. The Ryans, and various offshoots, had arrived when Denver was new and everything was up for grabs. They had started out as the proud proprietors of a tent saloon, and expanded from there. With her husband's encouragement, Annie's mother, Elizabeth, turned to the one business where she had experience—whoring. And she pressed her three daughters into service, hiring them out of the back tent flap. The sons of the family, Jim and John, were raised to become procurers and saloon keeps. If there was a shady dollar to be made, chances were the Ryans were in on it, or at least aware of its potential.

Their world in Denver was shot through with booze, rough morning-afters, and hookers. Fittingly, that's how they liked it.

Annie was glad to be back home and sure as hell relieved to be out of the mountains before winter set in. She knew she should track down the various factions of her family members, but decided against it. For the time being. The Ryans were not strangers to rivalry among themselves, and she wasn't set up in the way she wanted. Yet.

She headed down Market Street trying to get a sense of the other businesses, now that she had cast her lot in with Hollingsworth. As she passed by one saloon with a cockeyed awning, a woman wearing a ragged dress and a brazen look stepped out onto the boardwalk and gazed up at the weather rolling in.

She caught sight of Annie. "I'll be damned!" Abandoning her lounging posture, the woman fixated on Annie's face. "Is that you, Annie Ryan?"

Annie took a closer look, trying to see beneath the layers of face paint and rouge. "Francie?"

"That's me," the woman cackled, "but I don't go by that name anymore, for the love of Christ. Oh, what the hell, you can still call me that, if you like."

Annie had worked with the woman in Denver more than a few years earlier. Before she went up to the mountains. "I see you're keeping body and soul together and still working. That's good. What name are you going by now?"

"Rose. But I gotta admit the blush is off the bloom. What brings you back to the wilds of Denver?"

Francie had always displayed a good turn of phrase. She was also a frightful gossip.

"I got tired of being at high altitude. It does something to the brains of some."

Francie laughed, but looked shrewd. "You know, I'm kind of surprised to see you back here. You don't look any the worse for wear. You still hooking? And whatever happened to that sister of yours—the pretty one?" The woman kept her eye on the foot traffic, glanced down the street and then back over at Annie.

Annie tossed her head like she didn't care, like the questions posed no problems. Claire was about her least favorite conversation.

"Up in the mountains we had a saloon and ran girls off the side. I'm still hooking when the mood hits, or we get too busy. You know how it goes. I'll admit it's getting a mite hard on my bones. As for Claire, hell, I thought everyone knew about her. She's dead a long time now."

Francie turned that information over, glancing back into the saloon she'd come out of. "It's getting harder here than it used to be, you know. More fines and payouts—more ordinances on the books. The more settlers that come, the more they want it to be like home. It's damn near ruining industry, as far as I'm concerned."

Annie shrugged as she took in the street around her. The buildings looked like they intended to stay, especially the two-story ones. "Well, someone is making money. Things may change, but they stay the same, if you know what I mean. It's been nice seeing you again, Francie, and I mean that. I have a couple of cribs for rent if you ever decide to go that direction."

"Do I get a discount?"

Annie smiled, the regret only half faked. "You know how it is, darling. I have a business to run."

Francie's face fell a bit, and all of a sudden she looked tired and old. "No harm in asking, I suppose."

"None at all," Annie replied as she moved away. She figured, hell, she *knew*, that she had to be precise in her business dealings. If she wasn't, it would be her that ended up working in a crib. And she wasn't about to let that happen without one whale of a fight.

Denver was full of memories: some pleasant, some not. The wind picked up a bit—autumn was soon going to run out. Bumping into Francie like that had got her thinking about some things she would rather have left dead and buried. The memory of Claire needled her; she wouldn't have been human if it hadn't. That girl didn't have a backbone worth a damn, no matter how pretty she was. Nervous as a high-strung horse, she sure liked men and attracted more than her share. That might have been a favorable trait, if the consequences hadn't been so bad. Rumor had it she died in a Leadville gutter. All that flirting and crying and carrying on had led to nowhere good. It was the alcohol and the dope that took her in the end.

Thank God Annie was made of more practical stuff.

Nothing much remained of Claire, not even memories that anyone wanted. But she had managed to produce a living baby. And, while the arrival of that baby marked the point where things really went to hell, the girl still existed, although she nearly perished at the time. That she lived and breathed was no thanks to Claire, who had been out of her mind to the point that she was worse than no mother at all.

That was the part that got to Annie. There was no call to run things into the ground.

Autumn always made her see the worst side of human nature because winter was around the corner. Snow only looked pretty when it was fresh. It was only tolerable when viewed from indoors. Annie wasn't sure she trusted all this newfound prosperity. Just because Denver seemed to be booming, it didn't mean things were going to stay that way. Hard times could easily lurk beneath the surface. Annie had only been away for three years, but it was long enough for the early wooden structures to give way to brick buildings and façades built with swagger and optimism. For all their defiance, they would never stop the gusting wind that blew down from the mountains and careened through the streets. But it seemed pretty certain that the days were numbered for the untamed wildness: the scrub and the brush. Cultivating influences were coming. The wealth generated by the railroads and the silver mines might not stand it any other way.

There was no such thing as too much money—but there just might be too much of civilization.

Annie turned down Hop Alley, a dicey little district that never failed to do her spirits good. No matter what the busybodies and the reformers might say about Market Street and its morals, Hop Alley was bound and determined to make their hearts stop altogether. The Orientals sparked people's imaginations, which caused fear among the narrow-minded. The alley catered to strange and disturbing customs and tastes, including women. But it was the opium dens that really caused the consternation, scenting the air with a foreign and licentious smell, sweet and intoxicating. Dangerous to fragile and impressionable sensibilities, thank heavens.

Opium sure raised the hackles of the do-gooders, seeing as how its main consumers were bored and white and came from money. More precisely there was an alarming trend of white females darkening their doorways—women who were expected to remain quietly at home playing house. Hop Alley and the Celestials sure ran against the civilizing veneer that Denver was slapping on. But they provided a buffer between Market Street and respectability. And vice would always be there for anyone who wanted a good time and didn't give a rat's ass for what society thought. Just the type of crowd Annie liked.

Thank the saints in heaven for the baser qualities of human nature. Not that they would approve.


Annie emerged from Hop Alley and continued down Larimer Street, admiring the shops and gaming halls, approving of the raucous come-ons that punters drank for free. The greenhorns didn't seem to cotton to the fact that nothing was for free. Not in Denver.

She stopped opposite the Church of the Sacred Heart and experienced the predictable effect of feeling just a bit less certain. Churches got to her in that way: forcing her to think about choices that had been made, most notably the Home of the Good Shepherd. It hadn't done her girls any harm to speak of; in fact, it had even polished them up a bit for a while until they became hardened. It could even be argued that the girl children were better off because of it. All things considered, Annie might have left them in there a bit longer. She had gotten them out for sentimental reasons, even before they were of a useful age. Funny, she thought, that she had been so soft at the time.

Claire's daughter Pearl was approaching sixteen.

She considered the church's delicate wooden tracery in the arched windows. Those windows belonged somewhere softer than under the unrelenting Denver sky that offered little consolation. The whitewashed wooden steeple thrust high its cross and aimed to make a point or, more importantly, to mark a territory. The expanse between the spire and the dark cobalt mountains looming in the distance put them in separate and opposing worlds.

All things considered, it was for the best that God was remote, while Annie stood planted on the earth. At least in Annie's opinion. Defiant and unwilling to bend, she had been around long enough to know God drew lines.

And she had been around long enough to know she crossed them.

Reflecting upon family lines, she knew what the hell the struggle was for. All the procuring and boozing and whoring caused a rift between the siblings, each trying to guarantee their place in their world, such as it might be. Their relationships were marked with one-upmanship. The desire to not only survive, but to come out on top of the dung heap.

The Ryans labeled it as healthy rivalry among family members, but that didn't mean tricks weren't tried and advantages pressed. They often found themselves in direct competition with each other, and sometimes people got hurt.

In their minds, it stood to reason. In Annie's mind it was a foregone conclusion.

She eyed the church one more time, and resumed walking,

while making a note not to pass that way again. At least not for a very long while.

# Chapter 3
## Younger Women Need to Learn Their Places

Hollingsworth turned out to be just another huckleberry who thought that women needed instruction. He saw nothing wrong with proffering thinly veiled suggestions about how Annie ran her business and her daughters, and that was getting under her skin more than a tad. But what was worse, what was downright intolerable, was that Hollingsworth had been casting his eye about. And it wasn't in her direction.

Annie stood, elbow on the bar and hand on her hip, nursing a glass of whiskey. Watching Hollingsworth with that cow of a daughter, May. They were exchanging pleasantries and probably a bit more, judging from the way they were carrying on. Simpering.

Impatient and cross, Annie drained the glass. "The same again—although this tastes a bit off."

The barman shook his head and chuckled. But he poured her another drink. "I don't know what you're getting all sore about."

"Nothing that concerns you, darlin'. Just trying to keep the train on the tracks."

Hollingsworth was seated at the table he favored. May was half-lounging, draping herself—her ample self—across the other side. Her dress strap fell from her shoulder in a practiced way. Hell, Annie had *taught* her that trick. She couldn't hear what they were saying over the din of the customers, but she watched as May touched her breast, twirled a lock of dyed red hair around her finger. Hollingsworth responded by signaling for a couple of drinks.

That was it. There was no drinking on the job.

Annie squared her shoulders and walked over to their table. "The girls aren't allowed to drink while they're working. Is that what you think you're doing, May, working?"

"I'm taking a break," May's gray eyes were flashing. "Besides, you drink when you work. I saw you just now."

The girl knew how she felt toward Hollingsworth and was rubbing it in.

"You must be confused how this works, duckie. I'm the boss, so I make the rules and you jump when I tell you to. I'm telling you now."

May shrugged and rolled her eyes. "I would have said Caldwell was the boss. His name is on the door." She flashed him a smile and jutted out her breasts.

"And that is why I don't pay you to think. I pay you to turn jakes. Now if you're expecting any money, you had better get your ass moving." Annie grabbed her daughter's arm and wrenched her into a standing position, none too gentle. "There's some jakes over there, if you're having trouble recognizing them." She pushed May toward them. Hard.

"Take it easy, Annie." Hollingsworth seemed like he expected her to mind him.

Fat chance.

"You run your business, and I'll run mine. Unless you plan on paying for the time May spends pandering to you. Now, I need that girl on her back. Not lolling about like a side of beef." Pretending to consider something of importance, Annie came up with a nugget of truth that just might start him thinking. "She never was all that much in demand, come to think of it."

Let him chew on that. Hollingsworth did look a bit bothered, which suited her just fine. Maybe he would begin to think about where he was casting his net, when there were better fish to be had. Ones with more experience.

Maybe he was pondering his ability to run whores himself. Typical.

Annie was starting to wonder what she had seen in Hollingsworth in the first place. Oh yeah, his manners and his physique. Nothing she couldn't find elsewhere.

She walked back to the bar, picked up her waiting glass, and took a tiny, discerning sip. Ladylike. She was calming down, now that May was doing what she was supposed to—laughing it up. At least this time it was with a valid purpose. But there was no mistaking the fact that the girl would never be a top earner. She just was too damn sturdy. With luck, May might be unaware of her limitations. That could play into Annie's hands as well.

For the time being, May needed to be reminded who was in charge, and how they came to be that way. And the best way to do that was to give her a run for her money, just to put her in her place.

She walked up to the group of fellows May was working, and whispered in one jake's ear. "Let me take you into the tack room and show you how it's done, sugar."

The fellow ran his fingers through his greasy hair. "How much?"

"Five dollars for a whole lot of experience." Annie licked her lips, like she could hardly wait.

"It's a deal," the jake said, and hitched his pants skyward.

May cackled. "All that is required for experience is time. And she sure has had a whole lot of it."

"May's rate is four dollars *on account of the lard*," Annie announced to the group. "If you want her, that's what she costs."

The jakes exchanged glances, getting the impression something was wrong. The fellow May was pawing started looking skeptical.

"My rate's seven," May countered, tugging on one of the

jake's shirt buttons.

"Not today," Annie replied, holding out her hand for the jake's money. He handed Annie the four dollars and didn't look any too excited.

"You're just jealous," May accused, as she hooked her arm through her jake's.

"Actually, I don't give a continental what you think," Annie lied.

But Annie had fifteen years to be jealous of—fifteen years of passing time that she would never get back. She had a slight consolation knowing she could still pass as thirty-seven.

If she wasn't standing in direct sunlight.

Annie figured she might stick May out in the crib she had just purchased. Permanently. It would give the girl time to think about loyalty. There was nothing worse than an old dried-up prostitute with nowhere to go—or a young one that hadn't enough sense to be grateful.

Staying in a crib and paying rent might just drive that point home.

Annie took her jake to the tack room as sold. Fifteen minutes later he left with a big smile on his face. He rejoined his friends, said something, and a big laugh erupted.

She didn't fancy working her way through all of them, although she could.

She wandered to the back of the saloon, leaned against the doorjamb and surveyed the mucky domain of the blue row. Snow flurried on the wind, big flakes with short lives. The cribs sprawled along the alley, ragged. They were nothing more than single-room, clapboard shacks tacked together from discarded bits and pieces. Debris pressed into service beyond original expectations, like the women who inhabited them.

Cold in the winter, too.

Narrow, those dwellings provided a roof—with barely enough

space to swing a cat in. A bed, a chair, and a washstand were the usual furnishings. Maybe a picture or two. The lucky few were fitted with a small iron stove to fight against the winter, which was surely pressing down.

It was sad, looking at the names painted on a board that hung in the single window or door. All of those fallen Marys and Lizzies, Idas and Janes who found themselves on the losing edge of time. Women who would spend their final days looking upon nothing but mud, privies, and the backs of saloons and brothels that no longer welcomed them like they once had.

People threw up and defecated in those alleys.

Annie waited while May and her jake were inside the crib; figured with satisfaction that it was most likely cold.

Annie held few expectations for the future. If and when she could not hold her own in the business world, there wouldn't be any help coming. Her own daughters would spit on her when she was down. Hell, maybe they would already be dead of one thing or another. The thought of outliving her girls was accompanied by a prick of guilt, but it passed. It always passed.

May and her jake re-emerged. The jake was not smiling.

Annie grabbed May's arm as she reentered the saloon. "I'm thinking about putting you out in the crib and having you turn your tricks from there."

May yanked her arm from her mother's grasp. "Hollingsworth might have something to say about that."

"So he might, but it won't matter none. You need to learn to get along with me, or hope someone else takes you on. And they won't be as understanding as I have been. Mark my words, missy."

"Why are you so grumpy anymore?" May's color turned high with anger, and her bright red ringlets quivered. The girl appeared almost handsome when she was mad.

"Don't you second guess me. And I've decided you're done

for the day. That last jake you serviced looked fairly disgusted. Why don't you go back to the crib and let me know when you're ready to do as you are told."

Annie pushed May back out into the alley and shut the door. The girl's curses made her feel a bit livelier. She decided she'd take on another jake. Sometimes fighting made her feel young.

It was a hell of a thing, to realize the passing of the years. But she still had her wits about her. *Her* last jake had been happy as hell.

Still, the time was coming when fellows wouldn't want her—no matter how much she lowered her rates, no matter how experienced she was. They would always be looking for someone younger, someone fresh.

She wouldn't be able to compete with her daughters much longer, but that's just the way it was. She needed to bring a younger girl in. Pearl would fit the bill as far as that went. She should do just fine, if she hadn't taken to religion. It happened every now and again. Especially considering how the nuns were big into obedience and discipline.

Both were fine qualities as far as Annie was concerned.

And there was May standing in front of her, cackling and yelling like a lunatic. Some trail hand heard the commotion and cast disgusted looks in their direction, unamused by the scene unfolding. Of course, Annie laughed it off. Acting like she needed some pawing, she swaggered over to the seated man. She put her foot on his leg so he could get a good look at her calf. "Like what you see?"

The man's eyes grew wide and he spluttered—acting like her leg was too heavy. Jackass.

That was what she could expect. And she knew it.

Feelings bruised, she went to get another drink. But she laughed like his reaction was the funniest thing in the world.

When she was young and working in her father's saloon, her

head got turned by a railroad man. He high-tailed it to Cheyenne once he heard she was in the family way. Men came and went. And they all wanted one thing, and one thing only. Make that two. They would take a girl's money when they got the chance.

That was another lesson she had learned the hard way.

It would really irk Annie if May came out ahead. Hollingsworth might just do something as crazy as to set her up in the saloon. No man had ever set Annie up in a business. It had always been the other way around.

Never mind; Annie had plans of her own. Hell, it was a fine time to be trading in female flesh. She wanted a house that catered to the discerning, but not the particular. The bottom line was that she didn't have a big enough stake to get fancy. But she could do better than running whores out of another man's saloon. And she was ready to prove it.

The dalliance between May and Hollingsworth needed to be settled as soon as practical, once and for all. There was no sense in acting coy. If she needed to, she could cut her losses and move on. Simple as that.

# CHAPTER 4
# WHAT PASSES AS QUALITY—
# THE SOCIAL REGISTER

Fashionable circles might have frowned, but Lydia liked to work and enjoyed the chase of business deals. On days when laudanum didn't get in the way.

And she was having a very clear day as she drove over to Twenty-First and Market Street, where the property was located. Stanley figured it was worth "$5,000 or so," but Lydia knew better than to take his evaluation at face value. True valuations depended upon the customer and the intended purpose. It was a garish location, which provided a strong hint that the building would be used for something shady, something on the margins. Stanley never considered such fine points, content to rely upon surface appearances. If he had ever bothered to examine people and places at some deeper level, he probably wouldn't have married her.

She would still have been stuck in St. Louis. Denver offered freedom.

The residential streets blended into the commercial district, which slipped into the rougher area of lower Denver, riddled with vice. The dives and saloons were lurching to life, shaking off the night before. She should have been horrified. Instead, she felt a stirring in her blood knowing the rules of her world didn't apply on Market Street. Lydia recognized the chance to slip under the mask of propriety, thinking she would probably like what she found.

A catcall intruded into her thoughts—and was aimed in her

direction. Startled, she realized she was attracting unwanted attention from a bunch of whores and shiftless men. She pulled up in front of the building in question, a typical two-story brick square. The road was deep mud. Another rude call erupted from the building across the street on the second floor. She glared at the prostitutes in their white dresses leaning out of open windows, laughing and making fun of her. One of the especially bold ones waved at her and blew a kiss.

She stepped straight from the buggy into the mud. And slipped.

A passerby caught her as she sagged: grubby hands with dirty, broken fingernails on her sleeve. She clutched at him, appalled at the display. He held on to her a fraction of a second too long. She glared pointedly at his hands before he let go. Then she turned, hitched up her skirts, and squelched toward the building entrance, the women's coarse laughter trailing her.

"Mrs. Chambers?" A commanding voice accompanied a large man stepping out of the shadows.

She composed herself, forcing an out-and-out fake smile. "You must be Mr. Chase."

He gave her a nod, with a calculating look. "One and the same," he said, bowing ever so slightly.

About what she'd expected as far as charm was concerned. He was, after all, a major force in the seedy world of gambling. That element of danger made him more interesting. Dangerous people were good to know—if kept sweet and at an arm's length.

Lydia surveyed the property, starting at the top of the roof. The façade of the building was pleasing enough, in a Denver sort of way. The windows needed washing, and the weathered planks and framing showed the traces of the hard winters and hot summers. She had been under the impression that the building stood vacant, but there were signs of activity—muddy footprints going in and out of the front door. Men's footprints.

"It is supposed to be empty." Lydia turned the doorknob and found it unlocked.

She pushed through the tall door, entered into the rough front room—the walls created out of planks and lath and plaster. Banged-up wainscoting and a scarred bar ran the length of the building. The high ceilings were covered with pressed tin, the proportions good. But it wasn't a vacant building by any stretch. The dusty floors displayed scuffles and footprints, stains of liquids spilled and tobacco spat. It appeared for all the world to be a makeshift squatters' saloon, and none too clean.

Squeaky hinges from a door to the rear of the building protested, and the heavy tread of a man's boots approached. Without hesitance, as if he belonged. Lydia turned to face the newcomer, a heavy-set man with an unkempt beard and scruffy clothes. He pulled up short.

"*Who* are you?" Lydia demanded.

"I might ask you the same question." The man stiffened a bit when he got a closer look at Mr. Chase.

"No one is supposed to be in here, and the front door was unlocked. But I'll get back to you in a moment." Lydia turned toward Chase, searching. "It slips my mind what Stanley said you wanted this place for . . ."

Chase's eyes twinkled; he read her well. "I never told him, or anyone else." She took in the cut of his Eastern suit and tilted her head with grace. "The property could accommodate multiple purposes." She tallied up the square footage of the building, and reckoned it in the neighborhood of 1,800 feet or more.

"No doubt." Mr. Chase had sharp eyes and a cautious tongue. "Shall we go upstairs then?"

She considered the rough, narrow staircase that hugged the wall, and didn't flinch. "Why don't you take your time, while I straighten out a few things down here?"

"I'm sure the gentleman has enough common sense not to come back."

The stranger, although clearly displeased, nodded. Chase nodded in return, and promptly appeared to forget him. The stranger moved off and busied himself gathering bottles and glasses and setting them in wooden crates.

She stifled her irritation. No client ever need run interference for her. "I can deal with him, if need be."

When Chase disappeared up the stairs, she turned on the man. "Who's behind all of this setup?" She didn't want to appear weak.

The man sized her up. Blatant. "No one you know."

She stared back. "Squatters aren't tolerated here—you are trespassing."

"I don't give a rat's ass what you say, but I don't want to get on Ed Chase's wrong side." The man resumed putting items in crates.

She considered that, calculating. "Fine. Obviously this is a money-making proposition of some stripe. The question is which?"

"Mainly gaming." His smirk said something else.

Lydia focused on the dust motes that sparkled and drifted in the air, sunlight penetrating the dirty windows in streaks. Before long, she heard Mr. Chase's boots descending the staircase, slowing. "You still here?"

"I'm just clearing out, and won't be but five minutes. At most."

Lydia and Chase stepped outside onto the boardwalk. "Well, what's the asking price?" Chase said.

"Ten thousand," she replied, her voice steady and confident. "At that price, it will go quickly. Right now, Market Street has a shortage of double stories for sale."

Chase laughed. Almost in her face. "I'll speak to your

husband about the details." He tipped his hat and took his leave.

Lydia took care to remain expressionless. She knew a good deal when she saw one. When Chase turned the corner, she headed to the telegraph office on Larimer Street. Her dispatch to Georgetown was sweet and simple: *Have estimated Market Street Building worth $5,000. Have buyer for $6,000. Sell?*

And to her delight, the offer was accepted. *Her offer.* She now owned something that Stanley knew nothing about.

She aimed to keep it that way.

# CHAPTER 5
## STRANGE BUSINESS PARTNERS

There were more than ghosts in the Chambers's closets. There were bottles. The move to Denver was supposed to provide a fresh start, and so it did. Lydia moved from alcohol to laudanum. Her dependencies were made discreet that way, especially seeing how laudanum bottles were smaller.

And Lydia always felt fine about discretion.

It took two days for the bruises to fade enough that she could conceal them with makeup—and not with entire success. The face reflected back to her in the mirror appeared beset by gray shadows. It was a shameful thing, to be beaten by her husband. Society preferred that she stay out of sight while in such a state, and so did she. But the laudanum was running out.

She needed more.

Stanley had come home, drunk and spitting mad. "Ed Chase is livid that he wasted his time on a building that was not available. He said some operation was already set up in there. I don't know what that all is about, but he also inferred that I didn't have a clue about what was going on in Denver. The other fellows think I'm a heel!"

An accurate assessment if she had ever heard one.

Lydia, unmoved by his anger, was surprised it had taken him that long to find out. She stared at him, and couldn't help herself. "I told him it would sell quickly."

That earned her a sharp, backhanded slap that sent her sprawling across a wooden chair, landing on her ribs.

He wore a surprised expression that the blow had landed so well. But he made no move to help her—offered no apology. He left her in a heap, gasping while he shook out his hand like it hurt.

Good. She hoped it was broken. A spark lit inside of her— one that wouldn't allow her to cower despite the wind getting knocked out of her. She had no intention of being his punching bag for the next twenty years. "Jesus Christ. There are other places," she gasped.

Stanley continued to shake and flex his hand. "Then find them, instead of sleeping all the goddamned time! You know, this is your fault entirely. Why haven't you learned to act like you should? You shouldn't provoke me."

Lydia put her hand to her ribcage, flinching as she sank to a seated position on the floor. "He should have made up his mind faster."

Stanley lunged and grabbed her by the jaw. In one swift movement, he hauled her upright, looking into her eyes as he squeezed a fraction harder. "You're a very pretty woman, Lydia. Who would have thought you had a head with anything of value in it?"

Her breath came in short, jagged rasps. He didn't let go of her face, the violence in him still rising.

"Bruises are bad for business," she gasped.

That small tendril of logic registered. He loosened his grip and backed away, then fled the house. The door shut behind him with a bang.

She screwed her eyes shut, praying he might stay away and never come back. She sure as hell wouldn't have cared if she never saw him again.

Shaking, she got up and staggered over to the mirror above the fireplace mantel. Half-crouched from the blow, she tried to stand straighter. God, how it hurt. She checked her reflection.

The mirror confirmed tousled ringlets of brown hair, wild and escaping from the pins. Livid marks stood out against her cheek. Red fingerprints along both sides of her jaw. Telltale dark smudges under her blue eyes from the laudanum. She rubbed her face, forced her breathing to slow.

More laudanum would help. It was the one thing she could count on to always help, to replace the pain with a sensation of warmth.

She was interrupted by a timid tapping on the door. She knew that tap and hated it, almost as much as she hated the maid. The newest one that Stanley paid to spy. The one he was sleeping with.

"Go away." Her voice was clear, her diction upper-class.

"I heard a loud noise, a thud." Of course the woman wasn't concerned in the least, and she didn't sound it, either. She wanted to gloat—to rub it in.

"I fell. Satisfied?" There was no reason to lie to the likes of her. Lydia hobbled over to the door and turned the key stuck in the lock. Safe.

And she waited for the bitch to walk away, hating her smugness, her dishonesty. Her *stupidity,* for she actually believed Stanley was the master of the house. Lydia had handled the final negotiations for their fine house on Glenarm, while Stanley tried to act the big gun. She had heard the swirling rumors and moved in for the kill—the title transfer concluded at seventy cents on the dollar. She paid his club dues as well.

He had married her for her family's money, plain and simple. And that same money allowed Lydia to not give a tinker's damn about his preferences. Especially when she kept replenishing it with earnings of her own.

It was a good thing Lydia could make things happen. Her "little problem" was getting out of hand.

She retrieved a vial of laudanum hidden behind some books,

and added a few drops to a glass of water. She waited to take the drink, forcing herself to pause—to think for a moment, to plot out the next step. She needed to find a tenant for her building. Someone who could keep his mouth shut.

Then she drained the glass and felt the warmth hit her veins, lessening the pain in her ribs, the tightness in her chest. She lay across a fainting couch, and no longer cared about anything at all.

The following morning found Lydia shaky, nauseous, and desperate. She checked the empty bottle of laudanum, lifting it to her lips in an effort to suck out any remnants, without success. She had no choice but to go out for more. She had the gardener fetch her horse, which she mounted with difficulty.

"Are you feeling all right, ma'am?" He eyed her with concern.

"No, but I know how to fix it." There was a druggist on Larimer Street.

She urged the horse forward. Each step the beast took made her head pound. On the verge of vomiting, she pulled up in front of the druggist's and looped the reins through the ring on the hitching post.

She hurtled through the door, went straight up to the tall wooden counter. "I need laudanum."

A portly woman entered the shop and came up behind her, waiting. Suffering, Lydia didn't care. She was deathly sick, and growing sicker with each moment of withdrawal.

"Do you have a script?" the druggist asked with a smirk.

"What?" No one needed a script for that stuff. Lydia felt the sweat in her armpits; her hands started shaking. "Please; it won't do any harm."

He eyed her. "It looks like it already has."

She pulled herself straighter, perspiration soaking through

her blouse, down her back and between her breasts. "You are mistaken."

Her challenge sounded hollow. Her stomach heaved, bile rising. She rushed to the front of the store and burst through the door before throwing up in the street.

"He's always been a cucklehead."

Shaking, Lydia managed to glance at the woman who owned those words, who stood behind her. It was the same lady who had been in the druggist's.

"It's not what you think," Lydia lied, feeling horribly ill and humiliated.

"Don't worry on account of me. Here." A plump hand held out a small bottle. "I have some laudanum with me. For emergencies such as this."

Lydia's hand shook as she reached for the bottle. She pulled the cork stopper and poured a small amount onto her tongue. When the calming effects of the narcotic reached her veins, her stomach settled. She took a deep breath, nodded her thanks to the woman.

"Sometimes I have bad nerves." True enough, Lydia's thin hands were still trembling.

"He always was an ass. Doesn't like women any too well, either." The woman dropped the bottle into her fringed handbag.

If Lydia felt shocked at the language, she hid it. "You must be from around here, then."

The woman shrugged. "Used to be. But unless things have changed greatly—and it doesn't seem the case—you don't look like someone who rubs shoulders down here."

Lydia shrugged at the fair judgment. "I bought a building I need to lease. My name is Lydia Chambers. Mrs."

The plump woman studied the street, measured Lydia with shrewd eyes. "I'm Annie Ryan. As it so happens, I'm looking to rent a place. But it has to be on Market Street, or right off of it."

Lydia didn't flinch or flush. "My building is right on Market—a fine location. Care to take a look?"

The plump woman considered, shook her head slightly. "You probably don't even want to be seen talking to me, much less renting to me. I'm looking for a saloon that can double as a whorehouse. If you catch my drift."

Lydia did. And it didn't bother her one jot. "At least whores are honest."

"Whoever gave you that idea?" Annie snorted. "But you're right up to a point. They don't pretend to be something they're not—unless they can get away with it."

Lydia figured she might learn a thing or two from Mrs. Ryan.

There was also a good chance she just might know men who could get things "done."

# CHAPTER 6
## SOURED ROMANCES AND A BUSINESS TO RUN

Holding a tenancy on Market Street cost hard money. One thousand sultry dollars a month. That was a whole lot of screwing and drinking, and a few other things on the side. The notion of a thousand-dollar rent was astounding. It would take every penny Annie owned, plus more than a few that she didn't.

And she was getting a cut-rate price, at that.

Although it was a peculiarity in her world, Annie was different from the other sporting women in that she preferred to save money rather than let it slip through her hands. Intent upon making her mark in—or on—Denver, she would attempt to borrow money for the furnishings and booze. She didn't like holding debt, and she especially didn't like owing favors, but she would change her convictions for this rare trophy.

Annie's best chance was to turn to her brothers for a loan or a stake to get started. Hell, she didn't like them knowing what was going on with her—even informing them she was back in business went against her grain. But word would leak out. If it hadn't already.

Common sense dictated it was best to keep money in the family when they could. There was always the remote chance they would lend assistance, if things got pushed too far. Barring that, they would at least pick the carcass clean. It was a crap shoot either way.

Annie never considered that she was ruining her daughters by turning them into prostitutes. They were just selling a commodity they had. With success.

But now May was getting ambitions above her station and beyond Annie's control. The girl was still wound tight on Hollingsworth, and Annie needed to get that big trollop back on track. May wasn't working as much or as hard as required, which put a dent in everyone's finances, but most importantly Annie's. Thank goodness for the stable and steady Julia who caused far less trouble.

What the hell.

Annie stepped out into the busy street, pausing to let her eyes adjust to the blaring sunlight. Commerce flourished—commerce of *all* sorts. She braced herself, squared her shoulders, and headed toward the Monte Carlo saloon, one of her brothers' newer acquisitions. She had a few blocks to figure out the words to use. Family always required an approach, and there were some hard feelings. She had seen the building before—she checked them out like she would any other competition. For they were competition, even if they and she shared the same last name.

But she hadn't viewed them or their building with the intent of borrowing money.

With an assessing bent, she took in the fancy sign over the doorway, which must have cost serious money. They were doing well. Yes, a sign like that would lure the punters in. It also did a good job of framing the varnished double doors. The building appeared legitimate, though some of the proportions were a bit off. The upper portion was a bit too tall; there must have been rooms upstairs without windows. A definite drawback for the whores who were working up there, but it was one way of keeping things on the quiet.

None of which was her concern, unless there were some good girls who might turn more money for Annie than for her brothers. That was worth considering. Later.

She entered the saloon, a manly sort of place.

A sleek fellow she didn't know was working behind the bar. "Is Jim or John Ryan around?" she asked. "I'm their sister, Annie."

"And so you are," said a voice behind her. He didn't sound any too excited about it, either.

And there he stood when she turned to face him, a portly man with oiled-back hair wearing a tie. Her brother Jim. He made no move to hug her, but then again, he had always been stand-offish. That was why she almost liked him.

"That I am, Jimmy. And I was thinking it was about time I paid you a social call." Annie offered a dazzling whore's smile that got her nowhere.

Jim frowned. "You've taken your time about it."

So. Word had travelled. Hardly surprising, but not the way she wanted to start. She ignored the comment and surveyed the clientele. "Looks like you're doing well, Jimmy. Then again, I always knew you would."

He puffed up a mite with the compliment, but then grew guarded. "Rumor is you've been running out of Hollingsworth's. And why would that be, when you have us here?"

"Ah." She had expected as much. "That is a long story about a misguided affair of the heart and wounded pride. What can I say?"

He shrugged, largely uninterested. "Hollingsworth is competition. And, unless you've changed, you usually bounce back from misguided affairs just fine. What's different?"

Annie pondered that. "Prices. Denver's gotten expensive, and I'm tired of running second rate. Glad to see you're pulling in a fair amount here."

Jim surveyed the room and then returned his attention to Annie. Silent. He moved behind the bar, but gave no hint of offering any hospitality.

Annie waited a long moment and then pressed ahead. "You know, I've got the girls with me. The time has come to leave Hollingsworth's and set up on my own." She shifted her weight from one foot to the other, thought how a drop of whiskey might make this all a bit easier. "I'm leaving too much money on the table at that lark."

That got his attention. "Go on."

She licked her lips. Denver was damn dry. "Well, I got to thinking, that, being family and all, you could give me a loan. I need booze and furnishings and will pay you back. With interest, you understand. You know, come hell or high water, I keep to my word."

He eyed her straight, finally made a move toward the whiskey. "Drink?"

She nodded. He poured. Then he put the cork back in the bottle and slid the glass over to her. "That depends upon how you look at it. Usually you hold your end up—excepting, maybe, that whole business to do with Claire."

Annie felt her heart thump. "You don't still blame me for that, do you?"

"It's a pesky memory. At the time John and I thought you two would manage to sort it out between yourselves. You know, you weren't the only person that had to deal with her nonsense. She owed me twenty dollars, and I can't collect from a corpse. But it was a sad day when her baby was given away. She only did that because you made her. She said as much."

"Did she, now? Well, you could have gone to take the baby back, but you didn't." Annie stared him down, then eased up. On account of the money.

She tried to keep her tone level. "At any rate, it was the only decent option, Jimmy. Pearl will have been looked after and educated. All fine things. What do you think would have happened to her with us? You know about the muffs that go after the young girls. It was for her own good."

He shrugged, knowing her words held truth. To a point. "How old is she getting?"

"Not so fast, Jimmy. What would you be wanting her for, then?"

Jim frowned. "Probably the same as you. But that Claire business still sticks in my craw, especially since there was that baby girl involved. What chance did she have?"

Jim's maudlin vein would not get her what she wanted. "She had no chance at all with a drug fiend for a mother. Good God, Jimmy, Claire used to stand in the middle of the goddamned street screaming bloody murder for no reason whatsoever. And . . ."

Jimmy's eyes sparked with a light of acquisition. Annie paused, weighing her words. "I'm going to get the girl back—that's all part of my plan; never you worry. It's not as if I lost her someplace. Furthermore, I can tell that *you* haven't the first clue about her. So while you're busy blaming me for Claire's failings, at least I bothered to keep tabs on her child."

He looked at her, then at the ceiling. "Fair enough; I'll not bother to argue the point. But, all things considered, it might be best just to let the girl go. She might have a better life away from all of this."

Annie stared at her brother. "That's a lie, and you know it. You're just sore that you won't have the chance to get to her first. Her blood is the same as ours and she'll make it pay. It's not like any of us had much of a choice about how we stay above ground. Now, do you want to give me a loan, or not? I'm tired of flapping my gums."

"Twenty percent," he said, looking hard.

"Fifteen," Annie replied. "You have to leave me room to operate."

They sized each other up, spat in their palms, and shook.

Then they laughed, being family after all. They lifted their glasses and clinked the rims together, each wary of the other.

# Chapter 7
## Rivalries

Spurned affections and having the poor taste to go chasing after May amounted to one thing, and one thing only, in Annie's mind. She was quitting Hollingsworth. And he didn't deserve any notification of her intention to leave the premises, taking her daughters with her. The both of them. Annie threw her belongings into the same trunk she'd arrived with, feeling fully justified in her actions.

She pulled Julia aside. "We're leaving, so get your things together. Quick now. Where's your sister?"

Julia pointed at the tack room in the back, the door closed. "She's in there with Hollingsworth."

Eying the door that didn't lock, Annie figured the time was as good as any. She made a beeline for the door, skirting tables and customers as she went.

With force, she threw open the door. It smacked against the inside wall. If she hadn't stuck her foot out, it would have slammed shut again—in her face.

Undeterred, she entered. She found what she expected—May and Hollingsworth in bed together. Both looked shocked at the intrusion. Which was rich.

"That's seven dollars you owe me, Caldwell. May doesn't give pokes for free, even for you."

Neither of the bedmates said a word, so Annie kicked one of the bedframe legs just to make sure she had their attention. To prove she wasn't kidding around.

That surprised them, some—like a swift kick in the ass.

May looked a bit worried as Annie eyed her curls. She wasn't beyond pulling the girl from the bed by her hair, and the girl knew it.

"Not to mention that you owe a good explanation of this set-up in the first place. Now, how do you explain this situation? I would have thought you would have preferred your quarters upstairs." Her voice was clear, loud, and pointed. "Or do you not care about my girl enough to treat her decent?"

That caught May off guard. She looked at Hollingsworth, sheet held up to her chin. Like her goods hadn't been seen hundreds of times before.

Annie enjoyed their looks of confusion. "Let me help answer that for the both of you. You see, May: to Caldwell you're just another whore. One he even thought he could take for free. Isn't that right, Caldwell? Because really she's just a whore to you, isn't she? If you thought otherwise, you wouldn't care to take her where she's been had by so many others."

Hollingsworth started to protest, but Annie cut him off. "Look here, I'll cut you a deal. I'll sell her to you for the cost of her debts to me, plus ten dollars. No further questions asked. And we need to be clear about this; I won't take her back if you change your mind. Deal?" Annie stuck out her hand and waved it in Hollingsworth's face.

"Wait a minute! You can't just sell me." May's eyes were popping.

"The hell I can't! Now I was just doing up the accounts, and May hasn't been earning like she should. Her going rate is seven dollars, but then there were those days when she just earned four dollars per trick—meaning she got one lame-ass dollar per screw. All her expenses total up to three hundred and twenty dollars. That's what it will take for her to be free to pursue her own interests. You buying? 'Cause I sure the hell am selling."

"Hang on," May interrupted. "What if I don't plan on staying here?" The look on her face showed she was having second thoughts. About damn time, too.

"Well then, you better make up your mind pretty quick before I lose my patience. My stuff is packed and loaded. Now, I would have said Hollingsworth is a bit old for you—but there's no accounting for taste. But why, I still want to know, is he treating you like a two-bit whore in a tack room?"

May turned on Hollingsworth. "Yeah. Why is that, Caldwell?"

He looked from Annie to May and back again. "Well, I didn't think about it like that. But I'm not paying three hundred dollars to erase your debts. It would take a long time to get that money back."

May spluttered, indignant.

"Three hundred and twenty plus seven for this job," Annie corrected.

"And what if I don't want to work for you, you old cow?" May was sitting up straight, eyes blazing.

"Then pay me the money you owe me, and we're done." Annie acted impatient, hands on hips. "And if you don't, I'll haul your sorry ass into court."

"I hate the both of you," May said, barely pausing to pull on her shift before rushing out the door to gather her things. A couple of catcalls marked her passing through the saloon, only partially clad and giving a show to the punters for free.

Annie winked at Caldwell. "You made a good choice there. You wouldn't know how to handle her once things got rolling."

He didn't look any too happy, and somewhat confused. Annie turned on her heel and left the door wide open for all to see. Let Hollingsworth shut the door for himself. Asshole.

She stole two bottles of his whiskey on the way out the door.

The barman was about to say something, but caught the look on her face and wisely changed his mind.

The wagon was waiting outside. "I'm leaving now," she yelled—part threat, part celebration.

She ended up waiting a quarter of an hour, which was kind of a letdown. But at the end of that time, May was on board. Sometimes it paid to be practical.

Annie and her daughters were deposited in front of Lydia's building—the newest jewel in the Ryans' suspect holdings. Located two streets down on the other side of Market Street.

"This is it," Annie told the driver, and he pulled over in front of an impressive façade. Then, to May and Julia: "Now what do you have to say to your darling mother?"

The girls were gob-smacked, but they both hurried down out of the wagon.

Annie felt the surge of conquest. "Pretty fancy, isn't it? And doesn't the air smell just a bit better?"

May was still out of sorts. "The smell and the smoke still travel from the stacks and chimneys. But take a good look at it, Julia, because we'll probably lose it somehow."

"Over my dead body." Annie gathered up her skirts and swished to the front door. She fished in her purse, proud. "We have a key."

"You want the trunks inside or not?" the driver asked, ruining the triumph with his impatience.

"This is an occasion." Annie shot him a nasty look as she stepped over the threshold, skirts swishing against her ankles, May and Julia trailing. Some of their excitement faded as they took a good look around the interior. The dust lay thick, and the saloon felt cold and neglected. Too quiet by half. The floors needed scraping and washing.

"And who's going to do that?" May muttered, looking at the

evidence of spilled drinks and missed spittoons.

"We all are. Good honest work to remind us all why the hell we chose a different path."

Julia peered along the baseboards. Poked at something with the toe of her boot. "There are mouse droppings in here."

But at least the place had baseboards to begin with.

The driver was banging around with the trunks, thudding up the narrow stairs.

Annie opened one of the stolen bottles. "Here's to the future, and to hell with the past!" She raised the bottle in a toast and took a swig. She handed it to May, who did the same.

Julia shrugged and took a dainty sip. "Well, you don't actually own it, do you?"

Annie smirked. "Not yet. But as I see it, I'm helping someone out by taking this off her hands and keeping her name out of it."

The man came back down, eyed the whiskey.

Annie smiled, and pulled out a dollar. "Have a drink on the house, and come back when we're open!"

"I suppose you never know." He took a swig, then handed back the bottle and pocketed the silver dollar.

The women watched his departure. A bit deflated.

May reached for the bottle, took another swig, and pulled a face. "Nothing could go wrong with a secret landlady, I suppose."

Annie stiffened, then shuddered. Then she smiled and glanced upward at the pressed tin ceiling.

"Someone step on your grave?" May asked, giving her the eye.

Plenty could go wrong, and Annie knew it. "That's just superstition, and I'm getting a mite tired of you always complaining. Would you just look at that ceiling? Now, let's change our clothes and get to scrubbing! Tomorrow the liquor shipment comes in, and then we'll be open for business."

What the hell.

# CHAPTER 8
## THE WRONG SIDE OF DENVER SUITS SOME PEOPLE JUST FINE

Getting into business with a drug fiend was never a good move; Annie had no illusions on that count. But two days later, Ryan's saloon and brothel was starting to shape up—at least the building part of the arrangement. Her brothers had already come poking around, trying to horn in where they weren't wanted. "We're just making sure about our investment," they claimed.

"Hell, it's a loan at fifteen percent. Let's get that part straight once and for all." Annie felt her pulse quicken.

They found that funny. "We're just pulling your leg," John claimed. "Need any girls?"

Annie shook her head. "Not yet. And not if they're anything like the one you saddled me with all those years ago in exchange for Claire. You charged me five dollars, and all she did was cry. Hooker, my ass. Some farm girl was more like it."

Jim noticed the outline behind the bar. "What's that about?"

"Decorating." Annie puffed up a little.

The boys appeared a bit confused; plainly that notion had never crossed their minds. Annie was getting a picture painted—one of a naked woman. "Now run along, and let me get busy. I'm waiting on the liquor delivery."

"You should have come to us," Jim replied.

Annie smiled, knowing that would touch a vein. "A girl likes a bit of independence." The dolts actually had to look at each other to come up with an opinion on that. Annie almost laughed, but they would be back. Especially if she started doing well.

She watched them walk away, then turned to the sketch on the wall. It would be a touch of class—another one of her veritable improvements. Then Annie caught herself. The landlady might not exactly approve. Still, it was odd that a woman like that owned a building at all—much less one on Market Street. While she appeared a better class of drug fiend, puking in the street wasn't the mark of gentility as it was widely understood.

Annie turned away from the sketch and peered out of the saloon window. Her liquor delivery was running late. It was one thing if she cut her whiskey; it was another if the liquor agents were doing it. Adulterated goods caused problems. She ought to know.

Everyone was out to make money, honest or otherwise. The partially completed naked lady on the wall kind of looked like Annie sometimes felt. Half floating, half finished. She laughed. And often with her clothes off.

Market Street was slowly coming around to another morning with a bad hangover. Last night's dregs were sallying forth, and her own head was pounding as well. She brushed her brown hair back, then placed her hands on her hips and squeezed. There was more padding than there used to be, but then again, Annie wasn't young anymore. While she might not have youth, she had a business. And that counted for quite a bit, to her way of thinking. If it didn't, hell, there wasn't anything else worth admitting to.

And she was still above ground, in decent surroundings. Bully for her. Both against the odds.

She surveyed the interior and liked what she saw. Once the naked woman got done, and a couple of small naked pictures were added—well, a new life would be given to the place. She thought about women's "touches" in her line of work and laughed. It was more like groping and fondling.

No checkered tablecloths for her.

The situation was downright fortuitous. She had a twenty percent advantage on rent over the competing houses. That was what the fancy woman was offering to keep everything quiet.

There had to be a far sight more behind that story.

But it worried her—how drug fiends had a habit of changing what was left of their minds. Annie had seen it before, the glassy eyes with underlying dark shadows—the way they would get feverish in even a cold breeze. Those people would go through their money in nothing flat if the craving was upon them. Something was off with Lydia and her situation. Annie figured it was probably a man, and felt a rare spark of sympathy, which she promptly squashed.

Her liquor shipment rumbled up, distracting her from those unhappy considerations. Eagerly, Annie burst out the doors, bellowing. "Don't leave them sitting there—bring them on in, boys! And that stuff better be untouched. Is it?"

"Don't we look sober?" the driver asked.

Annie studied him. "Hell if I know. Some men hide it better than others."

The men seemed to find that amusing. Jackasses.

As the supplies were being unloaded, Lydia Chambers herself walked in through the front doors like she hadn't a care in the world. Like she owned the place.

The men unloading the liquor stared at her. She noticed, all right, but ignored them—a neat little trick in the way she dismissed them with the tilt of her head.

"Good morning, Mrs. Ryan." She glanced up at the partially completed painting. "I see you're getting set up, and . . . making improvements."

By the way Mrs. Chambers eyed the naked woman, Annie could tell she didn't exactly approve. "The rest of the body should be filled in today—it's a bit unnerving with her head just floating around like that."

Mrs. Chambers smiled, but appeared a bit aggravated, although she tried to hide it. "I was hoping for a word with you."

There it was already. Annie inhaled, sharp. The laudanum had already caused her to change her mind.

Lydia interpreted her expression. "Nothing like that, Mrs. Ryan. I wanted to talk about rent collections, and to ask you a personal favor."

Annie exhaled. "Of course, after all the liquor is unloaded. Booze has a tendency to go walking on its own if no one is watching. Would you care to wait in the office?"

"No need." Lydia chose a table in the far corner of the saloon and sat down. How touching. Then Annie noticed some of the porters staring at her.

"What the hell do you think you're looking at?" Annie snapped, as one fellow put a crate down. "Why don't you come back when there are girls that might just be interested?"

He just smiled, and pushed his hat further down on his head. The fellow in charge handed Annie a receipt.

Annie studied the chit: Four hundred and eighty dollars. She pulled a bottle out of a crate and held it up to the light for inspection, then opened it and took a deep whiff. Appeased.

"Furniture is arriving as well today," she said to Lydia as she set some of the bottles on the bar. "Care for a drink?"

"Maybe a sherry." The woman was too refined to be in such a rough place.

"How about whiskey?" Annie carried a bottle and two glasses to the table. "I'm not fully stocked yet."

Lydia seemed to find that amusing. "I wanted to run a couple of things by you. While I know discretion is in your line of business, for my own peace of mind I must reemphasize that who owns this building remains our secret."

"Understood." It suited Annie just fine if people assumed she was the owner. "But if you don't mind me saying so, you coming in through the front door is bound to get tongues wagging."

"I doubt I would know too many people down here," she murmured.

Annie looked at her square. "There's probably more than you think, Mrs. Chambers."

Mrs. Chambers flushed. "Perhaps. And please call me Lydia. I wanted to set up the rent collection details. Say each Tuesday morning around eleven o'clock? I can come through the back door then."

Annie nodded, wondering what the visit was really about.

Lydia took a sip of her whiskey, held a gloved hand up to her lips as if it burned. "Now for the part that is a little more difficult. I have reason to believe that my husband might be unfaithful."

Annie tossed back her head, but tried to appear sympathetic. "Most men are."

Lydia opened her purse, took out a photograph, and handed it to Annie. "This is my husband, Stanley Chambers. If you see him in this establishment, or any like it, I would consider it a favor if you let me know."

Annie considered the picture in passing. She thrust it back in Lydia's direction. Lydia shook her head and closed her purse with a snap. "I know what he looks like all too well. Keep it for reference—to be certain it's him."

Annie narrowed her eyes, sensing she was getting involved in something she shouldn't. "Most women don't want to know, when it comes right down to it. Can't say I blame them."

Something was wrong. Very wrong.

Lydia shrugged, took another sip of her whiskey. "I have my reasons."

Annie glanced away, entangled by her past feelings. "Fidelity is a bit of a horse race. The good ones don't always finish first, and the bad ones don't always finish last."

Lydia frowned at the comparison, but didn't dismiss it. "But would you agree that husbands are supposed to earn money, and not latch on to a woman and bleed her dry?"

"That I would," Annie replied. "Unless you really love them. Sometimes that happens. When someone loves a man so bad she foots his bills. It normally doesn't work out real well."

The way Lydia's stare didn't falter told Annie all she needed to know on that matter. There was little point in arguing the details when a foundation wasn't square.

# PART II
## SPRING 1892
## WHORE WITH A HEART OF GOLD
### (A DODGY STORY AND A DUBIOUS TRAIT)

★ ★ ★ ★ ★

# CHAPTER 9
## A CROOKED BUSINESS FOR A CROOKED FAMILY

From the beginning, Pearl hadn't trusted her aunt, perhaps with good reason. Maybe it was because Pearl, reasonably assuming she was an orphan, had been placed in the Home of the Good Shepherd. Maybe it was the silence and lack of affection that characterized her time there. Or perhaps the distrust stemmed from the fact that her aunt lived a pitiful seven miles away and had never once bothered to visit. Like many others in the orphanage, she had longed for what she didn't have—a family and a sense of belonging. She was shocked to learn, from the home's scrawny groundskeeper, who smelled of liquor and sweat, that she had a living relative.

Against the rules, the groundskeeper sidled up to her one afternoon when the opportunity arose. "Your aunt, Annie Ryan, asked me to give you a message. She said when you turn sixteen you should go to work in the family business, Ryan's Saloon on Market Street and Twenty-first. Why, she's even keeping a place open for you."

"I have an aunt?"

Before he could say more, one of the sisters came out and shooed him away. Grounds men were allowed neither to talk to the girls nor to be within twenty feet of them.

Pearl had, at first, been grateful for what appeared to be divine intervention. Yet something was wrong. Why hadn't her aunt ever come to see her? Pearl spent more than a few days turning the question inside out in her mind, worrying it from all angles. It was possible that this aunt had been ill or hadn't known where to find her. Or perhaps the aunt had been traveling and had just arrived back in town. But none of those invented situations explained why this newly discovered relation would relay messages through a scruffy groundskeeper. There was no mention of love or concern.

After that strange, brief encounter, she had many more questions to ask and details to seek. She looked for the man repeatedly, but never saw him again. She later found out he had been dismissed for breaking the rule about distances.

More than anything, Pearl wanted to belong in a family. So she ignored the warning signs that something about this aunt of hers didn't ring true. As everyone with a lick of sense knew, beggars couldn't be choosers. They had to take what was given. And the fact was that Pearl didn't have a dollar to her name. Risks were all she had going. She would have the choice, upon turning sixteen, to either enter the convent as a novitiate or hazard the secular world. Well before March twenty-seventh, the date assigned as Pearl's birthday whether it actually was or not, Pearl decided to chance it. She didn't feel holy—that much was fairly certain. A whole world awaited beyond the convent walls.

Besides, a saloon sounded heady and daring, and came with a family. Her family. It was enough to cause shivers down her spine.

The morning of her approximate sixteenth birthday might not have looked like much, but it sure felt big. Gathering her meager possessions, she approached the reverend mother's office for the last time, determined to leave the home once and for all.

"I would like to say goodbye." Pearl clutched her bundle and felt small.

The aging nun took off her glasses and gazed at Pearl. "Are you sure that's wise?"

Pearl smiled. "I've received word that I have an aunt in Denver. She wants me to work for her."

The nun frowned, not yielding to the good news. "Where does this woman live, and what does she want?"

Pearl knew better than to lie to a nun. "She runs a saloon on Market Street, but I promise not to drink liquor."

The nun's eyes widened. "That is a scandalous location. It is no place for decent young girls."

Pearl felt the nun's opinion exaggerated, hard. "My aunt will take care of me."

"You had better hope so." The nun looked sharp. "Do not shut your eyes to decent work—hard, honest work. Your good character is all that you own. Guard it well."

Pearl didn't know what to say to that. So she said nothing at all.

The nun pulled out an envelope from her drawer and opened it. "This is for you. We've kept it safe all these years so it didn't get lost or stolen." The nun held out a battered enamel and gold pin in the shape of a violet. "Your mother wanted you to have it."

The existence of a relic, and the accompanying information, was a betrayal. "You have met my mother?"

The nun tilted her head, gauging the effect of that information. "She left you with us."

"Then she wasn't dead." Pearl felt the fabricated history she had created snap inside of her like an old dry twig. *She had never been loved.*

The nun appeared resigned, and unsurprised. "I looked up your admittance record, which noted that your mother was an inveterate when she left you with us."

"Inveterate? What does that mean?"

The nun sighed. "It means irredeemable. Your mother was sunken in vice."

Turned out, Market Street was a sewer of vice.

Seven dusty miles from the Home of the Good Shepherd stood another world—a world of a different tempo and smell. The stench of the stock yards competed with the roaring smelters that belched fumes and smoke into the air. The breeze had a sickly sweet undertone that was new and unidentifiable. But no one cared about her impressions as Pearl stood on the corner of Market and Twenty-first—a rollicking, dirty expanse that had an off-key music to it. Amidst the swell of commotion and humanity, Ryan's Saloon was bold and easy to locate.

The name *Ryan's* was painted across the windows in unflinching black and red letters.

Jangling songs from pianos, on-key or otherwise, floated out from open doors to lure the unwary inside. The jumpy tunes were irreverent, impious. Men bellowed and came on from doorways about "straight" three card monte, and "players drink for free." Loud and unkempt, saloons lined both sides of the street—along with various other establishments of questionable purpose. Market Street sprouted from the dirt as a riotous jumble of wickedness and booze that masqueraded as a good, rip-roaring time.

It caused the blood to race and the pace to quicken.

Among the throngs of men were women—strange, brash women. In a peculiar and brazen manner, they spilled out from windows and doorways wearing as little as they could get away with. Some of them cut fine figures. And, Pearl noted with shame, what little they had on was still nicer than her orphanage dress of a durable gray. Those Market Street women made a game of playing with their untied laces and low-cut bodices in a suggestive manner . . . offering even ruder gestures if a man passing by broke his pace to admire. Obvious strangers exchanged laughter and banter. Pearl tried not to stare.

It was a spectacle by intent, and Pearl started getting the idea that she shouldn't be there. A drunkard came staggering out of a saloon and stopped at her side. Smelling blatantly offensive, he swayed with tottering movements. He pulled off his hat, his forehead marred by a red, sweating indent. His hair was brown and greasy and matted down. He caught her looking at him. Encouraged, he hitched up his pants and tried to formulate words. Spooked, Pearl bolted toward Ryan's.

Misgivings poked at her, just below the surface where her conscience was supposed to be.

Men loitered around the saloon entrance, leaning against the building spitting tobacco or eyeing the street with calculation. All of them should have been working. Dirty or clean, the men appeared restless, shiftless, and rude. One of the idlers winked at her.

There was no music coming from Ryan's—an omission that hinted at inferiority, a telltale sign that was not lost on Pearl. But of course she entered, pausing for her eyes to adjust from the sun. The first thing to come into focus was a large pair of painted breasts jutting out from a painting behind the bar. A reclining nude with red hair and a lewd expression stared at her without shame or remorse.

Pearl took a step back. She felt flushed. It was hard, if not downright impossible, not to look at the woman.

A warning went off in her brain. If she couldn't make it work with her aunt, Pearl had nothing of value to sell.

She tore her glance away from the painted woman's nakedness and concentrated on the staggering variety of liquor bottles on glass shelves. Square bottles, round bottles, short and tall, brown, blue, green, and purple; Ryan's certainly had booze. And another distinctive odor. The saloon smelled unclean and musty: the musk of liquor, tobacco, and unwashed males. The sawdust scattered on the floor didn't do much to improve matters, spilled or otherwise.

The bleached and scrubbed scent of the Good Shepherd faded into a distance much greater than simply across town.

Scattered on the far side of the room were battered and gouged tables with various ill-assorted chairs. The walls were dirty, the wainscoting battered, and what was visible of the floors under the sawdust appeared stained and uneven. Certainly dirty. The saloon's ceiling was the only redeeming feature: patterned pressed tin that needed another coat of paint. Gas lamps hung at indeterminate intervals, the chimneys protruding from chipped milk glass shades that cried out for washing and repair. It took a moment for the sound of a clearing throat to register—a sound coming from a man polishing glasses. A man who didn't look any too pleased to have her in there. Pearl figured it was her dress, which clearly failed Denver standards.

"Can I help you?" he asked, annoyed.

"I'm here to find my aunt, Annie Ryan."

The occupants in the bar stiffened, and the drinkers gave her a second once-over. She felt nothing of the desired welcome that had played in her imagination.

"Are you sure? Oh, what the hell. Come with me," the barman said, and led Pearl through a black painted archway and into a dark hallway. More pictures of women in various stages of undress were nailed to the walls—the subject matter absolutely unsettling.

The man knocked on a door, leaned toward the crack that separated it from the frame. "I've got a girl who says she's your niece, Annie. And she's standing right here beside me, so watch what you say."

A chair made a rude sound as it scraped the floor. Boards

creaked underfoot. The black china knob turned, the door opened by a large, brown-eyed woman swathed in ruffles and plaid flounces. She gave Pearl the once-over.

"So, you must be Pearl. You have the look of your mother about you. Like her, you're just skin and bones. How are you going to get a man, looking all skinny like that?"

The barman made a scoffing sound. Annie Ryan—for this had to be her—shot him a nasty look, then returned to her chair behind the desk. "Bring us a couple of beers. I'm not just paying you to stand around and gawk."

The man slung the towel over his shoulder and sauntered back toward the bar, his manner casual and unhurried.

"Yes," Pearl said like nothing was the matter, "I'm your niece."

"Take a seat." Annie's eyes were calculating, but she smiled— which was not altogether a pleasant experience.

Pearl took the offered chair, but kept her bundle on her knees. Annie folded her hands, index fingers pressed against her lips, large rings sparkling. Assessing.

"That dress is godawful, but we can get you something better. This is my establishment, the family business. I'm glad you had the sense to take up my offer."

The barman returned with the beer. Annie handed Pearl a glass and nodded at the man. "That's Michael; he's a second cousin of sorts. Now, bottoms up."

Pearl took a swallow, already breaking promises. Annie's fat cheeks puffed out as she drank. She watched Pearl with darting, dark eyes that took everything in. "I'll be damned; you drink like a lady."

Pearl felt insulted somehow, but Annie laughed, appraising her bust.

"Did my mother look like you?" Pearl felt uncomfortable with the way her aunt stared.

Annie's eyes flashed, the question distracting her from Pearl's figure. "Smaller."

"I thought she was dead all along, and that's how I ended up at the Home of the Good Shepherd. She *is* dead, isn't she?" Pearl leaned forward, eager.

"Of course she is," Annie replied, a bit sharpish. Then she attempted another smile to smooth her words over.

Pearl sensed something unpleasant, but pressed ahead. "What was she like?"

Annie snorted. "She was a boil on the bottom of humanity." Each word was enunciated, bitter and clear. "Just leave the dead well enough alone, will ya? The rest of us are very much alive—for the time being. And so are you."

It didn't sound like a desirable condition—the way Annie said it. "But, I want to know about her . . . about my father. My last name is Kelly, as you know."

"Oh, *that*. It was just a name chosen out of thin air for the admittance papers to the home. Having a different last name made it all seem more respectable somehow. As for your mother, I'll tell you that a bit later. Once you've had time to adjust." Annie slapped her desk with the palms of her hands. "Don't put on such a long face—and let's not go lamenting her absence. It was all so very long ago. You're here now, and I'll see you right, or close enough."

Pearl's brain was lurching, uncertain.

"I know what you'll like," Annie exclaimed. "You'll feel better knowing you have two girl-cousins—May and Julia, my daughters. They're only a couple of years older than you. They work for me, too. Now, did you do well in school?"

"Yes," Pearl replied, sensing safer ground. "I got good marks, and the sisters said I had ability."

"There're all kinds of abilities, some of them more profitable than others. Now, I know I sound hard about Claire, may her soul rest in peace. It's just that we have our hands full, running things. We could use another pair of hands and a body to go with them."

That was something she could understand—her mother's death was causing a hardship for the business. "I like to work," she said.

Annie launched away from the desk. "That's the spirit. Come on. I'll put you in my house for the time being. We'll stop at one of the stores to find something nicer for you to wear—something with a bit of color in it. You know how to wash glasses?" Annie asked as she opened the door and headed down the hallway.

"Yes." Everyone knew how to wash glasses.

"Well, that's just dandy," her aunt said.

Pearl wasn't certain it was dandy at all, but she followed her aunt. A bright new dress would be just the ticket to fit into Denver like she belonged.

It would all just take a bit to get used to.

# CHAPTER 10
## BOTTOM OF THE PILE

Straight away, Pearl learned that cleaning glasses was actually hard work.

It wasn't so much the strain in her back as it was the customers. Each morning Pearl entered the saloon to find the living dregs waking up, or starting over. Some hadn't slept at all, others had vomited and their hands shook until they had a glass of whiskey. The air was putrid, first thing in the morning. The sawdust helped . . . some.

She needed to pay her aunt for the dress bought on credit. And the skirt and blouse she wore for work.

Pearl found the monotony of collecting the glasses, washing the glasses, drying the glasses and setting up the glasses numbing. Worse, the job turned revolting when gobs of phlegm or tobacco spit lodged at the bottoms. Brimming spittoons were no joy, either. The dregs were flung out the back door of the saloon, and into the alley that backed onto the row—an area inhabited by old whores on their descent into the gutter.

She knew she was lucky, being trusted to run numbers as well. Sometimes she got tips, which she stored in a small tin. The glasses didn't earn her anything special at all. But the gambling hells were one street over on Larimer. Every time Pearl stepped out into the street her pulse quickened and she felt alive—the surge of youth and inexperience, although she didn't recognize it as such.

She grasped, almost instinctively, that the street was far better than the world that lurked behind the saloon. The alley was a rutted dump where things got cast aside, both living and otherwise. In the shadows of the night, it could be difficult to make the distinction. Daylight didn't help all that much. Pearl had learned that lesson early on—confronted by a specter her first Friday morning, to be precise. A woman with matted hair and an open bodice had staggered toward her, bent and gnarled. One of the woman's breasts was exposed.

"Give me a drink, for Christ's sake," she begged or threatened. Pearl couldn't tell which.

Revolted, Pearl stepped back, retreating into the lean-to that held the sink. "Wait! Don't come any closer, and I'll get you something."

She slammed the door, shaking, and debating what was right. But there was no one out in the saloon, and the bar had been left unattended. Pearl poured out a glass of whiskey as fast as she could from one of the cheap bottles, knowing full well she was stealing. Stealing from her own *family*. Still, she took it to the woman outside as an act of charity. The woman snatched the glass from Pearl's hand, and gulped, tracks of whiskey trickling down her chin. She stopped, stood without moving for a second, eyes closed and head twisted, before she gathered herself and wiped her face with the back of her hand. She licked the whiskey off of it. She wasn't clean; her hand was none too clean, either. Bleary eyes tried to focus.

"I've got fuck-all for money," she said, then drained the remaining contents, and stood a bit straighter once the booze took hold. "You work for her—that Ryan woman?"

"She's my aunt," Pearl replied, "but I just take care of the glasses and run numbers. None of the fancy stuff."

The woman nodded. "It starts out that way, or something like it."

Pearl eyed her, shook her head.

The whore handed back the glass and tucked her breast away, out of sight. Almost. "I thought the same thing, once. Look at me now, will ya?"

"I don't think my aunt would want me to do anything like that," Pearl replied, but as she was speaking, a doubt clanked loud in the back of her mind.

"You might want to think again." The mauk walked off, limping and talking to herself.

Pearl watched the alley swallow her up. She shrugged off the developing uneasy feeling.

The woman's words were only the mutterings of a drunk.

While downstairs was disgusting and rude, upstairs was nothing if not mysterious and dicey. But there were still those damned glasses that needed washing and bottles discarding. The girls' rooms were upstairs, full of strange and loud goings-on behind closed doors. Pearl was allowed up on the second floor only during the morning hours—with the admonishment to knock before *ever* entering any room. And if she heard any sounds or movements from within, she was to make herself scarce. She knocked on May's door one morning, but no one answered.

She opened the door and was halfway inside when she saw two inhabitants lying in the bed—May's fat rump and a sprawled out, snoring jake. His naked prick lay against his thigh, sprouting from a dark patch of pubic hair. Horrified, Pearl gasped and took a step backwards. The floor creaked as her weight shifted.

May heard her and lifted her head off the pillow, looking the worse for wear. "What the hell do you think you're doing?"

"Collecting empties," Pearl stuttered, panicked—not to mention caught red-handed.

The man snorted and opened his eyes. Startled, he grabbed the sheet and covered himself. "What the hell is going on? Say, is she old enough to be in here?"

May acted put out, brushed her straggly hair from her face. "It's not exactly like there's an age limit."

She gave Pearl another nasty look. The man cast aside the dirty sheet and wiggled his prick at her, and it hardened. "Like what you see, girlie?"

Pearl bolted from the room and slammed the door shut. She had seen something she didn't understand, but things were piecing together.

Half an hour later, a hung-over May was back down in the saloon mighty unhappy. She cornered Annie. "Did Pearl tell you what she did?"

Pearl felt trapped, and wanted to slink back into the washroom. But she was hampered by a flat of beer, which she set down behind the bar.

Annie looked at Pearl. "Something happen?"

"Lovely little Pearl came into my room when the jake was still there." May's hands were on her hips, and some of the punters were listening.

"I didn't mean to." It had been shocking, but now she had to worry about what Annie was going to do.

"Malarkey. You're trying to horn on in where you don't belong." May was coming closer to Pearl, pointing her index finger at her like she would poke her in the eye.

Pearl was sensitive about where she belonged, and she flinched. A flinch Annie noticed.

"Settle down, May. Pearl's not trying to steal your customers, if that is what you are insinuating."

"He didn't have any clothes on." Pearl flushed, miserable. "I saw his, his . . . member."

"Is that what we're calling them now? Oh, good heavens. Haven't you seen one before?"

Pearl shook her head; tears welling.

"Looky here, she's going to cry!" May jeered. "You wouldn't have to cry if you knocked before you barged in. Like you're supposed to!"

A knowing look came over Annie. "Let her be, May."

May continued on, acting indignant. "It's not my fault if she learns what's going on."

That caught Pearl up a bit. She had seen what she wasn't supposed to, therefore had learned what was going on. People went upstairs and took their clothes off. And they got paid more money for doing *it*.

*It* still looked fairly nasty and raw.

"I knocked; they were sleeping it off," Pearl said, holding her ground. She was beginning to sense an advantage—that May was somehow jealous of her. She knew she was prettier, bad clothes and all.

Pearl wanted nicer things, and she wanted an affection she just didn't feel toward these women, family or not.

Annie shrugged. "This was all bound to happen sooner or later. I'll bet you don't even know the facts of life, do you, duckie?"

Pearl frowned. May was only half listening—her eyes were fastened upon her next target.

Annie waited for Pearl's explanation.

"Well, I know it's a fact May makes more money than I do."

Her aunt started laughing, but looked pleased. Although Annie's reaction was odd, Pearl was relieved to find she wasn't in trouble after all.

Jakes tried to kiss her all the time. Secretly, she knew she would like a sweetheart. With all the men Denver had roaming about, it shouldn't be too hard to get one. Men came in and out through those saloon doors all the time, and as sure as anything. Maybe one of them, preferably well-scrubbed and shy, would take a fancy to her. Anything was possible, Pearl reasoned. But that simple desire would be elusive. She already knew nothing came easily to her.

# CHAPTER 11
## IN HOCK FROM THE START

It was remarked upon in the street, and especially in the alleys, that the Ryan family never backed away from a fight—never let feelings stand in the way of business. While Annie and her brothers held a grudging respect among the Market Street populace, that didn't make them good people. The family was nothing like what Pearl had longed for growing up—that much was for certain. Annie was a hard woman, uninclined to share stories or confidences when sober. And she was the only link to Pearl's mother—well, other than her uncles. Annie had warned her to steer well clear of them. She said they would press Pearl into prostitution in a New York minute. And how no one wanted that to happen.

Pearl still wanted answers with desperation so strong that she felt like sobbing. Her mother *must* have been different from the rest of them. She wanted so desperately to believe that—yet it was growing more difficult with each passing day. The undeniable fact remained that her mother had left her. But surely she must have had a compelling reason—women didn't just leave their babies behind. She longed for an explanation, for, as it stood, she couldn't make sense of any of it.

Canny enough to bide her time, Pearl waited until Annie took a bit more of the whiskey than she should have. Drunken confidences were almost as good as sober ones, and sometimes they were more revealing. And while not in the habit of imbibing more than she should, Annie did every now and again.

Especially when she had to help with "the hooking."

Late one afternoon, as the day drifted aimlessly into the evening, Annie sat at a table waiting for the evening rush to begin. An open bottle was in front of her, a sure-fire signal that she was up for hire that night. Annie's face was painted and she didn't look too appealing. She looked old and tired—her face puffy and her eyes small. Pearl was finishing up for the day, carrying her last crate of glasses to put behind the bar.

"You look like Claire used to, once upon a time. And that ain't a compliment, but a warning."

It was an opening, and Pearl took it. " 'Ain't' isn't a real word."

"Is that a fact," Annie drawled, helping herself to another splash of whiskey. "Then how come everyone uses it?"

Pearl was well aware that direct questions about her mother fell to the ground like dead birds. So she tried another approach. "Because they don't know any better, I suppose. What's the warning for, anyhow?"

"About how the truth is seldom what we would like it to be." Annie spoke to her glass more than to Pearl.

Her words hit a nerve. "You know, I spent my whole life thinking I was alone in this world, but it turns out that wasn't true. What do you have to say about that?"

Annie stiffened and looked hard. "Some things are better left alone, if you catch my drift. So let me put you straight on one count. Claire had to clear out of Denver. She went up to the mountains, and I'll be damned if those same mountains didn't chew her up and spit her back out. She caught something up in Leadville and died. That's all you need to know."

Pearl studied her aunt, distrust creeping in. "Were you the one who sent her away?"

Annie's eyes narrowed further. "So, what of it? She was attracting too many fines for being drunk and disorderly."

Pearl mulled that over. A lot of whores drank. "She probably ended up freezing to death."

"Screw that. She probably died of a bad dose of regret and a case of the clap," Annie said, tugging on her too-small bodice and stuffing down her bosom, which fought its way back up. She gave up and pointed her forefinger at Pearl. "I sure hope you have more sense than she did."

Annie took another swig of booze, and started fiddling with something under her skirt, adjusting her stockings. Pearl watched with distaste. "Do all the girls start off with the glasses and the numbers?"

Annie stopped whatever it was that she was doing. "I'm giving you a choice. I'm not pushing you into anything."

Pearl wasn't so certain. Annie had probably pushed her mother into something she shouldn't have.

"Seeing as how you've always been in charge," Pearl began, "I've been told I'm too pretty to be wasted upon washing glasses."

The challenge hung in the air. Pearl checked the looking glass behind the bottles. It was true, she believed. She actually might be something special.

"Maybe," Annie replied, sobering a degree. "I always said we could use another girl. Hooking is wearing on my bones."

Pearl kept her face expressionless. The truth was, fellows kept asking if someone younger was available. "May said all it takes is lying still."

"Well, maybe that's why she don't have too many repeat customers. Lay still my ass. It ain't a bloody game of possum." Annie sighed, took a slug of whiskey. "Do you know what brides do?"

"No. Do you?" Pearl doubted she had ever been one.

Annie cackled. "Not real ones, you pumpkin. You know about how a man puts his peter in the hole you pee out of, right?

That's where babies come from and money is made."

That was news to Pearl. Unpleasant and shocking news.

She recalled the morning she had walked in on May and the jake. But they all seemed to do it—and like it, even.

Julia said that was on account of them getting paid.

It didn't take all that long for Pearl to reach the pivotal conclusion that she was destined to become a whore. Besides being a family trait, common knowledge had it painted as the fastest and easiest way to get money. It wasn't that she was afraid of hard work—it's just that she seemed to be the only one doing it. It got under her skin to watch Julia and May get new dresses, and to sit around laughing and flirting while she suffered through washing the glasses and emptying overflowing spittoons.

And she was prettier than either of her cousins. Everyone said as much.

Her mother had been a whore, and she would be a whore. That was all there was to it, in Pearl's mind. It galled Pearl that she still owed Annie money for her yellow dress, the one she had assumed had been a gift. But she had been mistaken on that count, too. Pearl's first payday had been a bitter disappointment. Ten cents an hour was what she was owed. What she was paid was nothing.

"Well, Pearl," Annie had exclaimed with a faint twinkle, "you want to be a self-supporting young woman, don't you? I loaned you the money for that dress . . . with minimal interest. I don't buy your cousins' clothes, either."

Pearl had gasped. Her aunt had bought her a work skirt and a blouse as well. "How much money do I owe?"

Annie looked at her ledger. "Well, let's see. Fifteen dollars for the yellow dress, three dollars for the blouse, five dollars for the skirt, and two dollars for stockings. Altogether, that makes twenty-five dollars. With interest added, that becomes twenty-seven dollars and fifty cents. Your wages of thirty-five hours at ten cents an hour brings you to three dollars and fifty cents. That brings you down to twenty four dollars, plus interest of another two dollars and forty cents, which now totals twenty-six forty. See?"

Pearl saw—a little bit too well. And she knew better than to argue.

Annie glanced at her worn shoes. "And I'll bet you wanted to use your money to replace those."

Pearl nodded, not trusting herself to speak for fear she might cry.

"Well," said Annie, all chipper, "there's no need for you to go without. Just go to Fisher Daniels and have them send the charges here. And I'll add it back to your total."

Pearl felt upset, but new shoes would help.

Annie watched her for a moment. "Cheer up, duckie. The good news is that all of this money belongs to the family, and I'm just managing it for the time being. Now doesn't that make you feel better?"

Pearl nodded out of habit. While she had heard it was best to keep money within the family, she couldn't see what it got her at all. Nothing, or next thing to it.

She decided that had to change. One way or another.

# CHAPTER 12
## VALUATIONS OF FEMALE FLESH

The girls were all just commodities. Annie tolerated Pearl's presence, but she didn't exactly warm toward her. And the cousins were always working or sleeping, and had little time to spend with Pearl. Even if they had been so inclined. Which they weren't.

Pearl felt lonelier, in some ways, than she ever had at the home. At least there she had a friend named Lizzie for a while. But Lizzie's grandparents had come to get her one day. Pearl felt hard done by; even her cousins had each other when they were at the Good Shepherd. It was a pity no one had known or explained the family connection. Not that it would have mattered to them, but it would have mattered to her.

And it was true, Annie didn't really warm toward anyone—not even her own daughters. She sure wasn't like any imagined mother, and she never cared if anyone's feelings got hurt.

"Buck up," Annie would say. "A fast life beats a boring life any day of the year."

Hired out like horses, every pound of female flesh was assigned a value by Annie. Assessments, bartering, and money changing hands were symbols that defined their value. It was as simple as that, and as cold.

Pearl didn't know if she was living a fast life or not, but she knew she wasn't getting what she wanted. If she were honest, she was beginning to suspect her mother might have done the same as Annie, and been the same way. She might have been the one to press Pearl into the trade. Had she lived.

Had she *cared* one way or another.

Pearl would never know the truth on that count, but she was fairly certain she was wasting time, mucking about with the glasses and the numbers. She could be dressing a whole lot better if she just got on with it.

Men tried to get her to go with them and told her she was pretty—but she pulled away from their grasps. She acted like their clutching and pawing was all just a game. Pearl knew the jakes weren't all that choosy about girls when it came right down to it. When booze and baser nature took hold.

And a pretty face only had so many good years, or so Annie said. Maybe that was just another half-truth, the kind she specialized in just to keep everyone off balance. On edge. Pearl reckoned she could use the jakes just as much as they wanted to use her.

And maybe, just maybe, someone would fall in love and rescue her.

She was building up steam for her argument—to tell Annie her thoughts, as she set out upon her mid-morning glass and bottle collection rounds. She saved Annie's office for last, noting the door was opened a crack.

She cleared her throat as deferentially as she could manage.

Annie looked up. "Come in. It's not like you haven't been in here before."

"I didn't want to disturb you," Pearl replied, setting the crate of bottles down.

Annie didn't look convinced. "That would be a first. No one gives a rat's ass about disturbing me usually."

Annie had piles of money arranged in stacks on the desk in front of her. She was counting it out, and tallying amounts in her ledger. She caught Pearl looking at the bills and coins. "The wages of sin sure looks pretty good, doesn't it?"

"It would, if any of it was mine."

Annie eyed her, sharp. "Strong words from someone who's never been around the block. But hold that thought; I just need to finish this up before Lydia arrives for the rent."

"She looks out of place down here." Her very expensive dresses made from fine materials and cut to perfection stood out beyond a doubt. Whatever the cost, she sure looked nice. Envy was a sin, according to the nuns—but that seemed a bit overblown.

Annie shrugged. "It doesn't concern you, or me, for that matter."

Pearl found an abandoned bottle on the windowsill behind Annie's desk chair. There was a trace of whiskey left at the bottom, and Pearl held it up for inspection. "I don't know about that family fortune you keep talking about, but we sure have booze."

Annie stopped counting and tallying totals and considered Pearl over the rims of her glasses. "Booze isn't free, and money is tied up all around you."

"Well, I was hoping to become a full-fledged member of this establishment. Ten cents an hour isn't enough. Maybe *the Boyos* would pay me more."

"Leave them out of it. Nothing good comes from how they treat their women. And for that matter, no one's stopping you from earning more money here." Annie's voice held a note of caution. "But I'm not sure you have what it takes."

That got Pearl's gall. She had learned more in a couple of months about drunks, anatomy, prostitution, venereal diseases, bunko artists, gambling, stealing, and plain bad behavior than she had a right. "But this is all still second-rate, isn't it?"

Annie took off her glasses. "Second-rate my ass. And what would you know about that anyhow—have you been sneaking around to the other houses?"

Pearl had struck a nerve she hadn't intended, but there she found the hint of possibility. "I see how people look at me on Market, including the procuring women."

"Maybe you are getting yourself into mischief, just like your damn mother."

"It's a sin to speak ill of the dead." Pearl wondered if she were setting her sights too low. One of those fancier houses would be an improvement.

"That's a load of bosh. Didn't the nuns tell you it's a sin to lie?"

Pearl tossed the bottle into the crate she carried. It clanked hard. Almost broke. "Details seem to be a sore point in this family, but you've been a sporting woman since you were my age. And I know what a screw is now *because I asked*. My mother was doing the same, and she was your younger sister. And being as how she *was* your younger sister, no doubt you looked out for her. Isn't that so?"

Annie studied the rings on her fingers. "What are you driving at?"

Pearl attempted to look innocent. "Since we all share the same blood, I might as well earn decent wages. It's not like I exactly have someplace else to go—but I can find one. You promised to tell me about my mother, but you don't. You just skirt around the story. Someday soon I might reach the conclusion that you are leading me on a right old dance."

Annie sighed. "Everything with you is like beating a dead horse. Your mother drank. She took to the dope. When she got pregnant with you and started to show, she couldn't hook no more. We stuck her behind the bar, but that turned out to be a bad idea. We'd all try to keep her indoors when she got drunk, but she kept sneaking out and getting arrested. Satisfied? And if you're not, that's too damn bad, because I've got work to do. You do, too."

Pearl didn't budge. "You need a new girl. That is what everyone is saying."

"And they're probably right," Annie replied. "But I think you would get all weepy if you knew what was really involved."

Another insult. "I don't think I would."

"Then there's your attitude. You seem to have some pretty high and mighty opinions for a potential whore. Not even a real one. Your mother was that way, too, but it got her in the end."

Instead of changing her mind, Pearl was getting mad. "If Julia and May can do it, so can I. Easy money is easy money, and I am sick to death of the glasses. I thought you might be pleased."

Annie still had that calculating look about her. "The last thing I want is word getting out that I had anything to do with this."

Pearl shrugged, annoyed. "It's not like anyone is going to come and put me back in the Good Shepherd."

Annie's eyes narrowed. "Well, if they did, you'd be stuck doing the laundry this time around."

Pearl had seen some of those washerwomen. "And what about your own girls? Didn't you worry about what people said about you then?"

This time, Annie looked a trifle bothered. "Not that it's any of your goddamned business, but when I took them out of the home, we went directly up to the mountains. When word got out, even there as hard up as the miners were, it didn't set too well. Comments were made, but let's leave it at that."

Pearl could imagine. "Did you *have* to put May and Julia in the Good Shepherd in the first place?"

Annie sat, unmoved. "No. I got ambushed by a bunch of busybodies. And I was too drunk at the time to put up much of a fight. But it was all for the best and got you girls a decent education. Now, I'm paying you to work, not to bother me."

She turned her attention back to her papers and figures.

"But you left them in there a good long while."

Annie looked at her. "So I did. For their own good."

*No,* Pearl thought, *it was a convenience.* "Well, do I work for you as a whore or do I try one of those other houses? One of the fancy ones."

Her aunt inclined her head, recognition flashing in her face. "You know, Pearl, you can be the very Devil incarnate. Have it your way. If it's spread legs and money you want, I'll send you up to Leadville to get started with a clean slate. And before you ask, yes, your mother worked there, too. And don't you set off pestering Sadie about Claire, or she'll toss you out on your ear. I wouldn't blame her, either. We all have businesses to run, and don't have time to go chasing after damned ghosts."

And that was how Pearl got what she thought she wanted—along with the chance at better money.

# CHAPTER 13
## STATE STREET SIRENS

As the train to Leadville slowed to the point where she wouldn't get pelted by cinders, Pearl opened the window a notch and sniffed. The air smelled of dust and metal. The sounds of machinery carried and ricocheted over the noise of the train. The mountains around Leadville certainly looked and sounded active: mines, smelters, and stamping mills, all producing and spewing forth tons of dirt, pulverized ore, and tainted water. Dark plumes of smoke belched in the air, corrupting the breeze with an incense of burning wood, hot metal, and coal.

The man who had shared the train compartment watched her. "Smell that? That's the smell of money being made."

"I hope you're right." Pearl considered the mountains and felt small. Insignificant, even.

He didn't respond, but gave her a knowing look. One that conveyed he knew she was on the mash.

There sure were a lot of men of all shapes and sizes. For the most part, dirty.

Ore carts dumped raw minerals and rock into chutes that thundered along and spat from the thrumming mills, heading downhill. Machinery clanked and groaned—the effluvium from the mining and the ore processing stank. Pulleys winching metal ropes were bolted to the headboards, and heaved up iron cages of men and ore. Blasts detonated, whistles shrilled: the roar of machinery constant. And men. Men everywhere. Leadville was teeming with men.

A lot of men working meant a lot of money changing hands. While Pearl didn't know the first thing about mines or mining, she didn't care. She had seen enough to know the score.

When the train came to a full stop, the man tipped his hat in her general direction. She got off the train, and . . . waited. Other passengers disembarked and left her standing. Incensed, and then growing doubtful, her attention turned to a slouching man standing to the side of the platform.

Pearl waited, alone with her valise. Yet the man stood there for another extra moment, watching her like a hunter. She fidgeted with her hat, adjusted her sleeves. Every time she glanced in his direction he continued staring. She decided she could find Sadie Doyle's on her own. She picked up her valise and moved toward the depot.

The man called out. "You a chippie?"

Humiliated, Pearl turned toward him just as he spat a streak of tobacco.

"Not as far as you're concerned." Pearl hoped he noticed her disdain.

"That would be a yes. I've been hired to deliver you to Sadie's house." He motioned to a splattered, muddy buckboard downhill—started walking in that direction without any offer to carry her bag. Neither did he offer his hand to board and left her to fling her valise over the side of the wagon. She glared at him as she hauled herself onto the wooden seat. Rough and uncouth, he made her feel cheap.

A long five minutes later, the wagon pulled up in front of a building on a raucous intersection. Commanding a prominent corner, it didn't advertise, but everyone seemed to know what it was.

"Me, I don't hold with whores," the man said, "but there you go."

Annoyed, Pearl climbed down, careful to protect her skirts

against catching on the wagon and tearing. "I won't be seeing you again, then."

The building still looked to be a step or two up from Annie's.

The man drove off without a backwards glance. Pearl would have felt better if he had bothered to stare at her figure, or throw a proposition her way.

He was probably some type of zealot, anyhow.

The sound of music drifted into the street, nice and jaunty. Drawn in by the tune, she followed it through the front door of the saloon. An old colored fellow was playing the piano: another improvement over Annie's. Music cost money. Any establishment providing music in the quiet hours was doing well indeed. The walls were finished, and painted a soft blue. *Efforts* had been *made*. Emptier than in Ryan's in Denver; the front room had the usual card game in the corner and a couple of drunks propping up the bar.

The same male smell of spilled liquor and stale smoke, but with the addition of iron ore and machine oil.

A woman with tight, curly blond hair was standing behind the bar, counting the bottles of liquor. She caught Pearl's reflection in the mirror and turned.

"You must be Annie's Pearl. She said you were a looker!"

That surprised her. "She tells me I'm scrawny."

Sadie's eyes twinkled, not altogether kindly. She came around from behind the bar. "That Annie was a big lump of a girl, and I'm sure time hasn't whittled her down any."

Pearl guessed she should try to defend Annie. "She always says men like something to grab hold of."

"Of course she does. The timing of your arrival is good—we lost a girl yesterday. According to Annie, you're as pure as the driven snow. That right?"

The madam didn't bother to lower her voice one bit.

Hussies were hardened to such exchanges, so Pearl did her

best to appear unconcerned. "I suppose that's right."

"You suppose!" Sadie's eyes narrowed a bit. "Do you mean to tell me that she sold me old rope?"

Pearl could have sworn the volume of the music died down, and that everyone in the saloon was listening to their exchange. "I haven't been with anyone, but I'm not as green as people would like to think."

Sadie smothered a laugh, patted her bosom. "Groping men and letting them touch you doesn't count. Don't try to be making out that you're something you're not."

Pearl shrugged. "Annie said this was a better place to start out, than in Denver."

Sadie didn't appear flattered. "Maybe. It is a straighter business up here than in Denver, I'll grant you that much. Take a seat, and we'll go over a few things."

She motioned for Pearl to sit down at one of the empty tables, and brought over a bottle of whiskey and two glasses. Pouring out two substantial measures, she lifted her glass in a toast. Pearl saluted, tossed the vile liquid back and choked. Damn.

"Drink a lot?" Sadie asked.

"All the time," Pearl gasped in between coughs.

Sadie's eyes twinkled, and she shook her head. "Is that a fact? Doesn't seem like it. Just as well. I don't want you drinking on the job."

Sadie appraised her the same way Annie did. "You are about to cross the point of no return; make no mistake about it. If this is your way of finding a husband, you are on the wrong track. I want to be clear on that count. For all your nice speech, you might have some notions."

And so she did. Julia had claimed many marriage proposals, and Pearl wanted the same. Maybe her cousin was a liar, because Sadie seemed quite firm on the matter.

Sadie sized her up. "Now, I can be your best friend or your

worst enemy. But let us both be clear: this is a business arrangement. And I won't broker or tolerate any stealing, and there will be no holding out on me. Any tips you earn are half the house's. You get examined by the doctor monthly, whether you feel like it or not."

"I understand." Pearl wasn't a complete babe, as this woman seemed to think.

"Good. I'll set you up with one of the girls to show you some of the tricks, and how this all is run. For the time being, while you're young and fresh, you're *It*. But you'll be replaced by another new, fresh face once the next season comes around. It's best to keep that in mind, when dealing with the others."

Pearl disagreed, planning to shine through more than one season. And maybe all that shining would manage to procure someone who would actually love her. Sadie kept rattling on, unaware of any turmoil she was causing in Pearl's head. "Now, there are two ways to go about joining the club. The modern way or the old-fashioned way. Take your pick."

Finally, Pearl recognized a choice. "Which pays more?"

Surprised, Sadie swore under her breath, but nodded encouragement. "Good girl. But that was a trick question. It's always been the same with us. There is no modern way. Just hoick up your skirts and give them a smile."

There hadn't been much hoicking and smiling at Annie's, but maybe that was because they didn't know any better.

Sadie deflated a bit. "It's all about money. I've had enough of broken hearts this week to last me a year. Now, we're going to put you up in a discreet auction. And we will split the proceeds, fifty-fifty. How does that suit you?"

Pearl, feeling out of place, had never discussed finances with Annie: exact figures or the details of cuts and shares. "Is that the usual arrangement?"

"It is. And you owe me for a month's rent—normally paid in

advance. But seeing as how this is your first time out, I'll take it from the money you make. That means when payday comes around, you will be paying for this month and next month. Understand?"

Sadie's blue eyes turned kind of icy at the mention of money and business terms. "Furthermore, the wages you earn are confidential. Do you know what that means? Bragging about your rate leads to all kinds of unpleasantness—a fair amount of it coming from me."

Sadie's terms appeared hard, and the conditions strange. But, there was something in the madam's manner that didn't brook any negotiation.

Pearl looked down at her new travelling suit. She owed Annie for that as well.

# CHAPTER 14
# YOU CAN ONLY SELL YOUR VIRGINITY ONCE, CAN'T YOU?

Pearl was assigned to a miserable girl named Louisie to learn the tricks of whoring. Neither was happy about the arrangement. Louisie was a couple of years older, and didn't look any too friendly.

"Pearl doesn't know much," Sadie began. "But I don't want any funny business going on, ruining the deal. This will be her first time; let her know the rules and what to expect. No one touches her goods. Give her Pink's old room. Oh, and Pearl? Make sure you mind your belongings. Some people have itchy fingers."

"No shit," Louisie said. "Itchy other things, too. That cow Della has a pair of my stockings, and she won't give them back." She eyeballed Pearl, put out. "Come on," she said, and then mumbled something under her breath that didn't sound too complimentary.

Upstairs, Louisie pushed Pearl into a room furnished with a bed, an iron headboard, a washstand, and a battered chest of drawers. At least there was a mirror.

"It's fine." The room was much the same as at Annie's, although the mirror was nicer.

"La di dah and I don't care if it ain't," Louisie responded. "And I'll be damned if I'm going to be worried about what you do or don't do. You ain't got nothing that the rest of us don't."

Louisie had seen better days. She looked like she had been

ridden hard and hung up wet, as the saying went. Pearl considered making a face at her, but changed her mind. Louisie looked like the brawling type.

"I never said I did." Truth be told, Pearl felt far superior to the other girl.

That mollified Louisie a little, but she still took Pearl's measure up and down. "You know about stripping, don't you?"

Pearl shook her head.

Louisie smirked. "I'll leave it to you to use your imagination."

"You're supposed to be telling me. You're the one who's been around."

Louisie took it wrong, put her hands on her hips. "And that's another thing, Miss Fancy-pants. Quit your eyeing me. When it comes right down to the nekked truth, we're all the same if you get my drift. Just another hole, provided you ain't deformed or something."

"I'm not deformed . . ."

Louisie turned to leave. "You know that for a fact? Has the doctor even looked at you? 'Cause we know sure as hell no one's touched you. As far as I know, there's a reason for that. Something un-nat-u-ral."

Pearl watched her retreating backside. Her ass belonged on a horse, and Pearl shut the door hard, but not fast enough to avoid the nasty gesture Louisie made as she walked away down the hall.

Word travelled fast in whorehouses, especially if it involved quarrels. Sadie's house proved to be no different.

It wasn't long before Sadie sent for Pearl. "How you getting on with Louisie?"

Pearl shrugged. "Fine, pretty much."

"That a fact? She don't like you. But she's gone over things with you, right? What has she told you about?"

"Stripping. And the fact that she's jealous."

"I'd go easy on that kind of talk. Your popularity is going to depend on you and the prices you command. You can only sell your virginity once, unless you got a real sucker hooked."

That was an odd notion. "How do you figure?"

"Why, the blood! Don't worry so much. Relax and take some laudanum. It'll go just fine."

None of it sounded too nice. "Annie told me to stay away from the dope."

Sadie shrugged. "Tomorrow night is a special occasion. She wouldn't do it any different if she were handling this shindig herself."

There was little sense in arguing when she hadn't the slightest clue. "How much money are we getting?"

Sadie rubbed her hands together. "Sixty-five dollars! He's coming up from Fairplay and has a reputation to maintain. He might give you some extra, too, *if* he's pleased. Remember, fifty percent of that is mine."

Pearl smiled, thinking she would have to be stupid to agree to something like that.

Sadie gave her the once-over. "And remember, try to look like you like whatever it is that he does to you: that you're goddamned happy about the whole shootin' match."

And Pearl was pretty goddamned happy when she thought about the thirty-two dollars and fifty cents.


"Oh, for fuck's sake." Sadie's eyes bugged out when she told her.

Pearl was none too happy herself. Her only real option was to stand in front of Sadie and wait for the storm to pass.

A pudgy finger was pointed in her face. "And don't go spreading this around. We never disclose our customer's business, and he paid."

The jake also gave Pearl a five-dollar tip for doing nothing, but she didn't tell Sadie that part.

Sadie alternated between staring at her, and looking over her shoulder at the crowd of men in the saloon. "You've got more men lining up for tonight. What the hell was the problem?"

Pearl swallowed. "He just cried. He held me and cried for his wife who died last year. I offered to strip for him, which was fine, but that was it."

Sadie shook her head, mollified a bit. "That's still a problem. You've learned one important lesson. No one knows what a man's going to do until that bedroom door is closed. That's for damn sure."

Pearl felt she had to come up with something that might improve the bad situation. "Maybe we could try it again and get another sixty-five dollars—"

"Hell, no! Word will get out and people will think something's wrong."

Pearl recalled Louisie's accusation and started getting vexed. "There's nothing wrong with me."

Sadie was in no mood to spar. "Prove it."

Tears welled up. Pearl had no idea what to do. Sadie relented a bit.

"All right, no need to get yourself in a state. Now, not a word to anyone. I'll go get a jake to get the job done. Go back to your room, and wait there."

Sadie arrived in less than five minutes with a card sharp. He was clean, and his hands were nice, but Pearl didn't like his smug manner. The man eyed her in a dirty way.

"How long do I have with her?"

"Fifteen minutes," Sadie said, and didn't stick around.

★  ★  ★  ★  ★

It wasn't easy. The card sharp stuck his tongue down her throat, which was about the most disgusting thing that had ever happened to Pearl. He grabbed her breasts and slobbered on them. Then he pushed her back onto the bed, and left his long johns on when he took her.

And it hurt—laudanum or no laudanum.

Ten minutes later, the deed was done. She knew now what happened behind closed doors. She had become a bought-and-paid-for woman. She didn't feel as good about it as she had expected.

She thought about her first jake, the gentle one who had cried for his dead wife. He had spent all that money just to hold her and cry. Maybe that was how real love was supposed to be.

Pearl wondered if anyone would ever love her like that. And in the pit of her stomach, where it was uncomfortable, she already knew the real answer.

# CHAPTER 15
## SLUMMING ISN'T ALL IT'S CRACKED UP TO BE

Lydia started wondering about herself, and this adventure called Denver. Once she had abhorred prostitutes; now she viewed their *occupation* a bit differently. At least where the prostitutes were concerned, the bartering of their bodies was almost honest, if somewhat unpalatable. There was no getting around the fact that the Market Street building was her most interesting transaction to date. It was also conveniently located to Hop Alley. Now there was a surface she didn't mind looking under. But she bided her time. She didn't know if the operators or their dope were trustworthy. She didn't need her name dragged through the mud by strangers.

She had Stanley for that.

Stanley was a necessary liability—for the time being. He didn't work. Oh, he kept his office all right, which was just another expense for Lydia to pick up. In Denver, a man had to have a designated place of business. Worse, Stanley wanted to be kept in the style to which he had grown accustomed, which rubbed Lydia mighty sore. But her real-estate deals kept coming in. It was a good thing some men liked the novelty of doing business with a woman. But she always had to prove herself—to demonstrate that she was sharp and could do math. All that sharpness and calculating wore a bit thin after a while.

The fact that she could out-think a lot of the men raised Lydia's spirits a bit. "Let them put that in their pipes and smoke it," she would say aloud, and sally forth to size up another prospect. It wasn't her fault if they couldn't do sums and percentages.

But when things got her down, which happened more and more often, she would give Stanley fifty dollars to make sure he stayed away from the house for a couple of nights. She didn't care where he went, or what he got up to. As long as he stayed away from her, as long as he left her alone. She would take that purchased solitude and drift. Drift under her laudanum haze and dream of images that evaporated when the charm wore off. She had heard opium was even better.

The laudanum rendered her a bit unaccountable. Her male customers assumed her absences and omissions were caused by feminine complaints. She found that a trifle amusing, how little they understood. But it served her purposes just fine. And when the fog lifted, she would take a bath, dress in well-cut clothes, and make the rounds. Someone always had a transaction they wanted handled.

And Lydia was very good at keeping secrets.

These days, her absences were becoming more frequent. Her curiosity about the opium was growing stronger. Those "things that got her down" were really mere excuses. She knew that. She knew she ought to stop. But she didn't.

Maybe she would pay Annie Ryan a visit, to see what she knew. Lucid or floating, the bottom line on Market Street was usually quite attractive for investment return. A lot of cash changed hands down there. And that Annie was a sharp one— never late on a payment, never short on the amount. Maybe there were some additional places for sale with a discreet word. It didn't escape Lydia's notice that once she reconciled herself to the rather surprising fact of owning a brothel, any scruples she had on that matter fell by the wayside. After all, prominent men had been doing the same for centuries. And like those prominent men, she viewed the profession in the same way—

with a glimmer of added allure.

None of them wanted their names associated with such sordid dealings. But that didn't mean they shunned all the wares.

The proclivity of men was always explained in terms of wild-oat sowing. No one seemed, at least in public, to worry about whom they were sowing those with. Lydia reasoned that her wild oats left her person intact. But going to an opium den introduced a stronger element of danger into her life. Maybe that was part of the allure. The other was a growing dependency.

She wasn't a fool, and figured she could control her appetites the same way she controlled her business dealings. It was no one else's damned business.

Thinking of oats, she turned her buggy down Larimer Street, passing the varied gaming hells and saloons. There was the odd mercantile and greengrocer; how boring and mundane they were in the lawless town. The blood in her veins seemed to flow a bit faster as she neared the notorious alley populated by the Celestials. She slowed and peered down into the cranny known as Hop Alley. It communicated a foreign aspect to Denver; those with a more poetic bent might call it exotic or perverse. The laundries and dry-goods emporiums pressed in, blocking the wind and fresh air. The sweet, pungent smell of opium smoke wafted through doors as they opened and closed against the frontier town.

Lydia inhaled deeply, and felt a bit better.

The pleasant smell of opium was tainted by other, rank smells. The cloying odor of slaughtered poultry carcasses dangling from hooks corrupted any fresh air to be had. The bitter, strange Chinese herbs and spices scented the breeze, mingling with everything else. Hop Alley managed, as far as possible, to smell old, stale, and otherworldly.

Lydia decided to leave her horses and buggy on Larimer.

On foot she entered the tight, narrow passageway that all but shut out the sun. With interest, she watched a white man in a suit descend into a subterranean entrance. She masked her curiosity by pretending fascination with the area, until she drew level with those stairs. There was no sign on the door. Lydia looked around surreptitiously, then slipped down the stairs and knocked. The door was opened by a Chinese man with long fingernails. Repulsive.

"I must have the wrong address," she said, wondering if he spoke English.

"Perhaps," he replied, and moved aside ever so slightly, indicating that he would not block her passage. Beyond him the darkened interior was lit with small lamps radiating scant light, which only lengthened the shadows. But the scent of the opium that floated out was enticing, and boasted of intoxication of the very best sort. She hesitated before turning away.

The man quietly shut the door, but not without first looking into her eyes. Recognizing what she truly wanted.

Uncertain, Lydia knew the time was coming. For the moment, she felt satisfied, even relieved. But that satisfaction would pass.

# CHAPTER 16
# MEN WHO DON'T WANT TO PAY
# AUGUST 1892

Pearl became adept at entertaining customers, but the term "servicing" hit closer to the mark. There was very little laughter, and a whole lot of grunting. And it often hurt. There was no getting around the fact that she felt sore and didn't know what to say to the jakes. Almost worse, they seemed to find that appealing. But they coughed. A lot of the jakes coughed and spat. That part was different than in Denver, but no one in Leadville seemed to take notice—other than Pearl. Even if a man almost turned blue, coughing and gasping to get air into his lungs, the others carried on like nothing was happening.

Then again, they probably coughed, too.

"Is everyone sick?" Pearl asked Louisie.

The other whore shrugged. "Hard to say. They say it's the dust from the mining that settles into their lungs and chokes them. Whiskey works. For a while."

Whiskey was good for a lot of things, including numbing the senses to all kinds of physical experiences. While she wasn't supposed to drink on the job, Pearl did. She saw little reason not to.

Sadie's was one of the few houses that didn't sell watered-down drinks, or at least that's what Sadie claimed. And there was a whole routine that went along with the girls pretending to drink, or not. As the case might be. They were supposed to dump real booze in the spittoons if no one was looking. Failing that, a girl might sip it in a lady-like fashion. Pearl chose the sipping method and forgot about the others.

Almost one month in, nothing felt new.

It was as if Pearl had never been anyone else, anywhere else.

One Thursday afternoon, Pearl was the first of the working girls up and prowling. The saloon was populated with a bunch of no-accounts yucking it up. A blond fellow nodded at Pearl, but she noticed his dirty fingernails and walked on. She sat down at a vacant table, bored.

"Care for a drink?" Of course, it was a man's voice and Pearl was supposed to be enthusiastic.

Pearl glanced up. "Care for a screw?"

He was young, and blushed. "Kind of blunt, aren't you?"

She smiled at him, wiggled her foot in a suggestive manner, making sure to show a lot of leg attached to a tiny foot joined by a well-turned ankle. "Saves time. And I'll have a whiskey."

The fellow came back holding two glasses. Although missing part of two fingers he managed not to spill. He caught her expression as he sat down, self-conscious.

The professor started playing a spiritual on the piano, easing into the day.

"My name's Franklin, but people call me Frank. I've heard you were pretty, Pearl. And so you are."

Pearl smiled, checking the skin at the side of his neck, and around the back as far as she could see without attracting atten-tion. Passably clean, almost handsome. And close to her age. "What happened to your fingers, Frank?"

He shrugged, tugged at his collar. "Oh, that was last year. They've healed all right. Giant powder went off before it was supposed to."

Pearl nodded as if she understood what he was talking about. A lot of the jakes were mangled in one way or another. "Do you have a girl, Frank?"

He met her eyes with candor. "No. If I did, I wouldn't be in here talking to you. No offense."

Pearl tried not to flinch, but it was hard. "Maybe you would, maybe you wouldn't."

It was strange, but she wanted him to like her. Nice girls were in short supply in Leadville. Well, as far as she knew. She spent a fair amount of time wondering what it would be like to have a decent young fellow sweet on her. The longing kept pulling at her, but so did Sadie. The hard fact was that she was signaling to Pearl.

Ten dollars.

Pearl caught the tail end of what he was saying. ". . . the mine yesterday. A damn rock missed my head by inches; hit the guy drilling behind me. The foreman told me to take the rest of the week off, and not to come back until I had spent all my money. He said that cures damn near everything."

Sounded promising, the money part. "Spending money always makes me feel better," she purred, and tugged her bodice just a little bit lower to reveal more cleavage.

The fellow might have been rattled about the explosion, but his eyes sure lingered at Pearl's bust. "It killed him, but he took hours to die. At least we got him up to the surface."

Many things in life were dangerous and unpredictable. She noticed he had a small scar that ran along his cheek and set off his cheekbones to advantage.

"Best listen to that foreman of yours. My rate is ten dollars." Pearl finished her drink.

That drew him back. "Ten dollars? But I only have two and some change left. Honest—look." He laid out an assortment of coins on the table.

Pearl made no move toward the money, but scanned the room to see who might notice. Sadie was in the back.

It felt important that he understood she was worth more

than she charged. She leaned toward him, closer than she needed to, and whispered in his ear. "Men have to pay Sadie to go upstairs, so don't give me the money here. I'll go upstairs first; you follow in five minutes. Whatever you do, make it look like you're leaving. My name is on my door. And if I come back in and start hustling, we'll have to try some other time. When you have more money."

He picked up the change and dropped it back in his pants pocket, delighted as he finished his drink.

Pearl went in search of Sadie. "My stomach's bad all of a sudden."

"The bog's in the back."

"I'm going upstairs. I don't need assholes pounding on the damn door."

"This ain't a ladies' sanitarium." Sadie looked unconvinced. "And make sure you air everything out. I don't want to hear people complaining that it smells like shite in here."

Pretending her stomach was paining her something terrible, Pearl went back through the saloon, winked at Frank, and bounced upstairs to where the bedrooms were. She never saw Sadie watching her climb the stairs.

Frank sat with his empty glass, biding time as Sadie positioned herself behind the bar. He made a show of leaving as a poker game took a quarrelsome turn, distracting Sadie as he slipped back up the stairs.

He tapped on Pearl's door. She answered in silence, scanned the hallway and staircase before pulling him into the room. "Now, give me the money, and I'll give you a good time." Pearl twirled the hem of her dress, all coquettish.

And with a grin, he gave her all two dollars and forty-two cents.

Still, as far as Pearl was concerned, he was sweet and didn't grab or paw at her in anything other than what she considered a good way.

They arranged to meet the following Saturday, after he'd been paid.

Pearl felt sparky; thrilled that she might have an honest-to-goodness beau. Obviously, Sadie had been wrong.

# Chapter 17
## Graft, Liquor Licenses, and Miscellaneous Payments
### (Why being a landlady wasn't all it was cracked up to be)

A new lunk in a uniform came stomping into the saloon. Annie wasn't impressed, although she prepared to listen to whatever shit he was selling. It was best to pay attention when the law was being laid down. Then she could figure out the easiest way around it.

The cop hitched his pants upward as he bellied toward the bar. "Sorensen got reassigned. I'm in charge now. My name is Casey Harrigan, and I will be watching things. Closely."

Annie laughed—clearly a reaction he wasn't expecting, to judge from his expression. "Watching things do what? Sorensen watched the girls; that fella had a weakness for the ladies, no mistake. Want a beer?"

"I drink whiskey." Harrigan stiffened in a way that sure made it look like he had a chip on his shoulder.

Annie doubted he could tell the difference between cheap and expensive, so she poured him out a glass of the cheap. She poured out a measure for herself as well. Different bottle, of course. "To beneficial arrangements."

They raised glasses and locked eyes. Annie was certain there would be no love lost between them, but she didn't care. He didn't appear to, either.

"How long have you been out here?" Annie sized him up: a lot of bluster and ambition. A bad combination, without question.

Irritation crept into his voice. "I've been here long enough."

She doubted it. "Well, then. Let's get down to the brass tacks. I pay my licenses, and I pay them on time. Not early and not late. No doubt you've come to tell me that I need to pay you as well, for whatever supposed protection you're offering. Which I can stomach, as long as I get something for it. My family has been in Denver since it was worth mentioning, and maybe even slightly before. We know people, and can and will press influence for suitable outcomes. Do we understand each other?"

Harrigan stood up a bit straighter, sucked in his gut a fraction. "We do. As long as you understand that I don't tolerate any sass. The money you give me pays for your security. Sure looks like you could use it. And I'll be around plenty. I kind of like the looks of your place here."

"Bully for me," Annie swore under her breath, just loud enough so he could hear. She wanted to see what he would do.

He did nothing. Other than pretend that he didn't hear her.

She found a brown envelope and nub of a pencil, and wrote *Police—Harrigan* on it. Turning her attention out the window, she made a show of gathering her thoughts.

She waited until he relaxed a mite, then looked at him straight. "There are a couple of rules: my house, my rules. First, girls' favors might be discounted, but they do not come free. Second, you don't get drunk in here, although you can drink. And third, you will leave the punters alone, unless I tell you otherwise. Are we clear?"

Harrigan regarded her with wariness, like he might a rattlesnake ready to strike. "I'd say we understand each other just fine."

Annie figured there wasn't all that much to Harrigan that required thought on her part. But there was something kind of creepy about him. Something off. She scolded herself, thinking she was probably giving him too much credit. It was just that she hadn't slept well enough the night before.

She had more pressing problems than a beat cop on the take.

She'd paid Sorensen twenty-five dollars a month. "So, what's the fee? I presume the same amount as Sorrie got."

His eyes narrowed a bit. Annie could see he didn't know what Sorensen charged or how he had reckoned the sum.

"Fifty dollars," Harrigan replied.

Annie let loose with a belt of laughter. "Saints preserve us all! What a notion. I'll pay you twenty, and not a dollar more."

After haggling a bit, they settled on twenty-two dollars and fifty cents, which put Annie in a better frame of mind as he left the premises. "He'll be easy to manage," she said to herself, two dollars and fifty cents a month to the good.

But Ryan's still wasn't really pulling in the money she had hoped for when she started up. She ticked through the list in her mind: the rent, the loan from her brothers God-help-her, Michael's wages, fines, licenses, medical exams, liquor costs, and laundry charges—probably the truth was that she cleared more on those damn cribs she owned, and with a fraction of the trouble.

But she sure wasn't about to go shouting that around.

What she needed was a fancy girl to pull in some more money.

Just then Lydia walked through the front door, and Annie felt more than a twinge of anger toward her. What would she know of such matters? Nothing. And there was no reason she should, other than she owned a building that served as a goddamned brothel.

"Why don't you step into the office, where it is less public?" Annie said. If she told the woman once, she had told her five times not to just come in through the front door like it was a storefront. It caused problems—not the least to her reputation. Lydia didn't seem to grasp just how many men she might know that frequented the establishments along Market Street.

Lydia was opening herself up to blackmail. Especially considering that little habit of hers.

"You seem out of sorts," Lydia said, eyeing Annie almost like she felt bad or something.

"This way," Annie replied, coming around to Lydia's side and herding her toward the office in back. If Lydia wanted her money early . . . well, she didn't have it. She had just paid a spate of trumped-up fines. Obviously the Denver city coffers were running low, and they were turning to the brothel and saloon-keeps to make up the shortfall.

"To what do I owe this visit?" Annie used her most genteel speaking voice, which sounded false to her own ear. There was no denying her sentences grew a bit longer when Lydia Chambers was around.

Something in Lydia seemed to falter a bit. It was the first time Annie had seen that.

"I wanted to ask what you knew about some properties over near Wazee."

Annie looked at her sharp. "No reason for me to go down there. It's where the opium dens are, and the Celestials run their businesses. Why?" Annie had a pretty damn good notion why. But she wanted to hear Lydia say it.

Lydia colored a bit. "What do you know about those . . . opium dens?"

Annie shook her head, got up and poured out two drinks. "Only that you're a damned fool if you go into one of those places. You're on their territory then. Who knows what goes on in there? I sure as hell don't."

"I saw some vacant properties that might go for cheap. This investment here is turning out well, all things considered."

Annie smiled, but shook her head. "So you're thinking about buying a drug hell as well? My, my, perhaps I *had* better watch out for you!"

Lydia took a sip of her drink and set it back down all dainty.

Then she got a faraway look in her eyes. "Have you ever wanted something that seemed so elusive you doubted you would ever get it?"

That took Annie back, so she lied. "Sure, who hasn't?"

"And what would that be, in your case?"

Annie paused to see if Lydia was making fun of her. But she looked to be in dead earnest. Annie thought a moment about jewelry and fine dresses, and decided she didn't give a hoot for those. She thought about the men she had believed she loved, and predictably lost. Probably good riddance to each and every one of them.

"Respect," Annie said, after consideration. "Isn't that what most women want?"

Surprise flickered. "Respect? Probably most women would say they wanted love, or a nice home, or healthy children."

Healthy children. Damn. Annie had never considered that one.

It was a sure-bet winner Lydia had a nice home. "And what is it that you want, if you don't mind me asking." Annie felt out of her depth.

"Solitude," Lydia replied.

Annie considered telling her that solitude didn't cost a damn thing. But she caught the note in Lydia's voice—wistful and unhappy at the same time.

"Well there's no need to do yourself in over it," Annie advised.

Lydia rose to her feet. "The thought never crossed my mind," she replied, with added emphasis.

Annie wasn't entirely certain and was growing wary again. "If your husband doesn't work out, you still have your real-estate business." She opened the door to the office, and escorted Lydia to the *back* door.

"That's what I admire about you. Your ability to never appear surprised by anything at all."

A distant memory of Claire flashed through Annie's mind. "Unhappiness comes and goes, but the liquor and the drugs can kill you."

"I don't do any of that," Lydia said in a quiet voice.

Of course, they both knew she was lying.

# CHAPTER 18
## EASY MONEY IS HARD TO FIND ON THE ROAD TO RUIN

"Welcome to the day of reckoning," Louisie said, in a weary tone. Coming from her, it sounded almost friendly.

It was noon, and the time when the monthly wages were distributed.

That Louisie hadn't a happy bone in her body. Pearl felt excited, thinking of the money that was about to come her way. "Don't you like money?"

Louisie snorted.

Fancy Nell Brown looked over at them, appearing older than she normally did. But then again, noon was an early hour for them all. "You'll learn, as we all did."

The office door opened, and one girl came out and another went in. The door closed with a click.

Louisie stood with her hand on her hip, waiting. "It's a hell of a thing to learn that you're already in hock after spending so much time on your back and knees."

Pearl cast a look around—the last in the line of six girls. Dressed in a shift with a silk shawl thrown around her shoulders, she started playing with the ends of her brown hair. She had bought the embroidered shawl on credit. Like the arrangement in Denver, they sent the bill on to Sadie. Maybe that part wasn't so good.

The door swung open. One of the girls came out with an envelope clutched in her hand. She looked upset, although she tried to appear calm.

Nell glanced back at Pearl. "Remember to keep your money quiet and to yourself."

Louisie gave Pearl a nasty look.


Pearl's first accounting as a whore began with Sadie seated at her desk, going over figures and tallies. She wore spectacles, which rendered her almost harmless in appearance. "How are ye?"

Pearl tried to smile as she shut the office door. "Fine, but I'm the last in line."

Sadie ticked down her ledger. "Good girl. That way you can keep your business to yourself. You're doing well. I reckon you've got one hundred seventy-two dollars and fifty cents totaled, of which your portion equals eighty-six dollars and twenty-five cents. After deductions and the goods bought on account, you get twenty-one twenty-five. What are you looking like that for?"

"That's for the entire three and a half weeks?"

Sadie nodded. "So it is. We went over the rules, remember? Thirty dollars a month for room and board—you are paying for last month and this upcoming month. So that is sixty dollars and five for the clothing—and you get twenty-one twenty-five."

While it was a hefty sum, it wasn't as hefty as Pearl expected. "I just thought it would be a bit more."

Sadie's eyes sparked. "Good lord almighty, what do you think this is? It's a business. What the hell. Look darlin', this is how whorehouses are run. And before you start getting any bright ideas, you're better off here where there's protection. Them gals out on their own, well, they still have to pay the landlord and get provisions, don't they? Don't take it so hard."

Sadie looked like she might almost feel a tinge bad. Almost, but not quite.

Pearl supposed she would have to try to do better next

month—but there would be no sixty-five dollar times for her again. It was hard to imagine becoming wealthy at twenty dollars per month. Maybe she should just turn her attention toward finding out information; Sadie wouldn't throw her out for asking a question or two. That's just what Annie had said to keep her in line.

"Did you know my mother used to work here? Her name was Claire Kelly."

Sadie got a wary look, and then sighed. She motioned for Pearl to sit. "Annie said you had queer notions about things, and that you'd be asking sooner rather than later. I don't know that I should be the one to tell you anything at all."

Pearl pulled up a chair and placed it right across from Sadie. "Please, Sadie. I'll do what you want, and I'll owe you a favor—anything. *If* you'll tell me what you know."

Sadie's expression softened a bit. "You don't owe me anything on that account. If you had asked Annie nicely, I think she would have explained . . ."

That was not how Annie was. Sadie just didn't see it that way.

"I don't think my mother and Annie got along very well. Worse, I've only heard Annie's version so far. I actually think her real name was Mary, but Annie refers to her as Claire, so it's hard to tell anything at all. Annie likes to keep things to herself as to the hows and the whys."

Sadie found a little joke in Pearl's words, but the amusement faded as memories came back. "Ah, she does that, doesn't she? But I know enough—and I'm warning you that the story gets ugly, fast. Claire started out in Cripple Creek and came here later."

"Annie told me she was a wreck." The ticking clock got louder, or at least it seemed as much.

Sadie nodded, assessing Pearl. "That about covers it. You

sound like you're mad at Annie. Any truth to that?"

"Some," Pearl said. "But if she would just tell me what she knows, I might like her a bit better."

"I'd say Annie did what she could for her sister. Claire worked here before I arrived. By the time I got to town, she had already moved down the line and into one of the cribs. But she used to come around here, begging for this and that. It was a hell of an ending."

Light streamed through the window glass, illuminating Sadie's hair. The harsh light emphasized the wrinkles on her face, made her dyed blond hair vibrant. Obvious. Dust was everywhere, on the floor, in the air. In their lungs.

"Where is she now?"

Sadie sighed. "In the pauper's field—a ways apart from most everyone. A sad ending to a sad life, I would say. I'll take you some afternoon, when things get quiet."

Sadie held out the envelope with her pay. Pearl took it and felt bad, near to tears at the tragedy. "I would like to see her grave. Couldn't we go this afternoon? It can't be far . . ."

Sadie shook her head. "It's not like paying a social call. But no, darlin'. Not today. I've got too much to do."

"What's to stop me from going to the graveyard myself? I can ask where the damn cemetery is." Angry, Pearl swatted at forming tears. She was so close.

Sadie stiffened. "That you can, but it would be a wasted effort. Not to mention that I haven't given you the time off. You'll never find the grave by yourself—there's a fair amount of people planted out there, some marked, some not. I'll take you when you've settled down. You're not ready right now—the entire story is a shock to you. I can see it."

There was truth in Sadie's words, but Pearl didn't give a continental. "Annie tricks people and keeps them in line by withholding something they want. I didn't think you were like that."

Sadie arched her eyebrow. "You know, Pearl, you need to learn not to snap at the hand that feeds you."

Sadie then seemed to recall something, something that bothered her. "You know, Claire did come by here once, fairly crazed. She was telling anyone who would listen—not that there were many—that Annie forced her to give up her baby, or some such nonsense, and to sign a paper, selling the child off to the nuns. Which, for the record, doesn't happen. Nuns don't buy babies. So you see how bad off she was? All the same, I suspect she was talking about you. The worst part was she kept ranting about how Annie cheated her out of that money, poor delusional soul."

Pearl felt like she had been punched in the stomach. "The nuns said my mother brought me in."

Sadie gave a sad smile and turned back to her books. "Either way, I'm sure no one was happy that day."

But Pearl saw it differently—she figured Annie must have been pretty damn happy that day, killing two birds off with one stone.

Pearl no longer cared a jot about her pay, or the lack of it.

Her mother had died of a broken heart, and *Annie was to blame*. Sadie was just trying to make it sound a bit better, seeing how she and Annie were friends of a sort.

If Annie was any kind of a decent person at all, she would have kept Claire and Pearl together. Having a baby around usually cheered women up, Pearl figured. And then her mother wouldn't have taken to the drugs and the drink so badly.

It only stood to reason.

★ ★ ★ ★ ★

PART III
THE COEXISTENCE OF THE
DREGS OF DENVER AND THE
PATH TO RICHES
OCTOBER 1892

★ ★ ★ ★ ★

# CHAPTER 19
## MONEY PROBLEMS ARE JUST THE BEGINNING

Stashing away eight hundred thirty-two dollars a month was harder than Lydia anticipated.

Secrets could turn on the owner in unforeseen ways.

The underhanded bank loan she had taken to finance the Market Street building was proving no problem—but the building itself was. The rent that Ryan woman paid exceeded the loan installments by a significant portion. Eight hundred thirty-two dollars and sixty-five cents, to be precise. Some idiots might think too much money was a nice problem to have, as far as problems went.

But a problem was a problem. Nothing more, and nothing less.

Lydia closed the ledgers she had finished going through with a decisive snap. Of course, those records were the interesting ones—the ones she kept hidden from her husband. She returned them to their hiding place, safely secreted in a niche atop the wardrobe and away from view. She would be damned if she let them fall into the wrong hands—either Stanley's or that prying maid's he'd hired.

She opened the wardrobe door, considered her dresses in passing. Fashions were never much of an interest for her, other than she had to look presentable and sharp. Absently, she pulled out a wine-colored dress, but her mind kept turning over the building and its implications. Maybe she could just buy Stanley out of her life once and for all.

Any plan she came up with was a variation on escape, she knew that much. She had been seeking escape in one way or another for a very long time. She moved over to her dresser and checked the underwear drawer where she kept a secret supply of laudanum. She felt for a bottle, pulled it out to check its level, and then thrust it back among her frillies, hidden in the silk and lace folds.

Although she wanted the drug, she needed to come up with a plan.

She turned away and forced herself over to the window. Beyond, the garden withered in the dry Denver heat. Some of the vines were tied to stakes, which got her to thinking further. Maybe she should wire the excess money to her father for safekeeping. But that would signal that something, yet again, was wrong. Not that he would be surprised—his opinion of his son-in-law had soured when Stanley's embezzlement came to light. That discovery triggered her father's suggestion that they leave St. Louis and head west. While Lydia and Stanley didn't get along with each other in the conventional sense, the lure of adventure proved irresistible.

In hindsight, she should have just sued for divorce.

Restless and uncomfortable, Lydia peeled off her nightgown and tossed it on a chair. She pulled on her petticoats, fastened up her corset and struggled her way into the dress. In her father's home she had always had a maid to help her dress, and she had tried to be a good daughter. It was a trade-off, and her intentions didn't always work out. She hadn't intended on starting to drink, but she had all the same, and got sent to a sanatorium in New York to dry out. St. Louis society sure-as-shooting found that interesting, but her family did their level best to cover it up. When the socially inferior clerk Stanley Chambers came courting, they all heaved a collective sigh of relief.

Everyone, that was, except Lydia.

She felt like damaged goods sold for salvage value. Deep down, Lydia entered into her marriage with the full knowledge that something was fundamentally wrong with her, something that could not be fixed.

But she hadn't planned on getting smacked around, either.

The purchase of the Market Street property had been a knee-jerk reaction to what was clearly a good opportunity. She remained irritated that she had allowed her pride to goad her into such an impulsive purchase. She hadn't thought it all the way through—she hadn't counted on having to hide money. Then again, she hadn't counted on having a slinker for a husband. He was sleeping with the maid. She didn't need telling.

He had coerced that same maid into acting as his spy, collecting the laudanum bottles as evidence for her transgressions. Lydia hid them around the house—in the library behind books, in her dressing table drawers, under her mattress, and in the pockets of old clothes.

The maid only found a fraction of them, a point of pride with Lydia. But she was protective of her hiding places, and could not be at ease when the maid ventured too close for comfort. Dressed to begin her day, she slipped out of her room and glided down the stairs with barely a rustle and into the dining room. A pot of tea stood waiting for her. She felt it, still quite warm to the touch.

She wondered where the maid had gone off to, and stuck her head into the silent narrow hallway that led to the kitchen. Listening for any movement, after a moment she detected a creak from the back servants' stairs that led to the second floor. Lydia retraced her steps, back up the carpeted staircase. She managed to sneak up on the unsuspecting woman with no problem at all, and stood watching the maid pat down her undergarments in the dresser.

"What are you doing?" Lydia asked finally, tiring of the game.

The woman jumped, caught in the act. "I'm putting your things away."

Lydia smirked. "Is that how you would describe it? I would have said something different."

The maid gave her *the look*, jugular vein throbbing. "I'm doing what I am paid to do—my job."

Lydia noted with satisfaction that the maid hadn't very good nerves. "And your abilities are so very disposable."

The maid left the room, without meeting Lydia's eyes. Their shoulders brushed. Lydia had no intention of giving ground, of stepping away to let the woman pass.

Lydia had every intention of getting rid of the maid. That could be handled sooner than the ultimate problem of Stanley.

Hours later, Stanley entered the house. Lydia had been listening for him. Waiting, clear-headed, without a dose of laudanum to lessen her discomfort.

She met him halfway down the stairs. "I want you to fire Susan at once."

Stanley took off his hat. He didn't look surprised. "Not without a good reason."

"I caught her going through my things."

Stanley look a step closer, his hands on his hips. "So?"

Lydia took a step down. "I don't want her here, which *should* be reason enough. However, seeing that it is not, I have a proposition for you. If you do as I ask, I will introduce you to a man who could sponsor you into the Denver Club. But the next maid will be of my choosing. Do we have an agreement?"

"No," Stanley said. "We do not."

"Come now. She is a stealthy maid—oh, yes I've noticed— who isn't working out. You've set her up to spy, but spy on what? I don't really have a problem—other than her. You are going to have to concede on this point. Either that or I shall have to get my father involved."

This was no idle threat.

Stanley bounded up the stairs and wrenched her arm. Hard. "Since you need Daddy so much, you shouldn't have left St. Louis. You weren't this goddamned headstrong when we married!"

Lydia pulled away and tripped down the stairs, just shy of falling. She steadied herself on the level floor and shot him a look that she hoped conveyed the hatred she felt toward him. Hatred could often masquerade as resolve. "Don't get confused, Stanley. My motive was never love. All I ever wanted was freedom."

"You are insane." Stanley's voice, for once, was calm and measured. Like something had finally settled in his mind. The accusation was probably an opening salvo—a shot to have her committed and take control of the money and business affairs. Wives got shut away all the time when they became inconvenient. All it took was a quack diagnosis purchased under the guise of a medical consultation fee.

A contest of wills might be interesting, but it was too little, too late. A backbone might have once raised him in her estimation. Now it was just another obstacle to knock down. "No. I am not insane. All you need to do is stay out of my way and get rid of that horrid maid. That doesn't seem all that much to ask. *Not* when you consider that most of the income and position you enjoy comes from me."

Stanley turned away. "It's getting a little old, hearing that," he called over his shoulder as he headed into the library.

Lydia rubbed her arm, fuming, as she watched him stalk off. Maybe Annie Ryan knew people who could speed things along. Lydia was fairly certain she would.

# Chapter 20
## Missing Days and
## Unwanted Attentions

Lydia turned up seven days late. She came in straight through the saloon doors, in plain sight. Like she didn't care what anyone thought.

"What the hell," Annie muttered. If Lydia didn't care, there was no reason *she* should. Other than Harrigan.

Annie was behind the bar taking inventory—more of the beat cop than of the booze. She trusted Michael well enough with that—although it never hurt to double-check. Sometimes people's dependability changed over time. A truly trustworthy person was a rare commodity.

All that rareness was causing a definite feeling of irritation.

And then Lydia arrived like an apparition, in a dark-red woolen dress. Like she was out for a social call, which was more than a bit off-putting, with the cop sitting right there. He was bound to take notice. And Annie didn't want Harrigan to know a thing about the real landlady of Ryan's Saloon.

Lydia was vulnerable, even if she didn't know it.

"There you are, then," Annie said, as if her presence was expected. "Follow me into the back." She spoke louder than normal, for Harrigan's benefit and as a warning to Lydia.

Which worked. Lydia pulled up a bit short, gave her a strange look, and mercifully held her tongue.

Annie came out from behind the bar and indicated the way, as if Lydia had never been in the saloon before. Lydia shook her head ever so slightly, followed Annie to the office, and waited for the door to shut.

"You had me worried," Annie said.

Apparently, Lydia found Annie's comment odd. "Just now?"

"Now and last week. You forgot to collect my rent, which isn't a bad thing, I realize. Unless, that is, something happened to you."

Lydia frowned, looking almost embarrassed. "I had a bad week and got my days mixed up. Better news is, I sold a house as well."

Annie still felt off-kilter. "I sent a boy round to your house. Made him pretend to be selling newspapers. He got sent away without seeing you."

Lydia's eyes widened; Annie interpreted that look to mean she disapproved. Lydia cleared her throat, almost like she was going to cry. "I didn't know."

"Well, all's well that ends well," Annie said, conflicted.

The unreliability was starting. And where were this woman's friends? "You see Harrigan out there? He's the one in the uniform."

Lydia got hold of herself. "I did notice. Are there problems?"

"Nothing I can't handle, but I don't want him knowing who you are. That one asks too many questions—no doubt trying to leave his mark. I just want to make sure it's not on my backside."

Lydia looked a bit relieved as the conversation veered away from her. "Fair enough. I just sold the chief of police a house. Want me to have a word?"

That was fortunate, in terms of money and luck. Annie smiled as she pulled out the rent money from her desk drawer. "Not right now, but I'll be sure to let you know. Having connections along those lines is a mighty fine thing." She paused and held onto the envelope for a moment, hesitating. A long, silent moment passed. "Though it's not good if you can't get word out, if needed."

She stuck the envelope out. Lydia took it and put it in her purse. "So, what would you advise?"

"Get someone in your pay, someone who can be relied upon," Annie replied. "Now, I'll walk you out the same way you came in. But I'm not sure how to explain you, for there will be questions."

"What is he here for, anyhow? Are you sure there isn't any trouble I can help with?"

Annie shook her head. "He's here because he's a leech. What's worse is, I pay him. We always pay the beat cop. It's customary. But he's not what I'm talking about when I say to get someone in your pay. I was thinking an errand boy, or someone who lives nearby."

Lydia shrugged in a way that conveyed the point was taken. "Tell the policeman I'm in real estate, if he asks. If he ever comes into a fortune, I would love to know him."

Annie shook her head. "If he comes into a fortune, there's going to be something wrong with it. Worse, it would probably be at my expense."

"You worry too much," Lydia said.

Annie thought Lydia ought to worry just a bit more. Together they walked back through the saloon, Harrigan watching their every step.

Harrigan never bothered to ask who she was, which made Annie even more nervous. She didn't think Harrigan was as stupid as that. But maybe she was wrong.

The Denver Post—*November 1892*

*Late yesterday afternoon the denizens of Market Street were treated to an exciting spectacle, as twenty-six arrest warrants were issued by the police to "Mary Doe" and "Jane Doe." The "Marys" were charged with the keeping of bawdy houses and keeping disorderly houses rife with encouragement of drinking and fornication. The inmates of such establishments were served warrants to "Jane Doe" with the charges of being accountable for the declining moral conditions of the Market Street ward. Half of the third floor of the court house was required for the makeshift jail once the warrants had been served, and the miscreants carted away in wagons on hand especially for that purpose.*

*Many of the girls were still drunk from the night before and did not fully comprehend the significance of the charges. One girl, a wily denizen, even hung a "for rent" sign in her window, and hid herself in a large steamer trunk as the raid was in process. The women themselves displayed every style of dress imaginable. Some were well turned out; others were in little more than rags. Coarse and vulgar in speech and appearance, their painted faces, disheveled hair, and their disgusting appearances illustrated once and for all the depth to which women can sink in vice. This striking scene was a ruckus created by the women themselves, some babbling in French, others crying or shouting, some dancing and laughing all at full tilt. It goes without saying that all wanted beer and cigarettes, and were unimpressed by the proffered tea and coffee.*

"Jesus Christ," Annie swore. "What in the hell am I paying monthly license fees for, if we're all going to get run in anyhow?"

Michael the barman trudged alongside her and held his tongue. May and Julia trailed behind, greeted by a few catcalls and mocking applause as they walked back down Market Street toward Ryan's.

"At least it didn't take that long to get hauled in and released," May remarked, apparently enjoying the outing. Or the notoriety.

"You can thank Michael for that." Annie was in no mood for pleasantries. "There's a fair amount of work to make up, and that's if the punters aren't afraid it all might happen again with their pants down around their ankles."

"Who'd you leave in charge of the saloon—John?" Annie asked him, figuring that was one more disaster in the making.

Michael bit the side of his mustache before answering. "Well, Jim's boy is behind the bar, and Harrigan is keeping his eye on things. But before you say anything, I made sure your office door was locked."

Annie nodded. Thankful for that at least.

Of course, the first person Annie saw in the saloon was Harrigan, leaning on the bar. A little too close to the till for her liking.

"A word," Annie said to him, walking straight back to her office without breaking her stride. Harrigan followed. She stuck her key in the lock and turned. Glad it was bolted.

"Shut the door." There was no need to mince words.

Annie sat down behind her desk. She didn't motion for Harrigan to sit, but left him standing. "So, you had no warnings that a raid was on, is that it?"

Harrigan squinted, rocked up on the balls of his feet. "Yes and no. But I didn't think it would involve here. I thought you paid your licenses on time."

"I do." Annie's voice was as sharp as a steel blade. "And I want to know why I was targeted."

She waited.

Harrigan shuffled. "I don't know, but as you've no doubt figured out by now, you weren't the only one." He said it as if that fact would be enough.

"Maybe I should decrease your cut, since I can't see what you are doing to earn it." Annie's shoulders were tense.

"I wouldn't recommend it," Harrigan said as he left the office, not bothering to close the door.

"I've got a couple of recommendations for you, you son of a bitch," Annie yelled after him.

He didn't bother returning to tell her off, although he must have heard her plain as day.

Something wasn't right with him. Annie didn't like dealing with men she didn't understand.

# CHAPTER 21
## LEADVILLE DALLIANCES OF THE ROUGH VARIETY

The professor was banging out "The Old Gray Mare, She Ain't What She Used to Be" on the piano—just another Saturday night in the mining town. There was a manic feel to the song and the atmosphere. The streets were teeming with men looking to whoop it up. For Pearl, this night held different expectations than usual. She was waiting with a flutter in her stomach for her special fellow to come calling.

To "come calling" was a polite term for what they would be doing.

But his interest had been waning. He seldom dropped by for a chat, or even to have a beer to pass the time.

It would be hard to say why she didn't see his absence as a lack of enthusiasm, but somehow the finer points passed her right on by. And although they had loose plans in place for a Saturday screwing, that didn't mean she was free—either figuratively or literally. Friday and Saturday nights were busy and the bulk of where the money was made. Of course, they coincided with when the miners got paid. She had a lot of men to work her way through, and the night dragged on as she cast about the place, seeing who might be interested. But none of them was Frank.

She finished with one of the mining bosses who took far too long, but paid twice as much. Still no sign of Frank.

The bar was four deep with men at seven-thirty.

"Pearl!" Sadie had a brawny fellow in tow. "This is your next customer."

None too polite, he didn't even offer her a drink although he had a bottle of whiskey that was corked. "I'm going to make you forget about all the other pricks you've had," he bragged.

Pearl smothered a snappy retort. Men were such idiots about their pricks and abilities. Because she wanted a tip, she laughed like she was looking forward to it. Like she actually believed him. He grabbed her ass on the way up the stairs. Hard and bruising.

Upstairs, Pearl tried to keep a bit of distance between them. "Now, you just sit on the bed and I'll give you a private show."

She peeled off her skirt, and he grabbed for her. She jumped back, but he tried to get hold of her. Pearl couldn't keep him at bay and he kept on trying to take the pins out of her hair and unlace her bodice. She pushed his hands away, but he still managed to pinch her breast.

"Damn it, that hurt." She covered her breast with her hand.

He laughed and tried it again, and she slapped his hands. "Calm down, you jackass! I'll yell for help if you don't, and I mean it!" She backed up toward the door, her hand on the knob.

He eased up for a moment. Then he lunged again, trying to wrestle a kiss on the lips. She caught him off balance and pushed him onto the bed. She felt, and heard, a seam rip along the back of her bodice.

"Now, who's going to pay for that?" It was one of her favorite dresses that showed off her coloring to advantage.

"It's not like it was exactly new." The jake paused, considering the damage.

He uncorked his bottle of whiskey and took a swig. He offered it to Pearl.

She knew she should stand her ground, but he was offering

*whiskey.* No one would see her drinking, which tempted her fierce. If she couldn't collect on the tear, she might as well drink the cost in booze. She took a big swallow, and another.

"Damn, girl!" The jake was impressed.

Together they killed off a good portion of the contents, which calmed things down a bit. But it could have just as easily gone the other direction.

She abandoned the strip tease, as her balance was harder to keep.

The man was still rough—but the booze helped deaden the pain. He even tossed her a dollar when he was done. "To pay for whatever got torn," he said.

She was actually coming out a bit ahead, but didn't feel satisfied. It wasn't greed that drove her, but perhaps it was more like pride. Both were sins—not that it mattered any longer. She was committing the sin of fornication, and that had to be far worse.

Focusing upon how her world revolved around money, Pearl stared at that silver dollar for a long moment and thought of the bruises she was sporting.

One silver dollar was what he thought she was worth, and she was supposed to be grateful.

Maybe he was right, but it wasn't enough.


Pearl did up her hair again, consulted the mirror, and saw fingerprints on her breast. She also had bruises on her upper arm from an earlier customer. Men were rough by nature—some of them. She pulled on the same outfit she'd started out in, complete with the new tear. She had a hunch Frank wasn't coming.

Tipsy, Pearl made her way back downstairs, and surveyed the scene in the saloon from the relative safety of the staircase. More and more men kept piling on in. Every man in Leadville, it seemed, except Frank. She went up to the bar, and smiled at a band of men who wore nicer shirts than usual. One of them was looking for a go, so she led him back up the stairs.

He was quick and efficient. Just the way she liked them. Clean, too.

She washed both of them off and got re-dressed. Starting to sober up, she put on a touch of rouge and hoped that did the trick.

Back down the stairs she went. It was going on ten o'clock. She stood at the bar, hoping her next jake would buy her a drink. The music was still jangling, and the songs were repeating. As they did every night, as time wore on.

She was in luck; a drink was offered, and Sadie's back was turned. She shot the liquor back like a professional, relaxing as the initial burn faded to warmth in her stomach. Ladylike sipping never worked as good. She took the jake upstairs and asked, in a casual way which mine he worked at.

"The Mikado," he told her. But it wasn't Frank's mine.

She worked her way through another three jakes, realizing all the time that Frank wasn't coming. He might never come back again, and there was nothing she could do.

That night, drunk and the worse for wear, she cried herself to sleep, knowing that tomorrow was another day. But it wouldn't be any better. Tomorrow never got any better. It was all pretty damn much the same.

She was a whore, and her body always ached.


The week limped along. The following Saturday, Pearl came down the stairs with the jake she had just finished. Like every other payday, the house was jumping. This time, Frank was seated at a table with some other miners.

Her heart fluttered, and she advanced toward him, but was intercepted by Sadie, who was in no mood for guff. "The jake in the Stetson is your next trick."

"But I see someone I want to say hello to," Pearl replied, and tried to move past the madam.

Sadie grabbed her upper arm. "He's already paid his twelve dollars, and he's been waiting for you. Now you can say hello to your *friend* afterwards. And *only* if he's got twelve dollars." Sadie nodded, to make sure her point was driven home.

"Last time you told him the price was ten dollars." Pearl pouted.

Sadie didn't look inclined to budge on the matter. "That was a weekday. Oh, I get it. And you drive that notion right out of your head."

So Pearl nodded at Frank, and walked straight past him to the jake in the Stetson. By the time Pearl had finished with the Stetson and made it back downstairs, Frank acted a bit put off at being kept waiting. Pearl flounced over and sat on his lap.

"You didn't keep your word last week," she said, whispering it into his ear, trying not to sound quarrelsome.

Playing the big man, he didn't bother to lower his voice. "I don't owe the likes of you an explanation."

That hurt. Pearl turned away, cheeks flaming with shame.

"What's going on here?" Sadie materialized at Pearl's elbow.

"Nothing at all," Pearl replied.

"This girl of yours is getting ideas she shouldn't," Frank added.

Sadie looked from him, back to Pearl. "Looks like she ain't the only one."

The look Sadie gave him was hard. "If you two are planning on taking this conversation upstairs, the rate is twelve dollars. Otherwise, Pearl, there are other men that need attending." Sadie showed no signs of moving until the matter was resolved.

"Oh, what the hell," Frank swore, and dug into his pocket for the money.

★　★　★　★　★

They went upstairs, and Pearl abandoned any more harsh words. When they were done, Frank rolled over and wouldn't look at her straight. "Don't forget to give me some of your money," he said, buttoning his shirt and pulling up his pants.

That caught her short. But Pearl fished around under the bed and pulled out a small white pouch of coins. The tips she kept secret from the house. She held out four dollars. To her great disappointment, Frank took them.

He ought to have felt bad, taking a girl's money like that.

# CHAPTER 22
## DIFFERENT KINDS OF GRAVES

Dead people usually stayed where they were planted. Living people were not such a sure-fire proposition. And Pearl had set her hopes upon Franklin Bonnert with his soft Louisiana accent: a prospector in every sense of the word.

They had fallen into a routine—what passed as a slim, strange courtship common among the brothel types. Some of the girls had a jake they favored, and Sadie absolutely hated it. Human nature being what it was, sometimes attachments were formed. Hell, even madams sometimes supported a man on the side, but supposedly handled it better.

Tight with his money and his opinions, Frank never bought her a drink after that first time. He never brought her trinkets or candy, or anything a girl would want, other than the obvious hard-on.

And for working girls, one more prick wasn't that much to celebrate. But Pearl kept watch on him with a jealous, possessive eye.

Not that it made the slightest difference.

Saturday night was a rollicking old time of it. No one felt well when Sunday came around, so they all just kept on going. Drinking could be a hard business—arguments and squabbles, offenses and overlooked promises. Spewing, blustering, and laughing: a drunken farce was set off against an almost continuous tirade of circular piano music.

Despite ordinances against guns and firearms being dis-

148

charged, pour enough whiskey and hooch into the heaving mix and things went off. Then the music might stop, might not. But it always picked up again.

And Frank started casting his eye at other girls.

"Do you ever think about me with other men?" Pearl asked, one night along the line.

Frank didn't stop tying his boots. "Should I?"

He stood up and headed straight for the door. He opened it, allowing another jake to get a good eyeful of Pearl's naked body.

"Franklin!" Pearl squealed, covering herself as best she could with her cast-off garments.

"Just drumming up business for you," he replied.

Even Pearl realized there was something fundamentally wrong with his actions, if he had any feelings for her at all.


When Pearl rejoined the crowd in the saloon, Frank was back to drinking with other miners and gave her a wink.

Sadie grabbed her arm. "The old fellow with the beard is your next number."

"What the hell does he want with me? He's seventy if he's a day! I doubt he could even do something if he wanted to."

The grip tightened. "The old fella's paid twelve dollars, and you're going upstairs with him even if it's to play tiddlywinks."

"Jesus, Sadie."

Sadie's blue eyes didn't broker any more back talk. "I want you to know I don't *care* about your feelings. I care about running this business."

Frank was gone when Pearl got back downstairs. As much as Pearl had tried to hurry, the old fellow hadn't been satisfied with tiddlywinks.

Her next jake was already lined up—a tall miner with black hair and coarse tendencies. The fellow after that was one of the bankers in town, who was satisfied jerking off to a striptease.

The next was a miner with dirty fingernails who kept grunting in her ear.

The last jake was a flat-ass drunk who passed out. Pearl went through his pockets and found a five-dollar coin. Smiling, she deposited it in a hiding place behind one of the wall boards. She left him with some money, tempted, *sorely tempted* to take more. It stood to reason that drunks lost money, or drank it and forgot.

She had never stolen before, but it gave her a thrill. And with that, she was done for the night.

After she kicked the drunk out of her room.

The jakes' faces and their personal habits and preferences started blending together. Even her repeat jakes. The weather began to shroud the mountains, although people shrugged it off as best they could. The chill was settling into Pearl's outlook. She tried her best to ward it off. She wasn't successful. But then, so few were.

All the girls in the whorehouse were assembled for their mid-day meal in various stages of dress or undress, shawls over petticoats and bloomers to ward off the cold draft. The stove burned hot and radiated, but the heat got swallowed up in the empty expanse. Drafts still found their way in through the walls and windows with every gust of wind. The girls pretended not to notice, hardened to the conditions. Their talk centered on the jakes of the previous evening, trading stories about drunken exploits.

Laughing it all off. It beat the hell out of tears.

Pearl felt like she was sinking. She kept her face down; concentrated on worrying the food set on the plate before her.

". . . That fellow was special, wouldn't you say, Pearl?" Fancy Nell Brown tried to draw her out.

Sometimes silence was a whore's worst enemy.

Miserable, Pearl managed to catch the tail end of the conversation. "They're all special, good God Almighty." But what did they think of her?

And everyone at the table laughed, including Sadie, which actually made Pearl suffer even worse, although she joined in.

Then Sadie gave her a cold, clear calculating look that froze the laughter in Pearl's throat. Dead. Sadie missed next to nothing that went on in her house, and that included ill tempers.

She knew about Frank, and wanted Pearl to stop.

Dissatisfied, Pearl returned to her room when the meal was finished. Out of sorts, she reckoned being a whore was about as low as a girl could sink—unless she had a bent toward murder. Being a murderer might have meant the end was in sight. Murderers didn't get dismissed as easily as hookers. Pearl had already started to fear being overlooked.

Most harridans didn't even use their own names, for pity's sake. All those girl babies born with different names that somehow got lost along the way. And they ended up in brothels or in the cribs. At least she used her own name—her connection into the other world, such as it was, intact.

And she was popular. For the time being. But being pretty just meant she got pawed more than most. Tiring of patting hands and probing fingers, she closed her mind to it. She certainly didn't like getting bit. She had dealt with a biter the night before.

She went over to her trunk, pulled out the bottle of laudanum. Sadie had given it to her all those nights ago—a lifetime, really. Right before her first jake. She shook it, held it up to the window and judged the level.

She just needed something to fill the empty hollow inside of her—to take the edge off.

She uncorked the bottle, knowing she shouldn't. She took a

small swig, held her breath as the liquid burned going down, before the sensation of warmth.

In a few moments, things started to brighten up a bit.

She pulled on a pair of stockings with holes and lattices that could be repaired—if she cared. Which she didn't. The nuns would never have approved of such sloth. Sticking her feet into her worn boots, she laced them up with finality and donned her blue and black dress. The dress that was one step shy of indecent. The mirror reflected a pretty face, which she painted with angry motions. She piled up her brown hair and considered how her face had changed over time. It certainly had grown a bit thin.

The rouge might not have caused a sparkle in her eyes, but the laudanum sure hit the spot.

But it was already getting old, screwing around.

Tarrying on her way down the stairs, she paused and let the coarse laughter rise up to meet her. The noise carried and drifted, while the haze of the blue walls flowed on by. She wondered what on earth had possessed someone to paint them that color. Amidst the jangling music, she made a quiet entrance and sidled up to a jake who was wearing a suit. Without any encouragement, she ran her fingers along his lapel, tracing the outline. She didn't give a rat's ass about him—but the flirtation was all part of the game.

"Buy a girl a drink?" She sniffed to make sure he didn't smell too bad, but he eyed her with disdain.

"Where's your mother? Has she seen you like this?" He asked it as a joke, but it wasn't funny.

"In the graveyard. Where's yours?" She felt so damned alone in the world.

Disgusted by her, he turned his back. "Nowhere that concerns you."

She poked him in the shoulder blade, hard. He turned again, angry.

"What's the problem?" Sadie asked, coming up beside her and grabbing her hand so she couldn't poke the jake again.

"This slut of yours is bothering me." The man sounded like he had nothing to do with the situation.

Tears blurred Pearl's vision. "That asshole asked where my mother was."

Sadie rolled her eyes, pulled her away, and sat her down at a vacant table. "Not this again. You're being paid to show the men a good time."

"I want to see where my mother is, Sadie." Pearl's bosom heaved as panic set in.

"Fine. Tomorrow." Sadie eyed her, not altogether in a sympathetic manner. "Now, whatever you do, don't start crying. It's bad for business. And you had better act goddamned enthusiastic with the jakes. Got it?"

Pearl brightened a bit at the prospect of visiting her mother's grave. "Got it," she said, and dabbed at her eyes.

The sky was gray like the granite peaks; clouds overhead spoke of a storm gathering. The occasional beam of sunlight burst through before succumbing to shadow. The wind caught on the jagged mountain tops and was pulled down the rock slopes above the tree line, then forced through the bristlecone pines that rustled and swayed in the valley below. Forlorn in sound, the movement of the air felt clean and cold as water. Noises of the mines and dredgers at work carried, ricocheted against the mountain walls, metal scraping stone—monotonous and unremarkable. Fragrances of the extracted minerals mingled, scenting the air as the impending winter lurked, insistent.

A chill current passed over the cemetery where her mother's body lay, cast out and coffin-less. Another winter drew near.

Pearl's skirts whipped around her ankles and her hair streamed behind her. She had on her visiting clothes and looked respectable on purpose. She hesitated a few yards away from the mound without a headstone—the resting place of her decaying mother. Her intent was to introduce herself; she was open to signs and sought meaning. But the bone orchard only provided a pile of dirt that the mountainside had begun to reclaim. Kinnikinnick had started spreading, sending exploratory tendrils out, hugging the ground for a warmth that would soon die off, too.

Empty graves were already dug for the winter, when the ground would be frozen.

Pearl hesitated, turned toward Sadie, who remained seated in the wagon, her face set toward the peaks and into the wind. She was giving Pearl privacy with the truth. It hurt. The grave felt abandoned: a pile of dirt that withered with time. Seasons when no one had cared.

"Are you sure this is her?" The toes of Pearl's boots were at the edge of the mound.

Sadie's answer blew away in the cold northern wind that caught in Pearl's hair—brown ribbons of nuisance that tangled before her eyes and stuck to the corners of her mouth. It was just as well her facial expression couldn't be read.

"Which way is her head?"

Sadie shifted in the buckboard in a way that said she didn't know, but pointed north. "She's facing that way."

The cemetery was a jumble of graves, some of which were already sinking from neglect. Abandonment. "This is a shit hole of a cemetery, Sadie."

Sadie glanced over at Pearl. "Keep a sense of perspective, girl. It's just fine in the paying section."

Pearl memorized the mound and its location, and then slowly turned and walked back to the buckboard. She climbed in next to Sadie, and their eyes met.

"I knew this wasn't a good idea," Sadie said as she flicked the reins and pulled away.

# CHAPTER 23
## HORNING IN

The term "horning in" had so many connotations, but all of them amounted to about the same thing. Getting screwed. Annie scrutinized her brothers standing at the bar rail smiling, and felt the predictable tightening in the region of her stomach. She paused before she sallied into the saloon and took up a position behind the bar. *Her bar.* They had drinks already set before them.

"Ain't it a little early for the hard stuff?"

The boys seemed to find that funny. "And a rosy good morning to you, too, Annie!"

They wore clean shirts complete with vests and jackets. This was no social call. "You two here for a particular reason?"

She wasn't late on her payments. Jim looked around at the tables and the few lone patrons who weren't inclined to be sociable so early on. They stared down into their drinks or off into space, but they sure as hell didn't make eye contact.

Dust motes glistened in the sun that streamed in through the window. "It's a nice place you've got here. The location sure is central. How you ever landed this is a bit of a mystery, but never mind. We are here hoping to have a meeting of the minds."

Annie poured herself a small draught of beer. "That depends what the topic is, doesn't it?"

"Let's go into your office," John prompted, picking up his drink. He belted it down.

Damn. "Not sure I exactly want to. What is this about?

Specifically."

Jim and John exchanged glances. Jim cleared his throat. "We were thinking about reducing the interest amount you owed on your loan to us. But, of course, there is a business reason for us to consider that."

Annie shook her head, not liking the sound of it. But she headed to the office all the same. The boys followed closely behind her. Inside her office, she sat down behind her desk, enjoying the sense of discomfort that instilled in them.

"That's pretty formal, ain't it?" John and Jim exchanged further looks, which made one point clear—it had never dawned on them to set up an office.

Annie felt a mite better. But she didn't feel compelled to answer.

Jim cleared his throat. "Let's talk about the common ground we all share. The fact is, like it or not, we are family and all that implies, and a few other points besides. Sometimes we even manage to overlook each other's faults." He glared at John, then turned his attention back to Annie. "And seeing as how liquor and poor judgment sometimes go hand in hand, we've got some liquor we need to unload. On the quiet."

"Because there is something wrong with it, in so many words." That sure as hell brought back unpleasant memories she could have done without. Especially of Leonard.

The boys looked at each other. "Well, it's not exactly bad . . ." John started.

"But it's pretty damn close," Jim finished.

"Can't do it," Annie said. She was set on that matter.

"But you haven't heard our terms! If you can help us unload it, saying maybe that you only serve it after midnight . . . That way the punters are already loaded. Hell, very few know what they're drinking after that point.

"No."

"Now don't be so stubborn, Annie. We have your best interests at heart, along with our own. You see, we know this fellow named Maurice Lyon. He stumbled onto this good deal, which he presented to John. John took him up on it, after sampling the goods. But he already had too much to drink."

John lifted his eyes to Annie. "I'd say he slipped a good sample in, because what I tasted sure the hell isn't what we bought!"

"Regardless, John. The rest of the whiskey has been watered, no mistake."

Annie shrugged. "Just don't pay him, then. Tell him the goods are adulterated—that's a good word—and you have a reputation to maintain. Like I'm telling you two, right now."

"Well, that's where it gets tricky. He's a policeman, with inroads higher up, if you catch my drift. We don't need City Hall to take an interest in us or our operations. Now, seeing as how we let you have Pearl . . ."

"Let me have Pearl, my ass! You didn't even know where the hell she was."

"But when she comes back, she'll be able to get the punters to buy drinks easier than anyone else you have. They probably wouldn't even notice what they're drinking, if it's offered to them right. We'll give you a reduced price on the booze, and we'll take twenty-five percent of the dealings."

"It's a little too close for comfort, boys. Not to mention it's a whole 'nother layer of money to keep track of. I'd say you just have to push it through the Monte Carlo, or sell it to some of the Italians up north. Either way, I don't want to touch it."

"Now that's too bad you feel that way, Annie. Isn't it, Jim?"

Jim stretched out his legs, considering them like they were something new. "Well, it sure is. You see, we're starting to get the impression you're not really one hundred percent with the family. Oh, you use the name when it suits you—all that goodwill we've built up over the years when you were in the mountains. Didn't we give you a loan to get this all kicked off? Now I would say that puts you in our debt, more ways than one."

Annie shook her head. Typical. "I pay interest on that money, damn it!"

John stood up. "Well, I guess we're calling it in about now. Seeing as how you can't, won't, or don't help. We see assistance as a two-way street. We'll give you two days to sort it out. Three hundred eighty-nine dollars."

Annie tried not to show her panic. With measured movements she opened up one of the drawers and pulled out a ledger. She opened it, ran her finger down a page. "Three hundred and sixty is what it says here, and that is what you'll get."

The boys rose to their feet; John shrugged in an almost apologetic manner. "We'll take your word for it."

Annie didn't have all that money. She barely had part of it. Expenses were running higher than she had figured. She held no illusions on that score. If her brothers were suffering, they would make sure she did as well. They would start strong-arming her into signing over interests, liquor or future earnings if she didn't come up with the money on time. Annie supposed she could sell off one of the cribs, if she absolutely had to. Though she sure didn't want to.

Bastards. Her brothers were bastards in more ways than one.

Luck was rolling in Annie's favor. John came back around to Ryan's the following day, looking pale.

"You're one day early." She didn't offer him a drink.

"Yeah, well. That's all off. On account of what has happened. Jesus Christ, will you give me a whiskey?"

Annie shrugged and poured. "I'll decide whether or not I'm charging you for it, after I hear what you have to say."

John took out a tolerably clean handkerchief and wiped his brow, then tossed back the measure. "There was a shooting on account of all that diluted whiskey business, and another cop is dead."

Annie stared at him. "What? Which cop? I haven't heard a damn thing."

John glanced behind him to make sure no one was listening. "Of course it's been kept quiet! We weren't born yesterday. Turns out Lyon himself got sold a bad bill of goods, which he then passed on to us. At any rate, that other cop was the one who stuck Lyon with the bad goods. As such things go, Lyon was in the saloon when that other cop came in. An argument started and wham! Lyon drew and shot him dead."

"That's a problem." Which was precisely why she didn't want to get involved with shady liquor dealings in the first place.

"Of course it's a problem! That's what I've been telling you." John had commenced to sweating again.

"I don't see how that changes anything where I'm concerned."

John rolled his eyes. "Jim was fired up about Pearl. That's the real reason why he wanted to call in the loan. But we didn't pay Lyon all the money we owed him, and it turns out he owed that dead cop. Now no one is paying anyone, for the moment at least. But it wouldn't hurt to have the money set aside. You know how things go sometimes."

And so Annie did. "But where is the body?"

John cast around again. "At the morgue. Where else?"

Annie looked at him closely. "Having a cop killed on your premises can't be considered good luck, by any yardstick."

John shrugged. "Well. No one liked him, so as far as these things go—it might blow over."

Annie still wasn't convinced. "And no one is going to say anything controversial. Is that the plan?"

"Close enough. Now do you think you might be interested in

some of that liquor? Fifty percent discount, on account of the tragedy."

"I'll think about it. So you are selling stuff you haven't entirely paid for. Where does that leave your friend Lyon?"

"Why the fuck should I care?" John appeared indignant at the notion.

Annie figured he had a fair point. There was no reason why any of them should care. Other than it might involve City Hall.

# CHAPTER 24
## UNWHOLESOME HABITS DON'T COUNT, WHEN YOU HAVE ENOUGH MONEY

Drip, drip, drip. The drops of laudanum went onto the spoon, glistening silver in the morning light. It would be another day wasted, but Lydia didn't care. Experience had taught her that laudanum was so much easier than alcohol. All she did was take a few drops, relax, and then drift off to sleep—her dreams or imaginings filled with pleasant notions and receding cares. She had given Stanley fifty dollars the day before as a type of insurance policy. One that should keep him away for another day. At least.

She turned the conversation with Annie Ryan over in her mind, recalling her words about wanting respect. There were different shades and hues to all of that. Lydia put the spoon in her mouth, the liquid numbing and soothing as it passed down her throat. Annie seemed very alone in the world, much like Lydia felt. Oh, people could be around all right, but they were more akin to shadows that didn't really matter to either woman. Lydia could see the similarities, and felt that Annie held that same recognition. It should have disturbed her to find common ground like that with the demimondaine, but instead it was intriguing. They were both businesswomen, and both had others in tow. Lydia certainly would have preferred to be alone without Stanley. Annie seemed comfortable with her relatives, although not affectionate as far as anyone could tell. Annie took pride in her family name, as Lydia once had. Names could offer shelter and protection with the right backing behind them.

Lydia's maiden name had once sheltered her—her father's prosperity and business acumen had allowed certain privileges. The primary one being that faults could almost be overlooked. But then she married and her world changed.

Annie . . . well. Who knew what the real story was there. But she did have her daughters. Girls she had raised to be whores as well.

A fact interesting and disturbing in equal measures.

Lydia had the distinct impression Stanley favored whores over her. Although it suited her purposes well, it remained insulting. Maybe the whores were more enthusiastic for his attentions. As she had been. In the beginning.

Annie probably wouldn't say much if Stanley turned up at Ryan's. Just like Lydia didn't tell wives about their husbands buying real estate for their mistresses. Within limits, business was business. And Annie hadn't given her any indication that she had encountered Stanley. Of course, that didn't mean he wasn't going someplace else. Denver was littered with prostitutes and brothels. Or worse. She knew about syphilis, and hoped that Stanley did, too. It made men go insane. Most women just killed themselves before they allowed that to happen. Decent ones, at least.

It was another mark in their favor, she thought.

Such were her musings, before the laudanum really took hold. She heard a telltale rattling and a click. The front door latch and sound of the door opening. The new maid used the back entrance—there was a battle she had won—so it had to be Stanley. It went against her grain to let him think he caught her at anything, so she stood up, opened her bedroom door and ventured out to the landing at the top of the stairs. Stanley's overcoat was splattered, like he had taken a tumble. His hat was missing, his hair standing up in patches, ruffled. It must have been some night at the club.

"Back so soon?" She made no effort to go down the stairs.

He seemed a bit disconcerted. "Just to get cleaned up. But another twenty dollars wouldn't go amiss. Seeing as how you like your privacy."

Ignoring the reference, she viewed him more closely. He probably wouldn't be much good at fighting, but it sure did look like he had been in a scuffle: a handkerchief was tied as a bandage around his hand.

Lydia felt the languor ease in, and struggled to remain focused and clear. "Don't let me get in your way. There's twenty dollars in the box in the library."

He gave her a queer look, as if he was actually thinking about telling her something of importance. Then the moment passed.

Lydia returned to the confines of her bedroom, carefully closing the door and wondering whether or not she should lock it. Her intuition told her that might not be wise. Stanley's expression was . . . strange. She couldn't put her finger on it. Instead of bothering with the lock, which could easily be smashed, she splashed her face with water to reduce the effects of the laudanum. She brushed her hair, pinned it up, and hurriedly put on something more formal than a morning dress. If Stanley was going to be home, she would go elsewhere. It was as simple as that.

And she knew just where to go. The opium den. No need to ruin her plans, just because an unwelcome presence returned home.

The house—the structure and its contents—was hers. Stanley thought differently, but would find he was wrong when push came to shove. Provided nothing, like an asylum, detained her. That was a point she needed to keep foremost in her mind.

In lower Denver, something was going on—just as it usually was. However, this time it felt different. People were gathered in clusters, talking and looking over their shoulders. No one paid any particular attention to her, but they sure seemed interested in something. Curiosity gave way to jitters. Her nerves were getting the better of her, as was her craving. She didn't care what was afoot. She cared about finding relief.

Opium promised so much more adventure than laudanum ever did.

No one died from taking opium. At least, not that she was aware of. She had even heard tell there was a certain type of honor among the people who frequented such establishments. As long as she paid for the opium, she should be safe while drifting in the haze, dreaming of strange currents. She was driven to try it for herself.

She slowed her buggy in front of a stable near Hop Alley instead of tethering it to a post on the street. A gnarled man came out to her and held the horse's bridle. " 'Day, ma'am . . ."

"I'd like to leave my horse and rig with you for a while."

He patted the horse, although he looked at Lydia. "Today it's a bit chancy-like. How long will you be away?"

She hadn't the faintest clue as to how long she would be in the den. Nor was she in any mood for small conversation. "Does it matter to you?"

Looking a bit offended, he spat out some tobacco juice. "Well, not so much in that way. But if you think you'll be away overnight, it's best to say."

"Well, I really don't know what my plans are yet." She made certain to give him a firm look that discouraged questions or speculation.

"Just hoping you know what part of town this is."

"It is the part near the railroad station." And with that, she turned on her heel and headed in the general direction of Union Station. A few moments later, she turned a corner and ducked down an alley.

There, the Celestials were gathered in twos and threes, speaking in their foreign tongue. There was no denying that everyone seemed in a flap about something. But it was unimportant. There were other things that were so much more interesting.

She made her way to the steps she had encountered before, the ones that led off the street and into salvation. She knocked. She knocked again. She waited, admiring the red and gold Chinese pendants that rippled in the autumn breeze. Her heart was thudding and her palms felt wet.

It was probably nothing more than nerves.

The door slowly opened. It was the same Chinaman she had seen previously. "Bad day," he said, and closed the door slowly, silently, in her face. The fragrance of opium wafted out, an enticement just beyond reach. Not as strong as it had been the other day. Maybe they weren't allowing additional customers to enter.

She had never considered the possibility that she might be turned away. Especially not when he had seen her before.

Something was strange. What the hell. She might as well go over to Ryan's and have a couple of whiskies before returning home.

She never wanted to return home, when there was a chance her husband might be there.

Of course, she went in straight through the front door of Ryan's, just like a paying customer. It was kind of funny, the expression Annie would get when she saw her.

This time was no different, except Annie actually looked startled. Lydia hadn't seen her react like that before. She was talking to the barman and one of the girls. Maybe it was one of her daughters. The girl was obviously upset, so, while Lydia approached the bar, she stood at a distance.

A man she had never seen before, portly and with a thick

mustache, sidled up to her, acting far too familiar.

"Why Annie," he said. "Who's this new talent you've got here? You must be doing a far sight better than you're letting on, if you've taken on ones like this. Either that or she's trying to see how the other half lives. Which is it?"

Annie shot Lydia a silencing glance before addressing the rude man. "Stay out of my business, Jim."

He inspected Lydia up and down in a manner she hadn't experienced before. Lydia flushed at his insolence, although she felt almost flattered.

"Can't she talk?" the man asked, apparently enjoying her discomfort.

"And who might you be?" Lydia snapped, unable to stay silent.

"Jim Ryan. Annie's brother. You must be new to town, if you haven't heard of me."

"Well, I'm not," she snapped. "And you have the wrong idea. I deal in real estate, not the flesh trade as you so wrongly assume. I'm looking for property in the area. Know of any?"

Shocked, Jim Ryan recovered. "Well, lady, today's a good day to be asking around. One of those Chink whores has been found strangled in her bed. Dead. Some people might get nervous and want to offload a thing or two."

Julia, or May, looked like she was ready to bolt. Annie looked more than simply unhappy. "Those people have their own ways. None of that has anything to do with us."

The girl didn't look convinced. "How do you know what happened? You don't. None of us do."

"Julia, that girl was found in a crib. Do you work out of a crib? No, you don't. That's why you want to be in a house environment like this. If a fellow starts roughing you up, you scream for help, and we all come running. That's how it works. Now get busy."

Julia gave her mother a sullen look. "It's hard to scream with someone's hands wrapped around your throat, I'll bet." But the girl hitched up one side of her skirt in her hand, which she positioned against her hip. All the men got a good look at her leg, as was intended. She swayed through the saloon prowling for her next customer.

Jim Ryan ignored the girl and focused on Lydia.

She met his look dead on. "Do either of you have a building or land that you want to offload?"

Jim shook his head and gave her an unfriendly look, which was still nicer than the look he offered Annie. He left without saying good-bye.

Annie was none too pleased. "He'll remember you from here on out."

"Let him," Lydia replied. "Sometimes the truth is the best defense, and I am always in the market for another good invest-ment."

Annie poured out two whiskies. "That might be," her hand shook a little. "But that doesn't mean I want him getting involved in my private business."

"Understood," Lydia replied, figuring that she *would* start coming in through the back, as Annie preferred. "Despite your assurances to the contrary, I can see you are upset about this unfortunate event."

"Well, although the Chinese are nothing like us, the killing does put the girls on edge. The strangled one was found late last night. Rumor has it that another Chinaman killed her. But like I told Julia, it has nothing to do with us."

Lydia frowned. "There was no mention of a murder in the newspaper this morning . . ."

Annie leaned on the bar and lowered her voice. "There's a lot that goes on down here that don't get reported. And with good enough reason."

Lydia started feeling more than a shade uncomfortable, and it had nothing to do with the laudanum. It had to do with the suspicion that they were all on the edge of something violent, something dangerous. The saloon had never felt dangerous before, but for the first time she felt the current. Lydia finished her whiskey. On her way back to the stable she took more notice of her surroundings. She inspected the alleys and sized up the drunks and other unsavory characters lured to that part of town.

A murder that didn't even make the newspaper.

No wonder people had been talking. No wonder it didn't feel safe.

# CHAPTER 25
## DISCARDED LIKE MINE TAILINGS

Christmas was a terrible time to be hooking.

The weather blew cold, the cheer was forced, and melancholy prevailed, especially in whorehouses. It marked the time of suicides and regrets, and Pearl herself was none too rosy. She carried on whooping it up through the elements, hoping Frank might bring her a Christmas present. All the while, in her heart, she knew better. She knew she was acting foolish.

The faintest vein of hope was more elusive than veins of gold and silver. And she knew this for a fact.

Pearl sat in the cold window of Sadie's to draw in business, distracted by daydreams on that forlorn gray afternoon. Flakes of snow pelted the frozen brown mud of Fifth Street. The dull thud of an ignited mine blast carried. She had grown accustomed to many different things. The industry noises were better than the moans of rutting and the terse words of petty squabbles. Very little truly shocked or disturbed her now. But the music she had once liked so well sure could get on her nerves.

Like many things, her first impressions of the sporting life got sullied with a healthy dose of reality.

It was like the music, whose sole purpose was for egging jakes on. Those jaunty tunes tried to cover up longing hearts and sad, hard lives. For the most part, they failed.

She sighed, and pulled her shawl tighter against the chill that travelled through the glass. Her brown hair was piled atop her head in a fashionable way but her legs were apart, revealing the tops of dark stockings against white thighs for the entire avenue to see. What once had been white frilly undergarments now bore a gray tinge. Her boots were still nice, well, nice enough, and her ankles fine.

"You're supposed to be enticing jakes in, not warning them off." Sadie had come up behind her to look out at the street.

True, Pearl was lolling in the window more than flirting. She sat up a mite, and winked at a fellow passing by. Of course, he came in.

"See what happens when you apply yourself?" Sadie gave her a teasing nudge.

"What the hell." Pearl figured she might as well try to have a good time. Remaining in the window, she sat crossing and uncrossing her legs. Jutting her chest out from her bodice and twirling a loose curl around her finger. All in a suggestive manner, and it worked. More men came in.

When Pearl tired of the window game, she got up and approached a miner.

He eyed her with hope. "Are you the one known as Pearl?"

"Good news travels far." Although the opposite tended to be more likely.

He hitched up his pants, then twisted them around his stomach fat. "Care for a drink?"

"Sure. I'll take a whiskey." Manners dictated that she should ask the miner a question, but there weren't any answers she wanted to hear. Of course, she stood closer to him than was acceptable to the outside world, like any good whore with an ounce of sense would do.

He wasn't too clean, and she didn't care as much as she once had. Come to think of it, once upon a time, she never drank whiskey and never touched the dope. Her language had been refined, which had earned her snide comments a-plenty. Now no one noticed, because she had come down with the rest of them.

She consoled herself that at least she knew better, not that *that* provided much comfort.

The jake signaled for two measures, and then turned back to Pearl. "So, do you know Frank Bonnert, the one that works at the Independence?"

"I do." Pearl felt cautious. "Why?"

"He said you were a good lay and that I should try you out for myself. And from what I saw in that there window, he is probably right."

Pearl never could remember what she said next. But that night, after she finished with that jake, another, and the one after that, she went to bed with a whole bottle of whiskey. Which, in all probability, had been added to her chit with a mark-up.

She felt as discarded and used as last year's newspaper—the one that carried unwanted news.

And a broken heart didn't mean she couldn't spread her legs. But none of it made her feel anything that mattered.

Maybe no one could make her feel much of anything at all.

It was a bit odd, visiting her mother's grave daily, but it was as close as she could get to a sense of belonging.

A cold gust of wind blew from the north. The clouds rising behind the mountains were deep and dark. She pulled her shawl closer. Errant grasses sprouted through the brushing of snow, bending under its weight. Clods of dirt and stones poked through at intervals, serving as punctuations of remorse and loss.

Pearl worried that she was set square upon that same path.

She patted the mound that covered her mother. "I'm back again."

But her mother never answered. Yet the wind blew through the pines, and sounded as lonely as Pearl felt.

Her illusions were slipping away through her fingers. The fading light dipped behind the mountains and drew her back up the rutted tracks to Leadville. She picked up her pace as she neared the business district, managing to step lively and toss out a few sassy remarks. She entered the Fortune Club from the alley and found Sadie at her ledger with some whiskey in front of her. God, it was depressing looking at the older woman, and her mood took a dive. Pearl pulled up one of the rough stools and sat across from the madam.

Sadie raised her eyebrows a fraction and poured her a drink. "The dead don't have to talk, you know." She pushed the cork back into the bottle, a decisive and practiced movement.

Pearl considered the shadowy corners where the light didn't reach. The cleaning woman didn't reach there, either. She brushed away a stray lock of hair. "A clairvoyant woman once told me that if I ever found her, and that if I tried to talk to her like I would have in real life, she might manage to give me a sign."

Sadie snorted. "She wouldn't have been able to formulate a sentence, toward the end, much less send out any signs from the beyond. She had enough trouble making it up one side of the street and down the other. Now, do up your hair and paint your face. Try to look attentive, for Christ's sake. You should be pulling in more money."

Pearl tossed back the drink in one motion. "Fuck it."

"Exactly," Sadie replied, approving.

★ ★ ★ ★ ★

PART IV

DENVER

A COW TOWN OF GLORIOUS
PROPORTIONS WITH A HIGH
PERCENTAGE OF UNATTACHED
MEN, FOR ONE REASON OR
ANOTHER

LATE JANUARY 1893

★ ★ ★ ★ ★

# CHAPTER 26
## DOWNHILL TO DENVER

Life was just so much bullshit.

Pearl got off the train at Union Station, expecting a familiar face to meet her on the platform. Although the station was bustling, there was no one there for her. Why did everyone act like she was so goddamned expendable? She had to hire a porter and the weather was cold. Obviously, Annie still didn't give a rat's ass about her, seeing as how she hadn't bothered to send anyone.

"Screw her," Pearl muttered.

Pearl surveyed her surroundings and liked the surge of Denver, the familiar smell of cattle and smelters. The city was her ticket to be new again—as far as the row was concerned. She would be smarter this time around. She knew how things worked, and she knew the score about her mother. Pearl figured she was smart enough to avoid another brush with heartache in the form of a handsome face and a stingy heart. But she didn't want to abandon the dream altogether. She just needed to make stronger choices.

She sauntered into Ryan's with the porter trailing five feet behind, knowing she cut a good figure. Her purple travelling suit sported a fashionable and form-hugging cut, clinging in all the right places. That was a damn good thing, too—considering how much she owed Annie for it.

She made sure she didn't let the hem drag in the street.

"Howdy, boys!" Pearl exclaimed to all the patrons in the saloon. Just to shake up the clientele a bit. There was no sense pussy-footing around. She was the top of the heap and that's how she wanted it to stay. And it would.

For a time.

The porter set the trunk down, uncomfortable at the display and at the surroundings. Pearl opened her purse with a flourish and tossed a silver dollar in his direction. When he caught it, Pearl blew him an exaggerated kiss.

"Come back to see me when you're off work," she said in a voice that carried, acting as if every man in Denver had been waiting for her arrival. She laughed with a whore's laugh when the flustered man bolted. "Guess he's the shy type," she pronounced, still playing to the crowd.

"Well," said a woman's voice behind her. "That's quite the entrance. What else did Sadie teach you?"

Of course, it was Annie. She took in Pearl's measure, eyes glinting with approval. She was already counting the money Pearl would be making for her. As was her custom.

"She taught me to do my own goddamned ciphering." Pearl felt it important to get that out on the table.

Annie smirked, brown eyes sparking. "Did you fall for that bit, too? That's just a little game she plays. She's as shrewd as anyone when it comes to figures."

That about knocked the breath out of Pearl, and opened the door to all kinds of unsettling thoughts.

Annie eyed her. "Let it go. Sometimes you just have to overlook certain peculiarities."

Pearl smarted. "That's kind of rich, considering."

Annie headed toward the stairs. "Considering all she put up with from you? I heard about the clandestine romance. So, I'd say you probably owe her some money on that score. Come along, and I'll show you the room I set aside for you."

Pearl went to the bar rail instead. "I'd rather have a whiskey and a hot bath."

A jake in a wool suit eyed her. His expression changed, as if he liked what he saw. "I would be honored to buy you that drink."

*Honored my ass,* Pearl thought—but for the moment Annie appeared impressed.

So Pearl gave him a winning smile, and a glass of whiskey appeared. She downed it in one go, much to the jake's surprise. Annie's, too, for her smile faded and her eyes grew hard.

"Travelling," Pearl proclaimed, "is a mighty thirsty business. Cold, too."

She winked at the suit, and put an extra sway and wiggle into her walk as she followed Annie upstairs.

"No boozing on the job," Annie cautioned through clenched teeth.

That was plain unlikely. But she kept her sentiments to herself. If Annie thought she was going to push Pearl around, she had another think coming.

Pearl was going to make damn sure she took care of herself, before anyone else. And that included Annie and the bloody house.

A couple of hours later, Pearl flounced into Annie's office. "You know, Sadie's has a bath of its own."

"That's the next improvement." Annie gave her a sharp look. "Sadie said your rates were tumbling."

Pearl shrugged it off. "I wouldn't exactly say 'tumbling.' I was a known commodity. It's to be expected."

"Maybe," was Annie's reply. The way she said it got under Pearl's skin a mite.

So she retaliated. "But you know, *Annie,* Leadville was an interesting experience all the way around. Some details got filled in for me. About how my mother was real bad off near the end. Did you know Sadie and the other girls had to take up a collection to bury her? I presume that was for the coffin, *because she's still in the damn potter's field.*"

Annie didn't look impressed, or even bothered. "I don't recall you swearing before you left. As far as Claire's decline, well . . . Make sure you don't go the same way."

Pearl gave out an irritated laugh. "No intention of it. And the potter's field is only the half of it. Do you know she told people you forced her to put me in the Good Shepherd? Somehow money exchanged hands, and she didn't get a dime of it."

Annie slapped her desk out of exasperation. "What the hell? I gave them a donation for your keeping, and out of my own money, may I hasten to add. Of course she didn't get a dime of it! None of that had anything to do with her. It had to do with *you.* I'm kind of getting fed up with being blamed for Claire's going off the rails. If you're going to be a pain in the ass, I might just not want you here after all. Now, let's get down to the business side of things, instead of making this a hamstrung family reunion."

"Fine," Pearl said, off balance and angry. She had no proof Annie wasn't lying. Annie was known to make up things to suit her own purposes. They all did. "I know I'm the best bet you've got going, and you know it, too."

Annie sat in her chair, appraising Pearl. Unwilling to concede. If she was upset by the accusations, she sure didn't show it. The consummate businesswoman trading in female flesh.

Like it was the most natural thing in the world.

"The rules for hooking here at Ryan's are as follows. The house takes fifty percent of what you earn, whether we are talking about the going rates or tips. See that you follow that here. Sadie went too soft on you on that account. Room, board, and laundry cost one hundred-twenty dollars a month. If you take any alcohol up to your room that is not paid for by a jake, that goes on your monthly bill."

Pearl flinched. Denver rates were more expensive than Leadville's. "I'll bet May and Julia don't pay that much. I suppose you're going to tell me they get some sort of discount or something, for one reason or another."

For a moment, Annie looked baffled. "Why wouldn't I charge them the same? Their days of having me provide for them are long over. If anything, they probably eat more than you do."

"You're not very much for family," Pearl sniffed.

That set Annie's temper to flare. "The hell I'm not! I'm what stands between you and the cribs, and don't you forget it!"

Pearl flinched, but tried to cover. "Well, you must not do a very good job of it. Considering past history."

"Claire was out of her mind. If anything, she cost me even more money than I realized—before things fell to that point. Now, see to it you keep to the good. Drinking whiskey on duty is a hell of a way to start, and it leads downhill fast."

Pearl waved that point away, like an unpleasant smell.

Annie tapped on her desk with her fat forefinger, rings sparkling. "Don't think I'm going to fall for your airs and graces, missy. Denver ain't as friendly as the gold and silver camps, and neither am I. You pay your own fines if you get caught doing something outside of these four walls. There's nothing the city likes better than to catch girls out and slap them in jail."

"I didn't have any problems of that nature in Leadville," Pearl smirked, superior.

"Bully for you." Annie was leaning forward, ready to strike.

"But if I had ended up in jail, what would you have done?" For once, Pearl was actually interested in the answer.

Annie didn't hesitate. "Not a damn thing. Maybe some time in a cell would set your head on straight."

"Sounds like the voice of experience. When were you in jail?"

Annie gave her a look that said she still had a lot to learn. Pearl was growing mighty tired of it.

181

"We all got tossed in during one very expensive raid along the entire street. So you can take your airs and graces on that count, and smoke them. Everyone who is anyone has been in jail at one time or another, but there's no need to put roots down in there. It's a sloppy habit, and it gets damned expensive. How do you think those politicians afford all those fancy houses?"

Pearl shrugged, wondering how the hell she was supposed to know a thing like that. "The thought never crossed my mind because it has nothing to do with us down here."

"The hell it doesn't," Annie said, indignant. "They're on the take, you pumpkin. I pay for liquor licenses every month whether I want to or not. All those fees, fines, and licenses and God knows what else lines their pockets. That's how Denver's run."

Pearl sighed, to show Annie just how little she cared.

In response, Annie smiled in an unkind manner. "Since this is a business meeting, *Pearl,* I was going over your tab. I show that you still owe the house forty-three dollars for clothes. You'll have a doctor's exam in the morning, too. Just to make sure you didn't bring anything back from the mountains that you shouldn't have."

Pearl stood up, a sinking feeling in her stomach knowing she had only twenty-eight dollars in her purse. "I didn't catch anything. I know what to do and how to do it. Sadie was quite emphatic on that all along."

"Good. And, Pearl, I'm going to start out charging fifteen dollars or more a go for you. Keep that information to yourself, and don't go sharing it with your cousins." Annie looked over the tops of her glasses in that annoying way she had. Just to make sure her point was taken.

The women locked eyes, but neither spoke. In other words, Annie had won the round.

For the first time in her short career, Pearl felt a little less special and a little more common. The common part bothered her a deal. Pearl wanted admiration for having particular qualities that had nothing to do with spreading legs. She sat across the expanse of Annie's desk and it struck her just how naïve she had been.

Well. It was all too late for that now.

The truth was that her value to anyone centered on having a price tag slapped upon her. She felt like a common whore. And it was Annie's fault. Annie had steered her in this direction.

Being the prettiest provided cold comfort. Annie had probably never been pretty, but she was running things now, and Pearl was just another horse in the stable.

Annie had to be lying about paying the nuns for her upkeep. She was a nasty, horrid woman. Even if she was family.

"I'm done with this conversation," Annie said.

Pearl stood up. "Nice to see you, too, *Aunt* Annie."

With those words, Pearl vowed to get even with Annie for how she felt. One way or another.

# CHAPTER 27
## BULLIES AND NEW BEGINNINGS

Leadville damn near caused Pearl to question becoming a whore, especially when her rates started falling. But Denver wasn't shy about restoring her earning potential. Her rates, once again, rose to twenty dollars a go—and she had jakes lining up to sample what she was selling. This time Pearl had more of an eye toward bolstering her income when possible, some methods of which might be considered dubious.

Ryan's was a step, or three, down from Sadie's. But at least that damn piano was dead during the day. It didn't escape Pearl how her opinions had changed concerning music. Once she had liked it, but it had become almost a trial. Especially when the songs started repeating. They would get caught in her head, making it spin like too much cheap whiskey. Twirling and flickering out of control, drunkenly. Dangerously.

One thing was for certain, at Ryan's it was going to be harder to get a proper drink. Annie watched her like a hawk.

Her popularity might have done her heart good—as long as she didn't dwell on what she actually was doing. She hadn't had time to catch a breath and take stock until that second Tuesday. She strolled down to the saloon at one-thirty in the afternoon. The pickings were slim, and a trifle odd.

"Could you pour me a glass, Michael?"

"As long as it's beer," he replied, yanking her chain. "No one likes a drunk whore. Especially Annie."

She took the glass he offered, eyed the liquid. The wrong

liquid. "She doesn't own me." But Pearl knew Annie pretty much did own her. No matter how much money she earned, Annie's cut still took a fair whack out of it. Worse, as long as any of them were in debt to "the house," they were in debt to Annie. And that meant she was owned until she could pay it off. That thought didn't sit well with her, but it didn't slow her down, either.

Pearl cast about at the daylight clientele, consisting of a couple of scroungers and a clump of greenhorns. The atmosphere felt a bit chancy. Almost the way she liked it.

Ever since she got back, Pearl felt a tension that had nothing to do with her: something in the underlying current she could sense but could not see. The saloon and whorehouse rollicked along at a fearful pace—but maybe it wasn't earning like it should.

Annie had always been close-lipped about money and business.

Perhaps that fancy lady was causing problems; not that Pearl cared too much. But it got her thinking, wondering about Annie's weaknesses and what they might be. She wondered about the pall Annie cast, at least as far as she was concerned. She took a mouthful of beer, swished it around and swallowed, wishing it were whiskey.

Annie emerged from somewhere in the back, envelope in her hand. The first thing her gaze landed on was the glass in Pearl's hand. Pearl held it up in a mock salute, which, judging by her aunt's expression, didn't sit too well. Regardless, Annie placed the envelope next to the till, making sure Michael saw her. She nodded at him; he nodded in return. Strange, secret codes of which Pearl knew nothing.

Annie all but ignored Pearl, her gaze directed over to the beat cop sitting against the wall. Harrigan, they said his name was.

That was something different from Leadville, too. In Leadville the police seemed . . . busier.

Annie must have been paying more attention to her than she thought, for she moved over toward her and said on the quiet, "He likes to throw his weight around."

Pearl thought of how he wasn't the only one. But at the moment, it seemed like Annie was actually confiding in her. She wondered if she should give Annie another chance. Then she dismissed the notion as foolishness.

"Isn't he smaller than you?" Pearl asked, intentionally widening her blue eyes with a forged innocence. Annie knew she was calculating.

Her eyes narrowed. "You have a big mouth, and a nasty disposition, *darlin'*. I would sure hate to see you lose any teeth. Now there looks to be a couple of fellas that need relieving. I suggest you get pulling."

Pearl laughed, all happy and shiny and false. One of the greenhorns was making eyes at her. He didn't know it simply didn't matter. She grabbed his dick through his pants.

"My, my," she said, as the fellow turned crimson.

His friends roared with laughter. "Damn!" They guffawed and slapped each other on their backs, delighted and shocked in equal measure. "Denver sure is something! Did you see what she just did?"

She led the spluttering jake by the hand and took him upstairs for a twirl.

When Pearl and the greenhorn came back down, he sure had been relieved of any tension he might have been carrying. He had also been relieved of a ruby stickpin when he wasn't looking. It could have so easily fallen from his lapel and landed in the gutter.

The bulky beat cop, in the meantime, had shifted his position to the bar. Annie stood tense behind the counter. Feeling vindictive for no particular reason, Pearl went over to her, hoping to rub some salt in whatever wound there might be.

"He looks like a man's man," Pearl said, voice low, acting like she knew how to handle the type. She did, in truth, admire his bearing. Maybe he had been a street fighter. Bare knuckle brawling was always a fine way to raise a girl's spirits.

Annie clearly didn't give a flying continental about Pearl's opinion. "You'd do well to keep out of his way."

That was probably the best endorsement she could have made to capture Pearl's interest.

Harrigan seemed to sense the women were talking about him. He offered them a bored stare that conveyed his general disdain for women of their ilk. Underneath that disdain was a dare, almost a challenge to step out of line.

Which was highly likely, all things considered. That was what whores did. That was what saloons were for.

Weighing her options, Annie cursed under her breath but then acted like she was making a social introduction. "Casey, this is Pearl. Isn't she a dainty, pretty little thing?"

Although he continued leaning against the bar, he turned in their direction, tugging his coat down. Barrel chested and beer bellied, he indeed had weight to throw around. But he was clean, obviously particular about his grooming. Which made him better than most, as far as Pearl was concerned.

"Nice to meet you," Pearl said, jutting out her breasts and wetting her lips.

If Annie was afraid of him, that would suit Pearl just fine.

The man cast a darting glance in her direction, then ignored her. Offended, Pearl twirled her hair, making a show of it. She had decided he was an asshole. But that didn't mean she was going to give up trying to spark his attention. His admiration. Triggering just whatever it was he had that could do something for her.

"I already know who she is," he growled in Annie's direction.

"It's not like she just got here. And talk on the street seems to be favorable. Maybe that means you need more protection."

Annie stiffened. "Protection is about quality, not quantity. As it is, you scare away more of the punters than you should. And since our arrangement has already been agreed, you can't renegotiate. Especially not in light of that damned raid that caught you flat-footed, without even the slightest peep of a warning."

"I told you before, and I'll tell you again, no one knew it was coming. As far as your girl here is concerned, well . . . If she was really quality, she'd be over with Jennie Rodgers or Mattie Silks. Wouldn't she?"

He was a rude man, speaking about her like she wasn't even there. The fact that word was out on the street about her lifted her spirits a mite, but then his observation about the parlor houses struck her right back down. Because he was possibly right. But when his cold, blue eyes rested on her for a longer moment, Pearl felt something register in his expression. A kind of reluctant regard.

Anger was emanating from Annie. *Emanate.* Now there was a word she hadn't thought of in a long while.

Her aunt was defending her, in a manner of speaking. "No doubt Pearl is bound to set tongues wagging, and those parlor houses would take her on, if she were to consider it. But she won't because she's a Ryan. And she's glad to be back in the bosom of her family. Ain't that right?"

Harrigan didn't seem to care one jot about Pearl's feelings on the matter, and didn't give her time to answer. "Ain't that special. She's like any other whore, willing to be bought and sold. None of you are much in the way of family virtue, as far as I can see."

Annie gave him a nasty smile for that particular commentary. "You know, I would watch what you say, if I were you. Denver ain't all that friendly when it comes down to it. And you'll do what I pay you for: help spread the word. And keep your god-damned views about my family to yourself. Got it?"

Bull-headed, he refused to back down. "The parlor houses ain't running their girls out of a plank and rough-shod saloon. What have you got to say about that?"

That crossed Annie wrong. "I would say I only have to tolerate so much, if you catch my drift. It might be best to keep in mind that you aren't on any parlor house payrolls I've heard of."

"For the time being," the cop snorted.

Pearl could see Annie's back was up, and agreed he wasn't much in the personality department. But she wasn't about to share that.

As Harrigan moved away from the bar and headed toward the door, he brushed close to Pearl. Like he expected she would get out of his way. She held her ground, so he stepped on the toe of her boot. Not hard, but enough to get her attention. Enough to smart.

"Didn't your mother teach you any manners?" Pearl scolded, making a show of leaning down to rub her toe.

Harrigan kept walking, but called over his shoulder loud enough for everyone to hear. "I don't answer to the likes of you."

Pearl intercepted the look Annie gave Harrigan's back. Her eyes glinted like a knife's blade. For the first time Pearl wondered how dangerous her aunt could be, if provoked.

She smiled to herself. "Are you sure you can handle him, Annie?"

Annie glared as she marked the cop passing in front of the window. Then she looked Pearl over from head to toe, none too friendly. Like Pearl had gone a step or two too far.

Pearl thought she might just shut up and stay out of her aunt's way. For a while.

# CHAPTER 28
## JEALOUSIES—PETTY AND OTHERWISE

The damn Denver weather was fickle—snow one day, runoff the next, then back to snow, and then switching into something approximating spring. It wreaked havoc with the outhouses, bogs, and cribs in the alley. Snow froze anything damn near solid, and the runoff allowed it to thaw—but on those bright days when the temperature rose, so did the smells that had been frozen.

And it sure stunk like hell.

Of course, Harrigan made himself at home there, right in the middle of Ryan's, much to Annie's ire. Graft didn't come cheap with him lapping up the whiskey, and neither did the coffers of Denver. Both were intricately entwined. When City Hall started to feel a pinch for whatever cockamamie reason, the pressure was turned up on Market Street. Businesses got set back hundreds of dollars through arbitrary fines and payoffs, and Ryan's was no exception. There was no way to avoid it. And the powers of Denver sure were testing the limits of what Annie could pay.

Feeling stretched, Annie had started cutting a few corners, as much as it grieved her to do so. In the form of watered-down liquor served after midnight to those already the worse for wear.

It was four o'clock on a Wednesday afternoon, and the weather was turning chancy as snowflakes swirled down. March was a month marked by worsening cabin fever and the attendant rowdiness. Despite all the rebelling against the lingering cold,

March tended to be a flat month in Denver as far as the brothels were concerned. Claims in the mountains were often inaccessible, and the roads to Denver treacherous. The stockmen were forced to stay close to their herds, for fear of heavy snows and blizzards trapping them. Nothing was worse than a frozen herd of cattle. Other than a vein of ore that petered out.

Both were equally dead.

The citizens of Denver didn't spend as much as the out-of-towners. Greenhorns and miners on a spree were a sight to behold, and a force to be reckoned with. They did the saloon keepers' and the madams' hearts good. The whores were getting bored deep within the drifts of March, but Pearl was already stationed downstairs, dolled up for another night of carry-on. Her long brown hair cascaded down her back, the front pinned up nicely, a tattered shawl draped seductively around her shoulders. She wasn't doing anything more than just standing, looking out of the plate-glass window to the street beyond. Annie approved, but it was eerie just how much she looked like her dead mother. The same bone structure and all.

Claire sure had been pretty, Annie recalled with an uncharacteristic stab of melancholia. And dead for the past twelve years or so. Maybe more. Well. There was no reason that history had to repeat itself.

Blessed saints, Pearl was drawing customers in just by standing there, lost in thought, almost nice and innocent. Perfect for the lure. Loud, clomping footsteps lifted Annie out of those damned musings. Julia and May came in, looking large and common by comparison to Pearl. Nothing more than good-time girls, they would never have a chance in hell of being parlor house inmates. They knew it, and passed nasty looks in Pearl's direction.

"What's the problem?" Annie didn't expect an answer, and she knew full well what the problem was.

The front door commenced to swinging open with more regularity, men tempted by Pearl's pretty fragility. It was a bit early for screwing, but what the hell. First up for sport was a jake in a shaggy buffalo coat, the chill of the afternoon radiating off of him. He headed for the bar but was marking Pearl and her actions.

"Whiskey and whatever she's having." He tossed his head in her direction.

May was hovering beside him. Sensing a likely target, she pressed along his coat and pretended to shiver. "Pearl's a priss, not to mention all skin and bones and gristle. I have more to grab hold of."

The man gave May the once-over; considered her proposition. He turned to Annie. "You in charge here?"

"I am." Annie poured out the whiskey.

The jake looked from one girl to the other, and back again. Conflicted, he asked, "Do they cost the same?"

Son of a bitch.

Annie tried not to appear irritated. May was listening in, dead interested.

Annie pushed the drink in front of him. "Each girl has her own rate, and it is not common to discuss it in front of them. No sense getting them all wrapped up in each other's business."

The jake seemed to regard that as some type of scolding, but he got over it. "Sorry."

Annie decided to move things along. "That's one dollar for the whiskey, unless you still want to buy Pearl a drink."

"Well . . ." he stalled.

While he was figuring out his finances, Harrigan blew on in. Pearl turned toward the commotion he tended to create. More importantly, to Annie's way of thinking, Harrigan was directly marking Pearl. It wasn't a casual look, either, but an appraisal.

"I'll have the usual." Harrigan flung himself in Annie's direction without breaking stride, heading toward the table in the corner. He always sat with his back to the walls: probably worried that someone might stab or shoot him when he wasn't looking. The first of which, Annie thought, might be herself.

However, his lack of manners toward her had a price. Because of what Annie interpreted as his general chicken-shittedness, he got served a measure of the cheap stuff.

Annie shoved the drink across the bar counter. "Here, Julia. Take this to Harrigan."

May stayed planted by the fellow at the bar, pawing and dogging him. Annie watched Harrigan take a sip of the drink Julia proffered, and noticed with amusement that he couldn't tell the difference in quality. She turned back to the jake. No sense having them standing around flat-footed when they had money to spend. "Another drink to help you figure it out?"

Michael arrived, and took up his position behind the bar. "It's about time," Annie muttered under her breath.

"What's the matter with you?" He didn't appear to expect an answer, but made sure to look busy adjusting bottles and all.

"I think I'll take her," the fellow told Annie as she rounded the bar. "The thin one over there. Provided she costs less than twenty dollars."

Annie nodded and shooed her daughter away. "That's enough now, May. You heard the man. Get a move on."

Annie signaled to Pearl, but the damage had already been done.

"She'd better not cost twenty fucking dollars," May grumbled, jostling Pearl as she passed, headed toward the buffalo coat. Pearl gave her a pretty good shove in return.

When May was out of range Annie named the price. "That'll be fifteen dollars for Pearl. And that's a bargain. Another whiskey?"

The fellow deposited gold coins in the hand Annie held out

for payment. "I'll buy her a drink, too." Annie watched as Pearl sidled up to him, no doubt attracted by the flashing whiskey.

With Annie watching the proceedings, Michael made sure to pour her a drink that only masqueraded as liquor. Pearl's expression predictably fell a bit flat.

And that was a fine thing, Annie thought. She took care of her family just dandy, when they had enough damn sense to let her do so.

Bastards.

Bastards or legitimate, Annie didn't care. What she did care about was the legacy she hoped to leave behind. And more men were coming in. She congratulated herself on the part she played getting Pearl lined up in the business. It had been clear from the start that Pearl would pay off one way or another. If Pearl had gotten cold feet, Annie would have found another use for her somehow. But nothing would have been as profitable as having her hook for the family. Hell, Annie could use another one like her. Maybe her brothers had someone they didn't know how to handle. Her brothers found inmates by hanging around the railroad station and suffered the consequences on more occasions than they would admit.

Farm girls usually stayed sweet for the first year or so, before the hardness set in.

Annie had almost forgotten that Harrigan was lingering on like a bad smell, until she noticed him watching Pearl and her jake. With a little too much interest for Annie's liking.

When the pair cleared out and went upstairs, Harrigan bothered to get off his ass and come up to the bar. "What do you charge for time with Pearl?"

That caught her short. "You asking out of personal curiosity? I didn't take you for someone who cared much for that type of thing."

He snorted. "I don't frequent whores, if that's what you're

poking around about. But I did ask you a question. And it is reasonable to say I expect an answer."

"La-di-dah. I have no intention of discussing rates or the business aspects of Ryan's with you, unless you are purchasing wares or services."

He was getting under her skin to the point where she felt something might have to be done with him.

Harrigan stared at her like he thought that would make her back down. Fat chance.

"Got a problem, *Officer* Harrigan?" She lowered her voice, tone dead serious.

"I think I'll have another whiskey," he replied. "Make it a clean glass."

Michael looked from Harrigan to Annie before he lifted a finger for the whiskey. As luck would have it, two fellows started shouting at each other over something or other. Whatever the cause, one fellow hauled back and belted the bigger fellow, and before anyone could even utter an oath, chairs got knocked over, elbows stuck out, and general mayhem broke forth. The fellow who landed the first punch got thrown over the table, and cards and drinks went flying.

Harrigan sighed, like even looking at the men cost him a great effort. He took his billy club out of its holster and cracked one of the fellows on the shoulder. Harrigan lifted him up by his arm and booted him out into the street, where he landed in a heap. Harrigan returned to the fray, wading back in for the other miscreant. Sensibly, the man bolted out the front door.

Harrigan put away his billy club and straightened his coat before heading back to the bar. "That whiskey ready?"

Michael poured him a double measure, while Annie stood by and surveyed the damage.

"That," Harrigan said, "is what you pay me for."

"Do not crack the punters on the head with that club,

whatever you do. Unless they're set on killing someone." Annie couldn't let him get away with actually thinking he did something right. Truth was, she was kind of impressed, all things considered.

He took his whiskey and resumed his position at the table in the corner. Annie smothered her irritation as she went to get a broom. "Pick those chairs up," she called to the men as she passed.

Remarkably, some of them actually did.

After about fifteen minutes' worth of calm, Pearl and her jake came back downstairs and parted ways. The fellow headed to the bar. Harrigan got up.

"Let me buy this man a whiskey," he said to the barman. Harrigan turned to the jake with something approximating a smile. "How much did it set you back to go upstairs with her?"

"Fifteen dollars," the man replied.

It was clear from his expression that Harrigan started doing sums in his head.

Annie got put out by that, but there was little she could do as Michael turned to wait on the punters clamoring for drinks. Any good feelings Harrigan had fostered in Annie got wiped away by that piece of underhandedness. To Annie's way of thinking, Harrigan had once again returned to the point of having outstayed his welcome. By a long shot. To make matters worse, Harrigan knew she was watching him. And he didn't care.

"I'll be in later," he told her, making it sound something like a threat.

"Yeah, make sure you don't let the door hit you in the ass," Annie muttered. She remained leaning on the bar, watching Harrigan leave in the reflection of the mirror. Michael came over to her, took up position beside her.

"It doesn't add up that he has this beat. It pays too much for an outsider to just stumble upon," she told him. "See what you can find out, will you?"

"That I shall." Michael placed dirty glasses on a tray and straightened up around the till.

Annie stood, thrumming her fingers on the bar, surveying the expanse of Market Street as seen through the windows of the saloon. If Harrigan had backers, she wondered who they were and how dangerous.

Regardless, he might be able to cause trouble. It was just a matter of how much, really.

He sure was a gob-shite, and no two ways about it.

And there was little sense in her going off half-cocked. Although it might be tempting.

# CHAPTER 29
## INTERESTS, AMBITIONS, AND DEAD WHORES

Whores and half-cocked ideas were no strangers to each other.

"If I had a penis, I wouldn't do my job near as well," Annie was saying as she patted her hair, enjoying the shocked looks on her brothers' faces. Slack-jawed and bug-eyed, they were caught off guard by Annie's words. She tossed back her whiskey in victory.

"What the hell makes you say that?" Jim spluttered, crouching a bit toward the table like he just might spring.

It took a lot to fluster John and Jim, but she had actually managed. She surveyed the Monte Carlo, and what passed as the working girls in particular. "I'm just saying that having dicks blinds you two to some of the details about running whores well. You don't even know which lies they use to avoid doctors' examinations, and by the looks of things, that might be important."

The boys exchanged worried glances.

"Do you two even know how to tell them to check a jake for the clap?" Annie was all-out enjoying herself.

Both the boys turned red, appalled. Apparently they didn't like discussing dicks with their sister. John rushed behind the bar to get away, pouring another round of whiskey with the determination of a man who was going to need it.

Jim was made of a bit sterner stuff, and at least managed to keep eye contact with Annie. "Is that what you are here for, to tell us about the clap?"

"Nah, but I am kind of worried that you might not have heard of it. The reason for this social call is on account of how I want to help you two out. I've decided I'm willing to take some of that discounted liquor off your hands. The stuff you offered me at a fifty percent off the regular price a short while back. And I was thinking about seeing what your stable was looking like these days, but I've decided I'm going to pass on that count."

John approached the table with more caution the second time around. "We got some younger girls upstairs."

"I need, and am willing to pay for, someone on the level of Pearl."

The boys exchanged glances that spoke volumes. "We can see who or what comes into town, but our finders' fees have gone up. In the meantime, how many cases of the swill do you want?"

"I suppose two cases. But I was really here for girls."

It was like a card game, really. An enjoyable one, because her brothers didn't have good poker faces.

Annie rose to her feet. "Well, it sure has been nice visiting with you boys. So you'll send the two cases over?"

They nodded as if it was of little concern. "For a two-dollar delivery fee," Jim added.

Annie let that roll off her back. Things might be going better for her than for her brothers for once. There was no need to disgrace herself and her apparent advantage with a squabble over two paltry dollars.

She looked at her brothers. "That cop Harrigan is turning out to be a nuisance. He might end up creating a problem."

"Let us know." Jim's tone came across bored and level.

John perked up a bit, preferring this topic to the other. "That costs a lot more than a whiskey shipment."

"I didn't expect anything less," Annie replied, with a trace of affection.

★ ★ ★ ★ ★

The Denver Republic–*March 23, 1893*

> *Lena Tapper, another woman of questionable repute who plied her tired wares along Market Street, was found dead yesterday morning. Strangled to death, the murder weapon, if it could be called such, was her own skirt. Although a member of the frail sisterhood, she was a largish woman and a German immigrant. Found lying on her bed in an almost peaceful manner, she inhabited one of the cribs in the upper reaches of Market Street, reputedly enjoying a good disposition toward every man that she met. There was nothing indecent about the body, and nothing was stolen from her dwelling as far as anyone could tell. The crib was neat and orderly with no sign of a struggle or break-in. Of course, the police conducted a cursory investigation among the frequenters of that notorious part of town. Normally such inquiries reveal nothing more than shamed faces and claims of mistaken identity. However, in this event, two witnesses stepped forward: a porter at one of the more renowned brothels, and another frail sister. No suspect has yet been apprehended, although assurances have been given that the Boys in Blue are working on it.*

Obviously, it was a slow day for news in Denver proper, because a whore's death graced the newspaper columns. But this whore was white. Word had already been circulating along the dives and watering holes of Market Street like fire consuming wooden buildings. As with any conflagration, it caused fear, especially among the girls.

"That's the second one in no time flat." Annie kept her voice level, her expression neutral. But her eyes flashed.

It was early in the morning, ten o'clock, but the girls were all up and unhappy.

"I knew her by sight," Julia said, eyes big and voice quivering.

"She wasn't mean or anything and was probably nearing the end of her working days. Who would have wanted to do that to her?"

"That has nothing to do with anything. *Murderers* don't *care*, Julia," Pearl replied in a practical manner, disdainful of Julia's maudlin streak.

Unflinching acceptance of facts without embroidery was a fine trait in their line of business, Annie thought.

Julia ignored Pearl altogether, proving that the bad blood was continuing. "It could happen to any one of us."

Pearl was about to respond with something snappy, but everyone's attention was diverted when Harrigan came in. Whistling a tune, for the love of Christ. Unconcerned, he looked at them all assembled like they were sitting around to pass the time of day. Of course, he said the wrong thing. "It's like a wake in here."

A hell of a way to start a conversation on that particular day. Annie patted the bar with impatience. "And you can't figure out why, is that it?"

Harrigan stopped. "Oh, shit. You're not all spun up about that crib git, are you? The killer will get caught and hauled in, if he's still in town."

"That might be kind of reassuring, if your lot were actually looking. But I'll bet that hasn't crossed anyone's mind, has it?"

With that line of conversation, Annie abandoned trying to console the girls. What she wanted was for Michael to get his ass into the saloon so she could high-tail it back to the cribs she owned, and a couple of others she had her eye on. It might just be the time to pick up something on the cheap. Murders tended to shake things up a bit and lower prices. But for a limited time. She also wanted to hear what the word was along the row as far as particulars were concerned. Annie was smart enough not to trust the newspaper accounts worth a damn.

"We're looking," Harrigan claimed, but didn't appear too convinced.

"Well, I would have to see the proof of that to believe it. If the murderer is not some rip from down here, the entire event will get brushed under the carpet. It always does. Witnesses or no witnesses—it's their word against his."

Harrigan threw his shoulders back a bit, sucked in his gut, and moved nearer to Pearl. "No one will harm a hair on your head," he told her. "That's what I'm for."

Annie snorted. "That's just wonderful. You keep an eye out on what goes on behind closed doors now, is that it?"

"Would you like a cup of coffee, Officer Harrigan?" Pearl got up, flashing something akin to gratitude. Along with a bit of skin. The kimono she wore was too large for her; the silk slipped off her shoulder, revealing a refined bone structure. One that could easily be snapped in two. Worse, she gave Harrigan what passed as a shy smile.

Annie rolled her eyes.

"With a dash of whiskey," he added, never one to leave well enough alone.

Annie watched Harrigan assess Pearl as she crossed the saloon, over to the coffeepot on the stove in the corner. She sure as hell put some extra wiggle in her walk for his benefit. Murder or not, that girl was working it as she got two mugs of coffee and spiked them both with whiskey. Annie gave her a nasty look on account of the whiskey part, but held her tongue due to the men who barged on in and bellied up to the bar.

"What'll you boys have?" Annie sounded cheerful as she took up her station, ready to pour out drinks.

"Whiskey and beer!" they chimed in, all enthusiastic. Obviously, they hadn't heard the news of the murder, or if they had, they didn't care. Probably didn't care.

The day lurched forward on shaky foundations. The girls

returned upstairs to dress. Pearl took her time in leaving, banking on the fact that she was alluring, near naked as she was.

Later that afternoon, Pearl sat in the near-empty saloon, looking distracted. It was one of those dead hours, in more ways than one. Annie weighed up the outcomes, and decided it might just be the time to give Pearl something to hang onto, so she wouldn't get any fool notions. Something to cement her in place just a bit better.

Annie plunked down beside her. "Your mother wasn't all bad, you know. She had a few points in her favor."

Pearl lifted her head, sat a bit straighter. It was a shame how that girl wore her heart on the outside. Annie could see it. That was something Pearl might want to consider changing. Sooner as opposed to later.

"That's not how everyone makes it sound."

Annie shrugged. She wanted to tell the girl to toughen up. She started to dredge up memories—things that should have been long dead and buried.

She smothered certain of them down. "Oh, there were some good times. But now you know how it is in this world. I expect you can see why I didn't tell you certain aspects about your mother in the beginning. Women are competitive creatures by nature. Forget all that nurturing crap, for that is what it is. Crap. Just try to be sensible and businesslike in your dealings."

"Like you," Pearl murmured.

Annie watched a change come over her. Just like Claire used to look.

Annie didn't reply—there was no sense in getting too close. She got up with a sigh of relief as a group of men wandered in, nice and boisterous. Crowds like that always drew others in.

"Howdy, boys!" Annie counted five men, all suits. The blond one caught her eye, and stopped her. His face was familiar, but she didn't know how to place him. A cut above the mainstream crowd, he sure wasn't one of the regulars.

No matter what was said, not all jakes looked alike and whores could be always counted on to lie. All to make things a touch less personal. A little less damaging.

Annie belted out a laugh, coarse and practiced, just to get the ball rolling. Precise in its implication. Nothing at all was needed to spark it off.

The men gathered at the bar and ordered a round of drinks. Loud, cracking jokes and talking all at once, they were splashing money freely. All that splashing drew a lot of attention, some of it welcome, some of it otherwise. Annie wouldn't be surprised if a few things went missing through the course of the evening. Rich men on and about town, looking for sport. The exact kind of prey that all of the demimonde lived for—existed for.

But Annie's inability to place the blond's face bothered her a fair bit.

Pearl approached the mass of menfolk, drawn by the smell of silver. Just like she was supposed to do. And the clean-cut blond fellow sure was eyeing her, all right. Hell, Annie thought she might ask twenty-five dollars with a fair likelihood of success. Then it came to her.

*Lydia's husband.*

She had to make sure. She slipped into her office, hurried to her desk drawers and rummaged around for the likeness Lydia had left with her. She found it, half-buried under some papers and receipts that needed paying.

A fine portrait, without a doubt. Asshole.

She shoved the picture back in the drawer and felt irritated on Lydia's behalf. But only in passing. Her indignation didn't mean there wasn't a buck to be made by the house.

Still, Lydia deserved better. They all did.

Toward that end, Annie charged him thirty dollars and almost miraculously the deal was struck. Annie considered the likelihood that the asshole was paying with Lydia's money. Of course, that didn't stop her from taking it. Business was business, after all. Lydia would feel the same way. That's why Annie kind of liked her. Drug habit notwithstanding.

May was bending Annie's ear about some slight or another, when Pearl came downstairs alongside Lydia's rotten husband. He rejoined his group of friends while another of the band of revelers went upstairs with Julia.

Pearl set off looking for another target, unaware of who she had been with. Even if she knew, she might not have cared. Annie couldn't take the risk of telling her anything the girl might find valuable.

But curiosity is a strong lure. Although she knew better, Annie couldn't stay out of it completely and went up to Pearl just as she was conferring with May. As they both were about to pounce. "Did he say anything?"

May and Pearl exchanged glances. "Since when do we care what any of them say?" May asked.

Good point. Who the hell, normally, cared? Caught, Annie lied. "One of the crib girls said she thought the killer was a blond. Like him."

Pearl rolled her eyes. "Well, next time warn me if I've got a murderer in tow. And since you asked, he said his wife didn't understand him."

May burst into a peal of laughter, hard and coarse. "Like we haven't heard that one before. Hell fire!"

Annie smothered a laugh. "Quit your cackling, you two. Misunderstood men are our bankroll. Now get moving. This is a good time house, and we have a reputation to maintain."

Which was pretty hysterical as well. But then Pearl slowed down on the laughter. "At one point he started stroking my throat. You don't suppose . . ."

Annie shook her head, having bitten off a bit more than she had planned. "Nah, but hard to say. Now, this one time you can have a real glass of whiskey to settle your nerves. Then it's back to work you go. Those plums need a pickin'."

Pearl shuddered, yet she bellied up to the bar and knocked her drink back like an old professional. That part wasn't good, either.

Annie swore under her breath. Damn Lydia, for having dragged her into this. But that was a mere annoyance. Something somewhere sure felt off.

And Annie couldn't tell what it was.

# CHAPTER 30
## GUTTER ASPIRATIONS AND OVERLOOKED DETAILS

The cold weather lifted like a velvet curtain, which could just as easily be dropped again. The rollicking drunks weren't muttering as much as usual, but chances were that the good weather wouldn't last. Foolish weeds had begun to sprout and unfurl—tentative green blades that most likely would get squashed down in time. Denver was doing its best to shake off the winter and place its money upon the spring.

Of course, like so many other things, it was a sucker's bet. The snow would descend at the worst possible moment, rushing to freeze flowers and snap budding branches and dash everyone's hope like a bug.

Every afternoon the clouds hung behind the mountains, biding their time and building their strength. That particular day, everything should have been up and running at Ryan's, when Harrigan poked his head in. Of course, the rest of his body followed.

Pearl was sitting half-sprawled at a table, bored with life. Or at least that was the impression she gave. She saw Harrigan all right, but hesitated to offer a smile. In fact, she looked the other way. He kept watching her, pretending he wasn't. It gave her the creeps and set her on edge. No one had been charged with the death of the two prostitutes. Although theories and rumors abounded. No one knew if the murderer was lurking in the alleys or in plain sight. It didn't pay to take chances.

But chances were all a whore took.

"Officer Harrigan," Pearl said as he approached the table.

"It's fairly quiet in here. Then again, the entire street is kind of quiet today. Why do you think that might be?" He looked down at her and smirked.

Pearl didn't bother to force a smile. It was little wonder Annie could barely stand the sight of him. "The nice weather probably has something to do with it. Or maybe the murders are bothering folks for some reason. How the hell am I supposed to know?"

"People aren't still bothered by that the murder business, are they?"

Pearl gave him a half-shrug with a bare shoulder. "Well, that depends on what type of people you are talking about, I suppose. Punters, no. Working girls, yes."

Harrigan signaled for two whiskeys to be brought over. So she warmed a bit toward him. Whiskey would make the afternoon pass a bit more smoothly. And Harrigan knew the difference between genuine whiskey and the shit she was supposed to drink. Michael knew it, too, and brought over the real stuff.

Harrigan sat down, eyeing her with an expression she took to be distrust. "Maybe you would feel safer in a place that didn't have a saloon attached to it. Liquor and violence go hand in hand." He lifted his glass in a salute.

He was a queer duck, but Pearl returned the toast. "The saloon's not so bad. The more the merrier, as they say." Booze and safety were a fine combination.

Harrigan frowned, cleared his throat. "I was hoping you might have dinner with me, over at the Depot. On your day off, of course."

He was turning pink and wouldn't meet her eyes. For a split second, she felt a bit tender toward him. Or maybe it was the whiskey, hard to say. No one had ever asked her to a restaurant before.

"You mean it?"

That took him back a bit. "I wouldn't have asked, otherwise. But keep that to yourself. And whatever you do, don't tell Annie. I get the feeling she doesn't like the police around."

Pearl smiled, knowing it was nowhere near as general as that. "I would love to have dinner with you. And I'll keep it quiet."

Although a carefully slipped word sure would make the other girls jealous.


The Depot wasn't much as far as restaurants went. Even Pearl, with her limited experience, could tell as much. It housed the Union Brewery in the back, and had boarding rooms upstairs and an office in the front. The restaurant portion was unceremoniously tacked onto the side like an afterthought. Which it probably was. The Depot wasn't like some of the finer restaurants she had seen with nice, big windows to the street. It didn't even hold a candle to the ones she had seen in Leadville. But prostitutes were seldom asked to dinner, so she would make the best of it.

She stood on the battered boardwalk and looked over at the building. She wondered, with a professional curiosity, just who inhabited those upstairs rooms, and whether they were straightforward or crooked.

What the hell. She knew how to handle herself.

Her arrival was signaled by a bell rigged to the door. Harrigan was already seated, plucking absently at the checkered tablecloth that was almost clean. When he saw her, he partially rose to his feet. So he had some manners, after all. He just chose when to use them.

"How come there aren't any other women in here; is this a

men's only restaurant?" Without waiting for an answer, she sat
down.

The sparsely populated tables were claimed by men—railroad
workers and laborers, some of whom eyed her openly. But she
was dressed just fine, and better than she had to judging by the
surroundings. She had purchased a new dress for the occasion
on Annie's credit. The men's scrutiny strengthened her
suspicions about the rooms upstairs.

An expression of genuine confusion registered in Harrigan's
eyes as his glance darted around to the other tables. "I hadn't
noticed."

Another woman, a waitress, appeared from the back. She
handed Pearl a menu and seemed a bit put out. Pearl looked at
the woman's clothes, and then down at her own. Dark blue and
almost proper, if a little low-cut. The woman had an obvious
chip on her shoulder, and Pearl had a fairly good idea just why
that might be. But she wasn't bothered. Much.

"If you've been here before," Pearl remarked to Harrigan, all
nice and proper knowing that he had, "what do you recommend?"

Harrigan's eyes moved down the menu and then back up to
her face. "The steak is good, but so is the meatloaf. It's up to
you."

Pearl figured she would order the steak. It was more
expensive, anyhow. "So, are we courting now, or what?"

Harrigan got all bug-eyed and flustered. Pearl laughed to
show she was joking. At his expense.

Happily, he took it relatively well. "Don't scare me like that.
It's not funny."

"All right," she said. "But it would solve a few problems.
Mainly it would put Annie in her place."

"Well." He smoothed his mustache. "I can't help but notice
there's no love lost between the two of you. Why is that?"

"Have you met her?"

Harrigan smothered a laugh. He waited for her to continue, without comment.

"I suppose it's because she never came to visit me in all the time I was growing up. But to be fair, I don't think she really visited her girls, either. I had been hoping for her to be like a mother or something. That sure didn't work out like I had expected."

And that was the end of that story as far as Officer Harrigan was concerned. She had no reason to offer him anything further.

Harrigan studied her for a long moment. "I don't think you are appreciated at Ryan's the way you should be."

That was for damn sure. "Well, I didn't think anyone ever noticed."

"Well, I have. And you can consider this a business meeting, if you like. You see, although I disapprove of what you do for a living, I figure you can't help yourself."

She felt wary. "Can't help myself, how?"

"Whoring. It's obviously in your nature, considering your family background. But here's where it gets interesting. You see, everyone around us is getting rich, because they are enterprising. So I've decided the best way to go about improving my lot in life is to come up with something I can control and profit from. And that involves you."

She figured she had experienced enough controlling and profiting upon her person to last a lifetime. "Involves me how?"

"I was thinking we could join forces. Leave Ryan's and come to work for me."

A gust of wind could have knocked Pearl over. The waitress reappeared, and Harrigan, acting the man, ordered for the both of them. "Two steaks, rare. With the juices running red. After all, bloody is best," he proclaimed. "I have to make sure Pearl, here, is taken care of."

The look the waitress gave Pearl upon receiving that piece of information was more than passing judgmental.

Pearl had never told him what she wanted. Good thing he chose correctly.

Harrigan cleared his throat when the waitress headed off for the kitchen. "The way I figure it, all those people in the fine homes on Capitol Hill are about three steps up from the gutter themselves. Including that fancy lady Annie knows. What's her name again?"

"Lydia," Pearl replied unthinking. And flinched. No one was supposed to know about her.

"And what is it that Lydia does?"

Harrigan was watching her closely. Too closely. The hair at the back of her neck rose. She was treading on very thin ice. But Harrigan was mistaken if he thought she was stupid.

"I've heard her say she sells real estate. Kind of strange for a woman, but there you have it."

Harrigan sure looked interested. "Well, I'll bet she's not married, or she wouldn't be working."

"How do you figure?" Half of the row was married one way or another, and that sure didn't stop anyone from *working*.

"If she had a husband, he would put a stop to her going into saloons, and especially wandering around Market Street." Harrigan folded his arms across his chest. But he gazed upon her almost fondly.

Steaming plates of food arrived, and Harrigan tucked into his meal, abandoning the conversation. Pearl took a careful bite, and had to admit it tasted fairly good. The rest of the meal passed in silence.

When Harrigan was done, he patted down his mustache. "So, what about it?"

Harrigan sure wasn't much for small talk.

Pearl decided to play it straight. "You just want to make

money off of me, the same way Annie does. What would be so very different working for you?"

He thought about that. "Well, your surroundings would be better, which means you can charge more money. How would that suit you?"

"And where is this place you have?"

Pearl watched as his face fell a bit. "I haven't gotten it set up yet."

She shook her head and smiled. Relieved, if anything. "Well then, I suppose we can talk about this later. When you have your place all set up and ready to go."

Earning more money was always a good idea. Pearl was propping Annie's business up, if anyone were to be honest about it. Which was unlikely in the best of times.

Harrigan paid the bill and stood. For all his professed concern for her well-being, he didn't offer to walk her home. He sure didn't seem too worried about a murderer on the loose that killed her kind.

In Pearl's world, that meant he didn't care. And half of her wondered why anyone should bother to care about her, or the rest of them.

That didn't sit well. But it just might have been true.

One of the things about Pearl was that she was never content to let things alone.

She noticed Annie was sporting a new pair of diamond earrings that sure as hell looked real. Pearl would be damned if she could explain where all her money was going—other than into Annie's pockets. She had a couple of dresses, and a few bits and pieces besides. Fuck all to show for fifteen dollars a go.

Then there was her mother's brooch.

She thought of Annie's diamond earrings, and calculated they were the results of a whole lot of time on her back or on her knees. Those damn diamond earrings would ultimately hold up better than she would, and it all struck her as very unfair.

Nothing was turning out as she had intended. She thought back to her arrival in Leadville, and how she had tried to act as if she were already experienced. No wonder Sadie had laughed at her. But it sure held an undercurrent of sadness, and one she had grown to recognize.

Pearl pulled open a drawer in the chest and felt around underneath the tatty chemises for the bag where she kept her valuables hidden. At the back of the drawer she felt the reassuring lump, pushed up against the left-hand corner. She brought it out and carried it to the bed. She sat and shook out the contents onto her lap. It sure as hell didn't amount to much.

The brooch was nothing more than a dented piece of flattened brass wire with a small, chipped enamel violet soldered on. A glass pearl in the center. That was it, really.

Maybe her mother named her after the stone on the flower. But she would never know.

She ran her finger over the pin and its chipped enamel, and wondered what her mother looked like. There was no picture. There seldom was a picture of women like them. But at least she had a keepsake—something solid to prove her mother once existed.

Of course, everyone wanted to believe their mothers had loved them. But, in Pearl's case, didn't the pin prove as much? Annie had said there had been some good times. Pride had prevented Pearl from asking.

A realization was half-forming like a nagging question that couldn't be silenced. What if Annie had truly done the best she could to save Pearl's mother?

Pearl resented Annie for a multitude of reasons. But she was growing to suspect that the real problem had something to do with the fact that Annie was alive, while Pearl's mother was dead.

Pearl took a swig of whiskey straight from the bottle. Her manners, along with her vocabulary, were going to hell. She thought she ought to care about that, even if she was the only one that held such concerns. Maybe a fancy man would come by someday and overlook her past. But as it stood at the moment, no one really cared about her or her fading manners, one way or another.

The weather was turning.

She moved over to the window, hugging the bottle against her chest as she surveyed the world below. Market Street caught between winter and spring was a miserable, muddy place. Rivers of meandering water created gullies around horse shit. The street was made worse still by the drunks that threw up on the rough planks that passed as sidewalks, and worse again by the off-tune pianos. A whore's brutal laugh carried on the forlorn wind and penetrated the window glass.

Pearl continued to stare out her window and felt as drab as the wretched flat gunmetal sky that threatened to spew rain or snow. The entire process would repeat until they all died.

It was a bit like working in a whorehouse, when it came right down to it.

Pearl took another swig.

# Chapter 31
## The Opium Scrolls

Lydia was never one to give up, especially not on something she wanted to try. Especially considering how Stanley was acting toward her: totally without regard or sentiment, good or ill.

She slapped the reins lightly across the horse's back, urging it forward. The streetscape flowed by a touch faster, and Lydia sank back into her own thoughts. Indulging in speculation of a private nature, she reasoned that their marriage must be entering into a different and changing season. Abstractions lessened the sting of the failure. The partnership had eroded into a barrage of hard words and beatings that signaled late fall. Or even early winter. The desolate depths of late winter would mark the end of one horrible marriage of convenience. It was only fitting that it ended in a death of sorts, but the notion caused her heart to jolt. It wouldn't be a real death, she assured herself.

Like her marriage had become, that death would be merely symbolic.

She had heard opium was a bit like a symbolic death. All dreams and the sensation of floating. A relief from daily horrors was the closest she could come to imagining what heaven might be. Of a sort. She didn't expect to go to heaven in the afterlife— and that thought didn't bother her in the least.

She caught the bitterness in herself, and knew it hadn't always been that way.

In the spring of her marriage, she had been happy enough. The physical act of marriage and of loving suited her. But that spring hadn't lasted long and had managed to be tempestuous, similar to the windstorms that raged on the plains and destroyed everything in their path. The storms always passed. There were fine and pleasant days, but always another storm, then a brief period of glory, then blinding heat. The summer of her marriage had been burning and scorching when she came too near to falling in love, or thinking that she might, with her husband.

When she had actually tried to figure out what made her husband tick.

It had been a lost cause, especially in light of his embezzlement from her father. That had been the start of the beatings, and of the laudanum. The laudanum had been advised by a well-meaning doctor to mask her pain, but did nothing to hide the bruises. Recognizing the signs of manhandling, he had pressed a bottle of the tincture into her hand with a knowing look.

Men tended to stick together.

The horse had slowed again. Foolish beast, with no more gumption than Stanley. She was still puzzled by the manner in which Stanley's passion had cooled toward her of late. He hadn't even knocked her around for the last few months or so— and that was odd. She had never refused him in her bed, but he had stopped visiting. Which was just as well.

She knew he frequented whores. He spent too many nights away for it to be anything else.

She gave the horse another slap. Her mind started calculating, like it always did when lucid. Her thoughts followed the trail of money, which was as sound a place to start as any, and more solid than some. Her calculations ended with the predictable conclusion that since the money coming in was earned by her, she could do as she pleased. Stanley's lack of opposition was a curiosity. One that could change in a heartbeat if she stopped supporting him in the style he craved. Cravings could be such a nasty thing.

Conceivably the end of her marriage was drawing nearer.

And she decided not to give Stanley too much credit. He was hapless, not dangerous, after all.

The opium den would do more than solve the problem of a slow day. She had no deals to strike, no negotiations to navigate—although, truth told, she wasn't trying all that hard at the moment. She could do that tomorrow, or the day after. Maybe even the day after that.

Turned away from the opium den the last time, well, that was a once-off. There was no need to let superstition scare her away. She had expectations of an exotic experience amid Chinese silks and fragrant opium-scented air. By going this very afternoon, she would gain entrance. She could experience for herself the sensation opium provided. Since smoking opium verged on illegal, it had to be better than taking laudanum.

Legal medicine was so run-of-the-mill.

Besides, there was nothing dangerous about opium. People just distrusted the Chinese.

Then she thought about the prostitute's murder. Somehow the murder of that poor unfortunate was linked in her mind with the opium business. It had to be the coincidence of strange events. Annie's disturbing insistence that the incident would go unreported. She checked herself, wondering when she had grown so hard. The death was more than an incident. It was a murder.

Maybe Annie was just trying to keep her out of doing more business in what she considered *her* end of town. That was another unworthy thought.

Without a doubt, Lydia accepted Annie's advice more than she did other people's. The madam's concern for her had been touching when she had presented herself with all those bruises. Lydia had accepted Annie's advice to hire a yard boy who took up residence in the attic of the carriage house. He had instructions to turn to Annie Ryan if anything happened to Lydia. Unsurprisingly, Annie's name had struck a chord with the lad. Which was just as well. As far as the addition of the boy to the household staff, Stanley hadn't asked who he was or what he was doing. Running a well-oiled household was women's work, or so Stanley thought.

Who was out at his club, or some other place. It didn't matter where. She never cared where he was anymore. That thought made her a bit miserable again.

As fine a reason as any to go to an opium den. Only this time, for propriety's sake, she decided she could leave her horse in a different stable.

There were no extravagant trappings to the opium den in Denver, a melancholic discovery that Lydia found almost predictable. The imagined divans and silk tapestries faded from her mind, replaced with a sparse and makeshift Denver set-up. Admitted into a low, dark room Lydia strained to see through the smoke. Spaces were partitioned by rough planks barely large enough to hold a mattress and a stool. The sweet smell of opium was delicious and overpowering in the gloom: a small window near the top of the low ceiling was inadequate to permit dilution with fresh air. In the dark shadows and recesses small dots of burning red glimmered and glowed, opium embers cradled in the drug pipes. She could almost taste the stuff on the air, drawn like the other white women who were already arranged into sprawling shapes. An extended hand, a reclining body, pale faces adorned with dark, lackluster eyes.

It was a veritable cavern of vice, and Lydia couldn't wait to join in.

But only fools pretended to know something they didn't. "I've never tried this before."

The proprietor offered a slight bow in her direction. Solicitous. "Three dollars is the cost for four pipes."

Lydia pulled the silver dollars from her purse. The coins flashed cold and bright before disappearing into the silk folds of his gown.

He gestured with an expansive motion toward a berth, set up with a pipe, a spirit lamp, and a small dish with four balls of opium. "I will help you," he said, guiding her.

Lydia reclined on her side, like the other denizens. The proprietor lit the small spirit lamp and stabbed one of the balls with a long, thin opium needle.

"Your English is good," Lydia murmured, curious.

"We are not all the same." He handed her a long, thin pipe.

Lydia leaned in toward it, and watched as the bulb of opium caught fire, burning yellow and orange against the pipe's resin encrusted bowl. She inhaled, and then choked.

"Breathe deeply, and hold the smoke within."

Lydia tried it again, with better success. She leaned back, feeling light-headed as a wave of nausea rippled through her. She took a deep breath through her nose to quell her stomach and the sensation passed.

Almost immediately the effects of the drug set in, and she drifted off.

When she started to awaken, an unknown old woman appeared by her side, pipe in hand, a question in her face. Lydia nodded. And the pipe was relit. This second time Lydia accepted the smoke without problem, relaxation covering and warming her as her muscles relaxed. Heavy yet floating.

Finally, free.

She awoke five hours later, disoriented but content. She drifted off into the clamoring street to retrieve her horse, already longing to return to the serenity she'd found in the den.

She never saw the man following her.

Of course, she returned to Hop Alley again. And again.

Stanley receded into the background, less of a concern. Until the day she stuck her key in the lock and he was on the other side, waiting for her. As she crossed the threshold, he yanked her inside.

"I know where you've been, and who you have been seeing," he sneered, then walloped her across the face with the back of his hand, his knuckles bruising her cheekbones. She slammed against the wall in the entryway.

She could see by the look in his eyes that the beating would be bad no matter what she said. "Then what is the problem?"

His hand closed in a fist, and that was the last thing she recalled.

Lydia came to on the floor some time later, the garden boy tugging at her arm. "He's gone now."

Rolling over on her side, groggy, she hurt. Bad. Yet she managed to sit up somewhat, half-crouching on the floor. She opened her eyes to find the boy still there. He rippled in her vision. "Do you need me to go get Annie?"

Lydia shook her head. The motion started new pain throbbing. "No, I don't think so. But how did you get in the house?"

A note of pride carried along with the fear in his voice. "Through the window in the kitchen. I make sure it's left open, when I can."

Lydia patted him on the shoulder. God, how she hurt.

The boy continued to stare, and she felt something tickle at the corner of her mouth. She brushed it away with the back of her hand. Blood.

"There's a man who was following you," the boy said.

Although disoriented, that caught her attention. Stanley was collecting evidence. That was how he had found out about the opium den.

She needed to do something, and she needed to do it soon.

# CHAPTER 32
## DISILLUSIONMENT WITH THE GILDED LIFE

Despite the fact that spring had arrived, upstairs at Ryan's it was cold as winter. The wind streamed in through chinks in the mortar that almost held the bricks together. The narrow corridor that clung to the shared wall was dimly lit by a solitary window that overlooked the street. Light from the moon filtered through that dirty window, and the single sconce didn't dispel the prevailing gloom. Belying the raucous behavior downstairs, the corridor felt hollow. If drink or drugs hadn't numbed the senses.

In the shadows, Pearl stood by her window, hair escaping from pins and rolling down her back in a tangle of dirty brown locks. She wore a beer-stained chemise, shiny blue skirt, and black stockings. Her bare arms were thin in the blue cold of the room, a chill from the window. But she was too tired and numb to care.

She turned away from the outside world and flung the bed coverings over the wrinkled and damp sheet beneath. Then she sat on the bed, arm's length from the dented steel bedstead. She held her face in her hands, bone tired. Exhausted. She considered whether she ought to change the sheet before going to sleep, but her stockings drew her attention. Black netting with a couple of gaping holes. Her thighs and calves peeked through, indecent.

Sighing, she pushed off from the bed, headed to the pitcher and basin. The last jake had pissed in the chamber pot. She picked the pot up, wrinkling her nose. Unhappy.

She opened the door into the hallway, plunked the pot down and closed the door. "What the hell," she said to herself, but that didn't make her feel any better.

She poured some water into the basin, then stripped off her dress, chemise, petticoats, and stockings. Standing before the mirror naked, she dipped a cloth into the water and wiped off the sweat and semen. There were angry welts and bruises on her arms and thighs, the love bites and the roughness. Her ribs showed as ridges through her skin.

She dabbed some rosewater behind her ears and in her cleavage, then pulled a threadbare, ripped nightgown over her head. Most nights, she didn't even bother.

She yanked back the covers and tore off the dirty sheet. The smells of tobacco, sweat, and stale liquor rose. She flung the sheet into the corner, a disgusting heap.

She took some laudanum, knowing its solace was far better than crying.

The following day passed the same as any other, and careened into night. Pearl was still on the prowl, but the night was ending. She gravitated toward the man who looked like the best bet in the lot of sloppy drunk pickings. He was a scrawny guy with a big droopy mustache. Nothing special—that was for damn sure. Nondescript, even. His pants were discolored on the thighs, shiny from rubbing.

"Care to come upstairs?" Pearl asked, but her heart wasn't really in it.

"Might as well," he replied, equally lacking in enthusiasm. The way he said it struck Pearl as odd.

They went into Pearl's room. He grabbed her by the shoulder once the door was closed and tore the strap off of her dress.

"Look what you've done!" she cried. "That's going to cost

you an extra ten dollars for repairs."

"And you have a big whore's mouth." He backhanded her across the face. Pain shot through her jaw and eye. Caught off balance, she fell against her dresser, banging her ribs. The sharp crack knocked the breath out of her. She struggled for air.

There was no doubt she was in for a full-fledged beating.

Scared, she could have stayed down, but she struggled to her feet from instinct.

It turned out she should have stayed on the ground. Her show of strength raised the jake's hackles even further, so he kicked her in the ass. Which sent her sprawling onto her face.

She landed near her chamber pot, the closest thing to a weapon she was likely to have. For a moment, Pearl and the jake stared at each other, ready to spring or bolt. Then she threw the contents of the pot at him, and he roared.

Pearl lunged for the door, but the man was quick. Furious, he caught hold of her skirt, and pulled her back to him, ready to strike her down as hard as he could.

Somehow, she twisted her face away from him and screamed. The sound of a frightened or wounded animal.

May barged through the door. "What is it? What the hell are you two doing? I'm warning the both of you . . . ?" She pulled up short when she saw the welt rising on Pearl's cheek and jaw. She sniffed, and it registered that the jake was covered in piss.

She screamed down the stairs, "We need help up here now!"

Footsteps pounded down the hall. May's jake came up behind her and pulled out a gun, levelling it at the beater. "That's enough!"

Annie and Michael were rushing up the stairs now, in answer to May's alarm. The space was tight, congested. All this time Pearl couldn't get free of the room and kept hold of the chamber pot like a weapon.

May's jake remained in the hallway with his gun drawn and

ready. Annie shoved her way past him and into the room. She took a look at the runty little beater and walloped him across the face with the back of her hand. "Empty your pockets, nice and slow or I'll ask that man to shoot you as you stand."

The scrawny jake gave her a disgusted look, but emptied his pockets. Matches, a snot-riddled handkerchief, a battered timepiece, a pocket knife, and a wad of cash were thrown on the bed.

Annie scooped up the wad of cash and stuffed it down the front of her dress, then pushed him out the door and into the hallway. Michael grabbed him by the shirt collar and pitched him down the narrow stairs. The beater clipped a couple of spindles on the way down, breaking them. He landed with a thud at the bottom of the staircase and struggled to his feet, limping as he turned around.

Annie stood looking down at him. He spat in their direction. Michael rushed down the stairs and gave him a kick in the ass that landed him in the saloon. "If you've any bright ideas about notifying the law, don't bother. I pay them," Annie yelled after him.

He limped out the door.

Pearl was panting, almost sobbing, which only made her ribs hurt more. It had been a terrible, violent episode. She thought about the crib girls who had been murdered. No one was around to help them, when they called out. *If* they called out.

"Do you think he was the murderer?" she said, shakily.

Annie's eyes widened at the suggestion. "He didn't try to strangle you, did he?"

"No," Pearl gasped, as it dawned on her that her callousness toward those murdered women had been a mistake.

The women in the room exchanged glances. It had been a close call. Violence always lurked beneath the surface of their profession. May and her jake left, and order, for the moment, was restored.

Annie pulled the wad of cash from her cleavage and started to count the takings. She handed Pearl some wrinkled notes. "Here. For your troubles."

"You're taking a cut of that, too?" Although banged up, Pearl still grabbed the money.

Annie narrowed her eyes. "You're right. I don't have to give you a cut. You didn't do anything, other than act as a punching bag. Jesus Christ, Pearl. You need to learn a bit of gratitude. I'll send for the doctor to give you the once-over."

The doctor's verdict was that Pearl would be out of commission for a couple of days.

While she normally would have welcomed a few free days, Pearl was too banged up to be happy about much of anything. She lay in her bed, still shaken by her close call. But that didn't keep her from considering a few fundamental facts, about how her earnings would stop while she was laid up. Her expenses would carry on as before, mounting. And sporting a shiner and other bruises for at least a week meant she would generally look like hell, which would bring down her earnings for a while. Until the marks faded.

No jake would pay fifteen dollars for someone who looked like a two-bit whore.

All of which made her feel worthless. She alternated between feeling sorry for herself and getting angry. During her angry moments, she thought about how Annie paid Harrigan for protection. Apparently. As far as Pearl could tell, that sure the hell didn't work.

Her thoughts kept turning back to the murdered crib girls. They had taken someone in for the promise of pay, and he had killed them. They had let their own murderers into their dwellings by their own hands.

Most jakes wouldn't do that. Not even the rotten ones like she just had. Maybe. It was impossible to be certain, and that was the problem.

Pearl started to feel a type of vulnerability she had not known before. It truly plagued her, knowing she might pick the wrong fellow to bring upstairs. And that one mistake could kill her.

She wondered who would truly care, and she knew the answer. That answer hurt. No one. Not really.

★ ★ ★ ★ ★

# Part V
# Whoever Said You Can't
# Put a Price on It Had
# Never Been to Market
# Street
# April 1893

★ ★ ★ ★ ★

# CHAPTER 33
## ROLLING WITH THE PUNCHES

From the corner of her eye, Annie noted that Harrigan pulled up short when he crossed the threshold and saw the shiner Pearl was sporting. Pearl, just turning the corner to go upstairs with another customer, didn't see him. His reaction was pronounced. About damn time, Annie thought. That might get him thinking about taking his job a bit more seriously. And not just for what he could skim off the top.

There was no denying that cop was a parasite.

As such, Annie ignored him as he straightened his shoulders and hitched up his belt. Like he meant business. It might have been funny if it all wasn't so pathetic. If she didn't have to actually pay him for his lack of purpose.

The pitch of the saloon was louder than usual. Three trail hands were caterwauling in the corner, and the other punters—the ones that bothered to gab—were shouting over the din to be heard. The bright weather had turned warm, and threatened to spark off violent storms that would roll down from the mountains and out over the plains. The wind was already gusting. But inside Ryan's the day was drunkenly careening toward night. Like a powder keg too close to a fire.

Annie was joking with some shave-tails who didn't know any better than to wander on in. New to town, they were clean behind the ears and their shirts were pressed. Astonished at the general rowdy behavior, they tried to act accustomed. Like they fit in with the Denver dregs.

They were ripe for the taking.

"Trying to run a disorderly house here?" Harrigan butted in, without an ounce of manners that even a jackass could manage. He eyed the shave-tails for trouble, unable to distinguish the crooked from the straight.

Harrigan, to put it mildly, was getting on her nerves.

"This is the local law, boys," Annie told them, none too pleased. "He ain't so bad once you get used to him and his peculiar sense of humor." She would have a few choice words to fling his way . . . later. Once she got him alone and out of earshot from the paying customers.

It made her skin crawl the way the shave-tails, boys really, lifted their hats to him.

Feeling the big man, Harrigan actually had the balls to lay hands on her, pulling her away from the bar. "Get your hands off of me, and watch what you say in front of the punters," Annie growled through clenched teeth, then wrenched out of his grasp.

He didn't appear bothered, more occupied with surveying the interior. "It looks fairly raw in here. What the hell *is* going on—things getting away from you?"

Things weren't getting away from her. Much.

Annie pursed her lips and eyed him, in a way she hoped he would interpret as unfriendly. "Referring to what particularly? Boy will be boys, and rips will be rips. What of it?"

"Well, have you seen your niece's face? What have you got to say about that?"

Annie thought he was joking. At first. "Where the hell have you been? These things happen. Some no-account got drunk and treated her rough. Her ribs got the worst of it: not broken, but sorely tested. He won't be in again."

Harrigan spat and missed the spittoon. "The jake got a name?"

He must have gone soft in the head. "Joe. I believe he said his name was Joe."

The sarcasm wasn't lost on him. "Let me try that again," Harrigan said with a nasty look in her direction. "If that rat-shit comes back in, send for me. He'll feel the back of my boot before we're done, I reckon."

That day would never come.

Annie sighed. "He was a little fellow, too. Pearl lost her balance, or she might have been able to take him. It always seems to be the little guys that cause the most problems."

Harrigan eyed her up and down, none too flattering, either. "Hell, it might be worth pointing out that a fair portion of the city is small in stature compared to you, Annie."

"And don't you forget it, Casey Harrigan. *Officer Harrigan.* It takes money to get my figure this way. But no, this guy was scrawny and had a chip on his shoulder. I guess pounding on a girl made him feel more like a man."

"It's because they got tiny dicks."

"Not always." Annie wondered how much Harrigan knew, or thought about, dicks.

Discomforted, he smoothed down his jacket and picked up his glass. Almost like he was reading her mind. "Well, I don't want to debate men's peckers with you. Now, pour me out a whiskey and a beer, and I'll sit down for a while to help you keep this place in order."

Annie glared at him, but went behind the bar for his drinks all the same.

Harrigan navigated the bodies assembled in the saloon, knocking shoulders just to throw his weight around. She watched his back as he lumbered on through.

Harrigan had a thing for Pearl, but Annie didn't know what it was.

Pearl came back into the saloon with a swagger that drew the men in like flies. Damn. Just like Claire used to do. Annie watched recognition flit across Pearl's face when she figured out Harrigan was present. She even had the effrontery to sashay over to his table, collecting attention as she went. Well, from those that hadn't seen her before. But wasting her time on Harrigan got none of them anything marketable. Annie sure as hell would have a word with her about *that,* later. Some more punters blew on in, and Annie was kept busy serving drinks and making saucy comments. But she managed to track Harrigan and Pearl. No one was going upstairs for free.

Not that Harrigan was into that type of thing. As far as Annie could tell.


Pearl wasn't exactly having the fine time that Annie thought.

Harrigan pushed back in his chair, arms folded across his chest, looking down at her. "You look like a whore from the blue row. I don't suppose you need to be educated on the value of appearances."

And although that was pretty much what she felt like, it hurt to hear it. So she smiled with some sass just to show that the experience, and his criticism, hadn't gotten her down. "I ain't got many complaints."

He dismissed her attempt. "You normally don't need to drum up business, but that's what you are doing, unless I am mistaken."

"That just tells me you don't know the first thing about it. Of course I drum up business. Every day, rain or shine, come hell or high water. Picking up jakes *is* drumming up business."

Harrigan leaned forward in a conspiratorial manner. "Admit it. You know you are a cut above what is normally served at Ryan's. You would do better if you were in one of those fancy brothels. But tell the truth now, isn't it harder to lure men upstairs looking like hell?"

Pearl snorted. She wasn't up for Harrigan talking up a load of shit about how he was setting up his own place. He had nothing that would convince her to follow him into an untested establishment. Especially not if he was running it. He was probably less trustworthy than Annie—and that was saying something. Trustworthy was a fancy word that belonged to a different life. "What better class of brothel are you talkin' about? Is someone now paying you to scout?"

"No. That's not what I'm talking about, and you know it. I've heard a story about how Jennie Rogers got her place financed. They say it was blackmail."

Pearl had heard that, too. So had the rest of Denver a few years back. And he was just finding it out. "Good for her. The fellows probably had it coming."

Harrigan sat back, toasted her with his whiskey. "That's music to my ears, to hear you say that. There's another thing I want to talk to you about. That fancy lady who sometimes comes in here; what's her name again? Lydia. I want to know more about her, and how well Annie knows her and why. Something is wrong there—something she will pay to keep quiet. What does she have to do with Annie? That's the part I just can't puzzle out. And that's the part I want you to help me with."

"But I don't know anything," Pearl said, panicking a little. She steered the subject back to safer ground. "My ribs are bruised," she told him, like that mattered a hill of beans.

He focused on her face. "Well, I told Annie if that fellow comes back in here to let me know, and I'll straighten him out. Permanent like. Never could stand a scrawny bastard that beats on women. Say, did that rip have a little pecker?"

Pearl tried to act as if she wasn't caught off guard, but surprise rippled through her. "We never got that far. Why?"

"It's a theory I've got," Harrigan replied.

She studied him, sizing him up. "That's kind of an odd thing for a man to be wondering about, isn't it?"

He cleared his throat, shrugged. "I'm a student of the human condition."

She tried purring to avoid the subject of Lydia. "Why, Officer Harrigan, there is more to you than meets the eye." She put her hand on his arm, and he flinched.

Goddamn him, he *flinched.*

Like a rotten melodrama, the music began. Ryan's had engaged a new professor, the previous one having died of alcohol poisoning the week before. The man started banging out some clattering ditty on the piano, and the saloon responded by lurching into a more fevered pitch. Pearl belted out a loud peal of laughter all of a sudden. Nothing sparked the money like a whore having a good time.

It pleased her to see she had startled Harrigan.

To top it all off, she gave him a wink. At that moment, she felt anything but kindly toward him. The funniest part of all was that he couldn't see it.

Pearl got up from the table as sprightly as she could manage, having ingested a few drinks along the course of the afternoon. She twirled around, flashing her skirts and her thighs, and sashayed up to a cowboy. She put her hand on his forearm like she had just done to Harrigan. But this man did not pull away; instead he leaned on into her. She knew she was pretty, damn it—if the jake could see past the bruises. Which, evidently, this man could. It didn't hurt that she pressed her breast against his arm as well.

It was those other parts of her body that the cowboy was more interested in. He bought her an overpriced drink. And Michael poured her a real one.

"For your troubles with the law," he said.

For the moment, Pearl had no intention of telling Harrigan anything more about Lydia. Not unless there was something in it for her that was quantifiable.

Annie was watching her. Annie would never let her go.

# CHAPTER 34
## STRANGE BEDFELLOWS

The day Lydia arrived to collect the rent was notable for more than one reason.

In a complete departure from custom, she entered Ryan's through the back alley, using the door she eschewed as a matter of principle. As usual, she was well turned out in an outfit that drew attention to the cost. But in another departure from the usual, she kept her identity hidden under layers of black veiling. Denver seldom stood on that much ceremony, even for those in mourning. No one wore such heavy veils in spring—and they certainly didn't wear them over their faces. But there Lydia was, covered from head to toe. She had wandered in and stood slightly leaning against the wall, taking in Ryan's in all its tawdry glory.

More specifically, she was peering into the saloon at the men assembled, with more than a passing interest.

"Jesus Christ!" Annie came out of her office without looking and almost collided square into her. "You gave me a fright! What are you doing back here like that?"

Lydia chuckled. "It's kind of fun catching you off guard. But I'm here, collecting the rent. It is Tuesday, after all."

Annie could have remarked that sometimes Tuesdays came and went without a visit from her, but there was no need to go about rubbing salt in that wound. "You're dressed awfully fancy for it, too. Did someone kick the bucket?" Annie looked at the veil. "Or are you finally trying to be discreet?"

Lydia laughed again, but the tone was guarded and bitter. Strained. "It's far too late for discretion in some matters. How about you give me a drink in your office, and I'll tell you a story."

Annie cocked her head, almost certain she wasn't going to like it. Lydia sure as hell didn't pay social calls, much less tell stories. "If you're going to ask for sherry, I'll have to get it from behind the bar."

"No," Lydia said. "Today is not a sherry morning."

Inside the office, Annie closed the door. "So what's this story of yours, and what's the veil for?"

Lydia used both hands to lift the gauzy fabric and settle it on the brim of her hat.

Annie gasped. "Dear God in heaven, did your husband do that to you?"

Lydia's face was bruised across one cheekbone—the eye blackened and turning spectacular shades of purple, yellow, and dark gray. But worst of all was the regrettable fact that blood had seeped into the white of her eye, coloring it a vivid, horrible red. Not to mention another heavy bruise across the other side of her jaw. A man's punch would do that, but her face had suffered more like two or three punches. Maybe even more.

"None other than Stanley Chambers, my lawfully wedded husband. Impressive, isn't it?"

Annie poured two very full whiskeys. She pulled her desk chair out, dragged it around to Lydia's side, and thrust a whiskey toward Lydia with concern.

Guilt was a powerful feeling, and one she didn't have too often. Thank God for small mercies. Considering the state Lydia was in, Annie was leaning towards coming clean.

When Lydia looked toward her with that blood-filled eye and an expression of gratitude, Annie crumbled. "He's been in here, you know."

Lydia took a strong sip of whiskey and tears sprang into her eyes. "Don't look all worried; it's just the whiskey is stinging the split in my lip."

Annie waited for the moment to pass.

Lydia caught the expression on Annie's face, and offered a half-laugh at the situation. "I'll live."

"I suspect so. But if you happen to be a little upset that he's been with the girls, hell. Half of the men in Denver do that. It's nothing to get that worked up over provided he doesn't bring anything back home with him, if you understand what I'm saying."

Lydia gazed at some point in the distance. "Well, while I had my suspicions, it's nothing any woman wants confirmed."

"Well." Annie patted her ample bosom. "It's not like you are *any* woman."

Lydia flicked her fingers in a helpless, losing gesture. "Anything that keeps him away from home I view as a good thing. It keeps him away from me, and any attentions he used to show me are long since gone." Her hand shook, threatening the liquid in the glass, but her voice was clear.

Annie shrugged and pursed her lips, uncertain how much she should reveal. "Frequenting whores is just something men do, and how I make my living. Other than that, it doesn't mean anything."

She patted Lydia's hand and forced her voice to be calm. "But what he's done to you. Well. There's no call for that. None at all."

"Using me as a punching bag is probably the least of it, if he has his way."

Annie looked at her more closely. "What do you mean?"

Lydia poked at the floor with the toe of her boot. "He mentioned something about having me put away in a sanatorium a while back. Of course, he means an asylum. These days, I wouldn't put it past him, either."

That sure as hell didn't sound good.

Lydia's lip threatened to split again, and she dabbed at it with a fine handkerchief that would be ruined. "He had me trailed."

So. There was more to it than hurt feelings and a walloping. That was a definite problem. Annie waited for Lydia to come out with whatever was really bothering her.

"I went to one of those opium dens," Lydia conceded, knowing full well Annie's opinion on that matter.

Annoyance rose up in Annie. "That's one way to set people against you. Is that what your husband was spying on you for?"

"That would be the simplest explanation. And heaven knows Stanley is a simple man. But he's collecting evidence, I'm afraid. Evidence fit for a spell at a sanitarium. At best."

Annie stared at her. "I don't know how those things go, but I can tell you about how the state penitentiary goes."

Lydia leaned toward her. "I know I shouldn't have gone there, and I know you warned me. It's just that sometimes I get so damned mad, caution falls by the wayside. But those places are illegal. If Stanley finds two doctors willing to certify that I am a drug fiend, he can have me locked away with the full backing of the law. Then everything I've worked for will come under his control. I'll be ruined, and *you* will have a new landlord."

The last sentence was a hell of a threat, and one Annie could ill afford. No question a new landlord would raise the rent to the going rates, if not a bit beyond. "I'm kind of anxious to avoid that, if it's all the same to you."

Lydia met her eyes straight on. "I need a divorce granted on grounds that won't be contested, and I need to file for it first. In order for that to happen, I'll need your help. Either that, or Stanley needs to disappear. Permanently. Do you know of anyone in that line of work?"

The breath escaped from Annie in a hiss. "No one admits to knowing people like that, although they do exist. And they can be found if needed. But they are not nice people to deal with. Hiring them leads to all sorts of trouble, in line with the gates of hell opening wide. The divorce would be easier and cleaner. Less to remark upon or get tripped up in."

Lydia's voice went flat. "I don't want to get shut away."

"Have you considered going to city hall to file a complaint? You said you know the chief of police. Why don't you talk to him and see what kind of protection he can offer? Failing that, you can show him your face and swear out a complaint. I don't think there's a judge that would find against you."

Lydia shook her head. "We don't know that. Whatever else happens, I *must* be seen as the victim all the way around. If I get a divorce on the grounds of cruelty, Stanley will make sure the laudanum comes up, and the opium as well. Stanley will say he beat me to try to get me to stop. He will testify that I was incapable of running my business affairs, so he took control of the money, the house, and the investments. For safekeeping, of course. And after all that, I could still end up shut away. He will say I'm a danger to myself."

It was a bad situation, no mistaking it. Lydia's bloodied eye was galling and hard to stomach.

"Tell me, does he have a favorite girl?"

Although it went against Annie's grain to answer her question, the stakes were getting uncomfortably high. "I suppose that would be Pearl."

"That's good." Lydia forced a smile, which came out more like a grimace. She finished her whiskey.

For all the world, Annie thought Lydia acted like just another woman who wanted a way out. But that didn't mean she could control her husband. "You might consider not staying at your house until this all gets sorted out. The next time, he might very well kill you."

And with that, Annie had said her piece, and dropped the subject. For the time being. This was what happened when you got into business with a dope fiend, no matter how likeable they might be. They had the potential to drag others down with them.

Annie sure as hell planned on staying above ground and in charge.

Lydia rose to her feet and let the veil fall. "I thought you said you would tell me when he came in. If you had, it might not have gotten as bad as all of this."

Annie bit her lip. "Damn it, Lydia! I know that, and I'm sorry. Hindsight is a wonderful invention. But I'm willing to bet you don't tell the wives of the men who buy cottages for their mistresses, do you?"

Lydia shrugged, a bit of her old spark returning. "I see your point. Business is business."

"Exactly," Annie replied.


The Denver Republic–*April 6, 1893*

*The story of yet another unfortunate has come to an unhappy end in the lower reaches of Denver. Aged twenty-three tender years, Marie Contassot was already a hardened woman of vice. She came to this country from France, accompanied by her sister Eugenie, who also set upon the scarlet path to ruin. The young Frenchwoman was found strangled in her crib on Market Street yesterday morning. A popular figure along the row known for her neat figure and flashing eyes, it is sad to say that those flashing eyes have been dimmed forever. Two of her frail sisters similarly preceded her in death, but Marie's case is viewed as a bit more sinister. She was the consort of Antonio Santopietro, also known as Tony Sanders, of the Denver police department. Rumored to be in line for an inheritance, it has been speculated that she was murdered as a result of those very riches she hoped to gain. This third murder has led to all sorts of wild speculation in the demimonde, with madams buying bars to place over their windows, hoping to deter further murders. Speculation runs rife as to the identity of the murderer or murderers. Suffice it to say that none of the girls are sleeping tight, with visions of death upon their fevered brows.*

# CHAPTER 35
## SHE SANK TO THE OCCASION

Julia was spooked, no two ways about it. When she heard about the third murder, she went to her room and refused to come out. She wasn't exactly alone in her response. Everyone on the row was running scared. Annie decided to give her space, but the clientele in the saloon didn't seem to care about the upset one more dead whore caused. May and Pearl were kept busy—it didn't matter that their nerves were tattered as well.

Pearl had finished up with a jake, and was headed toward the stairs when she heard muffled sobbing coming out from Julia's room.

"Go on ahead," she told the jake, who was already almost all the way down the staircase. He gave her a look that said he had no intention of waiting.

It was a cause for regret, Pearl thought. Common courtesy was sorely lacking in a whore house.

She paused outside Julia's door and listened. They were almost strangers, when they should have at least been distant allies. Both sisters had put up with Pearl from the start, but that didn't mean they all liked each other. But Julia took things like murder to heart, and Pearl softened a tad.

"Julia." She rapped on the door. "Can I come in?"

Julia broke off sobbing enough to answer. "If you don't let anyone else in with you. I don't want to end up murdered in my bed."

Pearl opened the door and saw the tear-streaked lump of her

cousin lying on the bed. The room smelled of piss. Apparently unwilling to risk the outhouse, Julia hadn't emptied her pot. Still, Pearl sat on the edge of her bed and wished they had been closer.

But they weren't.

At the very least, Pearl wanted to come up with something that would make her cousin feel better and get her back to work. "How are you, Julia?"

"Rotten," Julia snapped. "How are you?"

Pearl looked at her red piggy eyes, and thought that being kind might not be so easy. "I know this all has you upset, but chances are nothing will happen to any of us. Now that three girls have been killed, the police will have to do something about it. It's in the newspapers, too."

Mollified a degree, Julia calmed down and sniffed. "I'm sick of this life. Killers don't go after decent women. If I went somewhere new, I could start over. Be a ranch wife or something. Take in laundry—I don't care that it's hard work. So is spreading your legs. And to put up with all this miserable life just to end up dead. That is a terrible fate to reconcile toward."

"So what are you going to do?" Julia apparently had more to her than Pearl originally thought. And a fat lot of good it would do her. "Your mother wouldn't like it."

Julia sat up. "Who the hell cares? It's not like she's gone too far out of her way to provide for any of us. The only thing she cares about is the family in its loosest sense, and she wants to come out on top there, mark my words. Not to mention that she's always done pretty much what suited her."

"Do you suppose the Boyos are any better?"

Julia tossed her head. "No. Absolutely they are not. They're good for a joke and a laugh, but there's a lot of shady business over there. They screwed Michael out of some claim, and now he's stuck working behind the bar. At least Mother is fairly straightforward in her dealings. She's the one who stood by him and bailed him out."

Pearl shrugged. "She told me to keep away from them."

"Oh, they'd take you on in a New York minute. But you wouldn't be happy. None of their girls are. Haven't you heard the talk?"

She hadn't.

"It's just as well. I would leave Denver if I could—if I had enough money for a ticket and a stake to get started. I could always hook again, if I needed to. So what?"

"So, nothing, I guess." Pearl had to admit Julia had a good point.

"Why did you even come here, Pearl?" Julia sounded disappointed and baffled. It was strange she had never bothered to ask before.

The question stabbed at Pearl. "I just wanted to belong somewhere, I suppose. But that might have been a mistake considering how things turned out. Most important was that I discovered I actually had a family. And I wanted to find out about my mother in the beginning. What she was like. That sort of thing. Later, I wanted to find out why she left me."

Julia gave her a knowing look. "And my mother strung you along in the beginning, and isn't coming exactly clean now. Is that it?"

Pearl frowned. "In a manner of speaking."

"For what it's worth, she's bad, but she's not that bad. I knew she had a sister that died, and that it still bothers her some. She would save any one of us, but she might wait to the last minute to do it. But she would still try."

Julia actually looked like she believed that.

"I wish I shared your confidence," Pearl grumbled.

Julia gave her a sad smile. "I wish I shared your looks so I could make more money."

It was a hell of a life.

"I always thought Annie let my mother down—let her die."

Julia frowned with concentration, finally shook her head. "For all her faults, she wouldn't have done that."

Pearl considered her cousin's tousled blond hair and felt a tug of something nearing affection. "Tell you what. I can share the money I've got stashed away with you, as long as you *never* tell your mother where it came from. She would have my hide. Pay it back when you can—that is, if you are really bound and determine to leave."

Surprised, Julia acted like she hadn't heard quite right. "Why would you do a thing like that?"

*That* was the twenty-dollar question. Unsure of which instinct she was operating on, Pearl hesitated. "For my mother, I suppose. And for the fact that there's no sense in everyone dying or being so rotten miserable."

Julia leapt to her feet and gave Pearl a hug that almost squeezed the life out of her. Why hadn't they become friends? Then Julia let go, and without hesitation commenced to throwing her belongings in an old, battered valise.

Her desperation to leave would have been comical, if it wasn't so sad.

"I'll be right back with the money," Pearl said, heading out the door.

In her room she removed a loose segment of board from the wall, reached in and found the cigar box where she held her money. She took out a roll of bills, and counted out forty dollars. She could have added a bit more, but there was no need to go crazy.

Returning to Julia's room, Pearl handed over the wad. "It's enough to get you started." Pearl managed a smile in her direction, and went on back down the stairs to see which jake she could hook for next.

Less than an hour later, Pearl caught a glimpse of Julia slipping out the front door.

She wished she had asked her to write.


Annie was hopping mad when she found the note the next day.

"Damn it!" she sputtered. "If I had known she was planning on pulling something like this, I would have kept her flat on her back. No, instead I show her some motherly love, and let her sulk, and look what happens! She's done a runner. Well, she might not get that far. She shouldn't have all that much money."

Of course, Pearl said nothing.

And Annie waited and watched for her daughter to return. But she didn't. That didn't set well with Annie.

Annie concluded it was that damn murderer who was to blame. And she gave Harrigan an earful. The poor cop looked like he didn't know what hit him.

Annie sure was mad. Pearl stayed on the fringes, and let the storm pass.


That Pearl wanted and needed more money was the logical outcome of her current situation. She regretted her fit of generosity toward Julia the next day. When it was too late. She hoped she wasn't turning all sentimental.

Harrigan wanted to know about Lydia. What the hell; so did she. Her mind started turning. If Harrigan thought she was stupid enough to set up Lydia for his benefit, she had news for him. There had to be some aspect she could work toward her favor, but she would need Annie for that.

It was an unspoken law that no one at Ryan's asked questions of, or about, Lydia Chambers.

Drunk or sober, Annie never let anything about the fancy lady slip. But most Tuesday mornings Lydia entered the saloon about eleven, dressed in her fabulous outfits. Her bearing spoke of confidence. Lydia looked about as far out of place in Ryan's as it was possible to get.

Her clothes fascinated Pearl, but Lydia's reaction to the interior of the saloon was somewhat telling. Lydia usually paused when she entered, eyes darting, and then she would sniff. With discretion, of course. It was as if she found the smell of corruption and booze pleasing. But then her eyes would stray to the paintings, and her expression would harden. Offended. Pearl recalled her first encounter with those same paintings. She could laugh about it now, although there was nothing funny about them, or that fateful day. No, not in the least. That was the day when a lot of her illusions got smashed to splinters. The memories and the broken notions still gnawed at her.

Pearl had been proper once. Like Lydia. It was a shame that hadn't lasted.

"Lydia doesn't seem to like the paintings much," she told Annie. It was as good of a way to start prying as any.

Annie didn't seem concerned in the slightest. "That's Mrs. Chambers to you, not that you should even know that much. As far as the paintings are concerned, she doesn't have to look at them. It's not like it's anything she hasn't seen before."

Pearl shrugged. "What does she have to do with us, anyhow? It's not like she's part of this world down here. You always take her back to your office. Is she the real owner?"

Pearl could see she had hit a nerve, although Annie was good at hiding it. "Don't go spreading that around, for Christ's sake. One day, I'm hoping we'll own it free and clear."

So her guess hit the mark. "And how are you going to do that?"

Annie tapped her temple with her index finger. She was sporting a new ring Pearl had never seen before. "As you pointed out, a normal woman like that has nothing to do with a place like this. She's just biding her time. She's a business woman, who will sell when the time is right and the fancy strikes her."

Annie knew something more than she was saying and Pearl wanted to land a blow. "Not to mention a dope fiend. You do know that, don't you?"

"Not to mention," Annie replied, with steel in her voice. "And how, might I ask, do you know about that?"

Pearl met her gaze full on. "I notice things, like that new ring you're wearing. As far as dope fiends are concerned, I saw them in Leadville and I see them in Denver. It's hardly a rare condition . . ."

Cross, Annie snapped, "Well, keep your opinions to yourself. Just remember, her fortune is our fortune, so to speak."

"Some of our fortunes appear to be better than others. Is she married?"

Annie was hiding something. She was always hiding something important. That was one of the things Pearl couldn't stand about her.

"Don't know, don't care."

And the subject of Lydia's husband was dropped. With a clatter.

A few hours later, Harrigan showed up. Pearl felt kind of bold, on account of Julia's bravery. If Julia could strike out on her own, so could Pearl. Pearl put her elbows on the table, and cupped her face in her hands like a much younger girl might do. Like she was mooning over him. "I do wonder who Lydia's husband is. I'll bet he is powerful and important."

Harrigan poured the beer down his throat and then wiped the foam from his mustache. "Do you have anything in particular that leads you to that belief?"

"No, but it stands to reason considering the clothes she wears."

"It stands to reason that she's a slummer for opium. I've seen her once in Hop Alley. That's the only reason a woman like that would go anyplace near the dens."

Pearl scratched her ear, then batted her eyelashes. "Why, Officer, I do believe you fancy her, since you are paying so much attention to her comings and goings."

Harrigan grabbed Pearl by the wrist, hard.

She yelped. "You're hurting me!"

"Not as much as I will if you don't stop hounding me." He threw her arm down. It struck the table with a glancing blow.

She rubbed the indents the table edge had left in her flesh. "There was no call for that. I didn't mean anything by it. I was just having some fun with you. That was all."

Harrigan's voice was low and bitter. "No. You were questioning my motives."

"That hurt, Casey."

Harrigan rose to his feet and looked down at her. "You need to learn when to hold your tongue."

Pearl wrapped her hand around her aching wrist, watching his back as he walked out of the saloon. She didn't want to be any man's punching bag; and from that moment she knew Harrigan ran mean.

She got up, walked over to the bar. "Michael, could you please pour me a real whiskey?"

Michael gave her a look. "You better watch where you step, Gumdrop. You might be playing with something you shouldn't."

"I'm not playing with horse-shit for no reason," Pearl replied with a toss of her head.

Michael just cleared his throat, but he gave her some whiskey. The real, unwatered stuff.

# CHAPTER 36
## EMPLOYERS' CHOICE AND CHANGING FORTUNES

Lydia checked herself into the Hotel Continental under an assumed name, Mrs. Rebecca Smith of Cleveland, Ohio. And that was just the start of a series of hard decisions she had to make.

She hired an attorney, first thing. And she picked the meanest one she could find.

She sat across from him now, her purse on her lap. "What is the best way to get an uncontested divorce? I need to appear beyond reproach, purely for business reasons."

He gave her a sharp look. "Candor is important in cases such as these."

Lydia met his gaze, level and with cool eyes. "My husband is unfaithful and an embezzler. He beats me when he becomes frustrated, which is often, because he is such a little, untalented man. Worse than just paying his club dues and fees, I pretend he's an active partner in the real-estate business I run. But I have reason to believe he will try to have me shut away in an asylum. If he is successful in that attempt, everything of value and merit will transfer to him by letter of the law. I cannot tolerate being shut away, or losing my holdings to his fecklessness."

The lawyer viewed her with a dispassionate stare. "Well, there are a couple of things that can be done. The first is for you to sign over to me, or some other male of good standing whom you trust, Power of Attorney. That way, should you be committed before the divorce goes through, the person who holds the

Power of Attorney can arrange for your release, without your husband's permission or assent."

That was promising. "My father is in St. Louis, and I would like to keep him out of all this unpleasantness. I will name you, in the event something happens, with the understanding that you notify my father as well, if it can't be avoided."

He wrote down some notes. "I'll have the paper drawn up."

Lydia handed him her father's business card. He looked at the name with what appeared to be recognition. "What hold does your husband have over you? Although not unknown, success is seldom grounds for such an action."

Lydia appraised the window in his office, the solid furniture and bookcases. No one liked to admit a moral weakness. "He has suspected for some time that I take too much laudanum. I use it medicinally. But . . . he recently had me followed to an opium den located along Hop Alley."

"Does he have any reason to suspect you of infidelity?" The question sounded strangely detached, but Lydia flinched all the same.

"No," she replied, thinking how that was such a pity.

The lawyer pressed his fingertips together and viewed her with a serious gaze. "If you can catch him in the arms of another woman, there will be very little the law could do, other than grant a divorce. Especially if she is of low character. And of course, you will need a witness, such as a police officer or someone of moral standing for verification. Preferably, someone who is not close to you. Someone who would be viewed as impartial."

Lydia rose to her feet. "That is convenient, since I have learned that he frequents prostitutes."

The lawyer took the comment as intended, rising as well. "And that is something you can prove?"

Lydia gave him a look that conveyed little doubt.

"One more thing, Mrs. Chambers. While those types of low characters can be bought, they can be dangerous as well. The difficulty will be in finding your husband in a compromising situation. Perhaps you should hire someone to follow *him.*"

Lydia smiled. "I'm sure it can be managed."

Pearl always checked her reflection in the mirror behind the bar, but lately had started noticing a chasm between what she saw and who she was. Her face had always been her fortune, but fortune didn't appear to be shining on the row—other than for a select few. In the reflection, a man caught her eye as he entered. A blond man with fine, tailored clothes. He stood at the bar and ordered a drink. Her heart skipped, and then fell. While the bruises were fading, they were still *there.* Her face was marred by them. She wanted him to find her pretty, for reasons beyond simple business transactions. She wanted to be seen as a woman worthy of consideration. The only way she would ever get that kind of consideration was based upon her appearance. Her desirability.

He had even spoken to her last time, really bothered to talk to her like she was a person with feelings. With a brain.

Something about him was different than the run-of-the-mill jakes, and it wasn't just that he could afford to pay more. He had asked her if she liked Denver—a queer question, but nice all the same. She felt drawn to him. It had been a long, long time since that happened. The lesson of Frank remained, and doubt crept in.

Maybe she was just being too careful, too cautious.

Miners were not her favorite jakes, considering past history and the fact that they tended not to clean up too well. She knew she had a hard spot where they were concerned. But this man was a gentleman. He said he was in real estate.

Pearl re-checked her reflection, tucked an errant lock behind a hairpin. If only she didn't look like a two-bit whore with the bruising. She put her hooking face on: the brazen, bold one without a care in the world. She turned and started toward him, trying to approach him at a favorable angle.

Annie was standing in the back of the saloon, watching all the comings and goings as she tended to do. Pearl glanced in her direction. She found it odd, how Annie was staring at the blond man. None too friendly, and Pearl couldn't imagine why. He was the type of customer they should be trying to attract, not scowl at. Annie should be happy with the money he brought in, because he sure didn't shy away from paying.

Well. She didn't need Annie's approval to make up her mind about how well she liked a jake.

Maybe Annie had developed a little crush on him. The notion caused Pearl to smirk.

Oblivious to Pearl and Annie, the man sipped his drink unwary, just beginning to look around and size up the companionship. Pearl could almost feel him stiffen when he saw her. Her heart tugged.

If only she didn't have those damn bruises.

She sashayed up to him, but he flinched when he saw her face. "What happened to you?"

Pearl shrugged, like it was of no concern. "A hard night a little while back." She twirled her skirt a bit to show she was still up for fun.

Annie circled. Hawking. Cagey.

The man frowned, and put his hand under her chin in a very familiar way. Just so he could get a better look, like a doctor might do. He turned her face to the left, and then to the right. "He sure did some damage, honey. I never could stand a man that beats on women." He let go of her face, gentleness itself. "Did the man at least get arrested?"

Pearl shook her head, and felt fragile and feminine in his

regard. "No. They don't arrest jakes for things like that. But he did get pushed down the stairs, and then Michael threw him into the street."

The man looked over at Michael. "That fellow behind the bar?"

Pearl nodded.

The blond man called Michael over. "I would like to buy you a drink," he said. "On account of the way you dealt with the rip that beat on this fine young lady. And what would *you* like to drink, my dear?"

Pearl smiled at him, thrilled at the way that the barman looked taken aback. "I'll have whiskey."

The blond jake smiled down at her, into her eyes. "Make that a bottle then, one that's unopened."

Michael went and got one from under the bar, came back to them, and broke the seal.

"Pour a glass for yourself," the jake told Michael, "the first one from the bottle as a token of my regard."

Michael poured out his own glass, and was about to pour two other measures, when the jake stopped him. "We'll take our glasses and the whiskey upstairs, if you don't mind."

Annie moved in for the money. "That will cost twenty-five dollars for her, and five dollars for the bottle." She held out her hand.

The figure caught Pearl off guard, and she recoiled in surprise. Ten dollars more than usual, and her with bruises to boot. It was too much. Her temper flared. Annie suspected she liked this jake, so was trying to ruin it for her. Of course.

Pearl expected him to balk, and felt her stomach sinking. It would be terrible when he said she wasn't worth that price. Like she wasn't standing right there. Like she didn't have feelings.

But the blond man, his name was Stan or something like

that, didn't argue or squirm. He pulled out the money and handed it over, like it was a drop in the bucket.

Pearl was delighted, as far as that word could apply to a whore.

Annie should have been delighted, too. Although she sure didn't look it. She had to be jealous; that was the only logical explanation. There was always plenty of jealousy to go around.

And if Annie was jealous, Pearl reckoned it gave her some sort of edge. But she would have to figure out how to play it. As any good whore knew, an edge needed to be played in order to pay.

# CHAPTER 37
## IT WAS NO ONE'S FIRST RODEO

The next day Harrigan blew in through the front doors like he owned the place. Pearl was mooning around like she hadn't a brain in her head.

Annie felt edgy. She didn't like the way the wind was blowing. That much was for sure.

Sometimes it was best just to let things unfold, but she wished to hell that Lydia's husband would take his custom elsewhere. That would eliminate a few worries on her plate. And now Harrigan was making a beeline toward Pearl. Just wonderful.

Leaning closer than common, he said something into the girl's ear. Stare as she might, Annie couldn't make out what he was saying, and his expression was that of a man intent upon something. Something she probably wouldn't like.

Annie sure as hell noticed the glint that came into Pearl's eyes. There was no mistaking the gleam of a whore on the take.

Then Pearl said something that set Harrigan off. That part made Annie even more uncomfortable, but she stayed out of it. Harrigan grabbed Pearl by the arm and dragged her over to one of the tables toward the back of the saloon. Annie rose hastily, her chair scraping against the floor. She had always been very clear with him on that count. The beat cops weren't to lay a hand on the girls. He had been warned.

Annie's back tightened, but she stayed put. Harrigan had a violent streak right below the surface. Pearl was an idiot if she couldn't see that much. For that reason, and because they were keeping secrets, Annie stayed out of whatever drama was unfolding. Things were aligning in a bad way when Harrigan wanted something and Pearl was leading him on. Neither of them knew what they were doing. Things would only get worse if some professionals got involved.

Pearl needed to learn to handle things a bit better on her own, but she was still healing from the last hiding she took. Annie would talk to Harrigan about it when he came to collect his pay. Maybe.

"Fuck it," Annie said to herself as she went behind the bar and poured herself a drink.

Son of a bitch, every single last one of them. And that list included her as well.

She had other things on her mind than whatever tango was going on. One of her cribs was vacant on account of the murders. She couldn't blame the woman, although she would pretend she did. Nothing, in her mind, was working out right. And she suspected more trouble was yet to come.

Tuesday was her standard afternoon and evening off, and Pearl had a bottle of whiskey stashed away. One with a few fingers left that she had stolen from behind the bar when no one was looking. It wasn't near enough booze to dull the boredom, or to quiet her mind. Whiskey was the one thing she could count on when her feelings let her down. She wanted someone to care about her, but no one did.

Once a whore, always a whore. Wasn't that it?

A knock came at her door and not a timid one, either. Hamfisted, it had to be Annie. The door was rough and warped, and it rattled in the casement. Pearl hid the bottle behind her pillow.

She didn't have to answer, but it wasn't exactly like she was doing anything. Yet.

She went and opened the door, none too friendly.

Annie gave her a hard stare and the once-over. "That skinny blond jake you're so keen on is downstairs asking for you. I told him it was your afternoon off, but he doesn't seem to think the rules apply to him. How about it?"

Pearl's heart skipped a beat, a feeling she wanted to keep to herself and away from Annie. "I know who you're talking about, but I never said he was anything special."

Annie lifted her eyebrows in that annoying way she had. "So you've gotten smart, is that it?" The way she said it left little room for doubt. She didn't believe a word Pearl said on that matter.

"Smart enough to take his money." Pearl stared her down.

"If only that were true. But I'll tell him you'll be down, unless you want me just to send him on up."

If she needed more whiskey, and she did, it was all downstairs. "I'll come down in a few minutes, after I pull myself together."

Annie grunted as she turned to leave. "Don't take too long."

Pearl shut the door, a near-slam. A glance in the mirror showed a woman suppressing a smile, the spark back in her eyes. She poured what was left of the whiskey bottle into her glass. The afternoon was certainly looking up in that aspect.

Stan treated her like a lady. Almost. Well, at least he asked her how she was.


Downstairs, Stan was outfitted with a bottle of whiskey and two glasses. Annie continued to look put out as she was chatting up some punters. Her glance kept returning to Stan. Pearl licked her lips, and thought she finally had one over on her aunt.

Stan's eyes glinted when he saw her, like flint igniting. Cold and sharp, with negligible warmth. Although the spark could still burn naked fingers.

It wasn't the exact kind of look she had been hoping for, but she would make do. It never worked to get her head turned by a paying prick. She recalled in the distant past, of at least two years ago, that she hadn't always felt this way. That realization wasn't entirely welcome, although it showed she was becoming more professional. Harder. Like she should be.

He sure made a production of seeing her. "There's the one!" he announced, loud enough for others to hear. She drew glances from some of the other men, and that lifted her spirits a bit. Not that any of them would ever bother to get to know her.

A general sense of distrust started to gnaw. She wondered why he made such a great deal about their encounter. She was, after all, a sure bet. For anyone who came up with the fee.

Annie nodded at the two of them. "The account is settled, so it's up to you what you do."

"Shall we have a drink down here?" Pearl wanted one. That was for damn sure.

He laughed as if the question was in poor taste. "I suppose, if you want to."

Annie stood nearby, eavesdropping and unhappy. Pearl put that down to the fact that she was going to drink real, unadulterated booze. A practice Annie hated.

"I suppose we could just go upstairs," Pearl said, close to getting her prize but feeling criticized by Stan's manner.

She didn't want Annie to see that she was a bit upset, that things weren't exactly going her way. After all, what the hell did it matter? She was letting her emotions get in the way, and she knew better. She knew that for herself, although it could be hard to do. She just didn't want Annie reminding her.

"I've got a surprise for you," Stan told her, picking up the bottle and placing his hand against the small of her back. Like she was a lady who needed escorting. Pearl enjoyed manners as much as the next woman. She picked up the two glasses. She could wait a couple of minutes for her drink. But, like all whores, she knew surprises were seldom good.

They went up the stairs with Pearl leading the way. She opened her door wide for him to enter. She followed, and shut the door behind her in the most seductive way she could muster. "Let's have that drink, shall we?"

Stan pulled the cork out of the bottle. After he poured, he raised his glass in a toast to her. "Here's to women that know their places and their callings."

That didn't sound quite right, but Pearl simpered and lifted her glass in return. She drained it, and held it out for more.

Stan's expression fell a bit, but he poured out another measure. She felt perhaps she was doing something she ought not to. But she drank it.

He slapped her across the face. Although the blow wasn't all that hard.

She put her hand to her smarting cheek. She had drunk with him before. She uttered no complaint. Not even a whimper crossed her lips. But that slap was a rotten thing to do.

"Damn it!" he said. "I didn't mean to do that. It's just that you reminded me of my wife with that infernal guzzling of yours."

Guzzling. She wasn't guzzling, was she? What the hell. "Oh? And who is your wife, who probably has nicer manners than mine."

He laughed in her face. "Someone you would never meet. She's a rich girl, nothing like you lot."

No woman wants to be referred to as a part of a lot. He obviously didn't think anything of her. Just like all the rest.

"Hey. I really am sorry." He turned her toward him, held up the bottle for her. She took it and poured out some more, and he stuck his hand in his pocket. She swallowed some of the whiskey in a non-guzzling fashion.

He pulled out a small box. "See, I brought you a present."

Pearl stopped dead and read his face to see if he was teasing her.

"These are for you," he said, flipping open the lid of the box.

A pair of pearl earrings that looked to be the real deal. So he thought he could buy her cooperation with earrings.

He was right.

Pearl took the box, using restraint not to grab. "They're beautiful! What are they for?"

A look came over his face, and Pearl could see he was deciding whether to tell the truth or to lie. "They're my wife's. She doesn't need so many, so I'm bringing them to you. I kind of like the idea of a harridan wearing my wife's jewelry."

Stan removed his coat and stood in shirtsleeves and suspenders. He paused when Pearl said nothing. "Does that mean you don't want them?"

Pearl shook her head. She wanted them, all right. She felt a stab of sympathy for whoever his wife was.

He walked up to her, gently put his fingers beneath her jaw, and turned her face toward him so he could see her fully.

His eyes grew hard. And that wasn't the only part of him.

Pearl set the whiskey aside, and set the box next to it. "Those earrings are the nicest thing anyone has ever given me."

But he didn't care. He was already fumbling with the buttons on his pants. "Just lie still," he said.

So she did.

He seemed to like it better that way, although she found his preference odd.

# CHAPTER 38
## BLACKMAIL IS SUCH AN UGLY THING

It was hard to miss the earrings, the way Pearl kept shaking her head like she was trying to get rocks out of it. She was trying to draw attention, and she got it. Annie grabbed her by the upper ear. "Where the hell did you get those?"

"From that jake, Stan. And before you say you get half, you don't. They were a gift. Not a tip, but a gift. You do know the difference, don't you?"

There was not a doubt but that they were Lydia's.

Annie felt like spitting. "Stan, is it? Those look expensive— like the real thing. Are you sure you should be wearing them around? Things like that tend to get stolen upstairs, or so I've heard."

Annie gave her a pointed look—one that said she knew how things sometimes went missing from jakes in Pearl's room. Not that the dupes complained all that much. They were usually drunk at the time and embarrassed later.

"Nothing is going to happen to them; don't you worry."

"Oh, I'm not worried, because I'm going to put them in the safe for you. Now, hand them over." Annie held out her hand.

Pearl tossed her head. "Not now. Nothing's going on down here and they'll be safe enough. Besides, I want to show the girls just what my fella gave me."

"You don't have a fella, as you put it. I'm surprised you haven't figured that out. What you're doing with those earrings is to spark envy and rub their faces in it."

Pearl and Annie glared at each other.

Lydia waltzed into the saloon, straight through the front door, having once again forgotten to use the back. Either that or she didn't care. She paused at the sight of the two women. "My, my. What is going on here?"

Pearl pranced up to her like they were old acquaintances. "Look what a *client* gave me."

The entire episode was making Annie nervous, as did the queer look that came over Lydia's face.

Annie stepped in and gave her a bit of a shove. "Not now, Pearl." She turned to Lydia. "Perhaps you would like to come back to my office?" Hands on her hips, Annie wasn't amused as she sized the two women up, focusing on Pearl, who didn't realize anything was wrong.

Pearl flounced off. Lydia turned on her heel, with a cross expression as she followed Annie out of the saloon proper. Once safely in Annie's office, she said, "Those are the earrings I couldn't find the other day."

That was hardly a surprise. "Your husband's been back in. Last night. And now this is where your earrings are today. Strange how things unfold sometimes."

Lydia flashed a wry smile. "Hardly. However, I have a plan to resolve my current situation. Those pilfered earrings are going to make it all that much easier."

Annie didn't exactly like the sound of that. Nor did she want any details, but she figured she was about to get them. "Go on."

"Well. Let me ask you a question first, about Pearl. Is she trustworthy?"

Annie almost laughed. "Not where you're concerned."

It was strange how that didn't seem to bother Lydia too much. "Fine. But do *you* trust her?"

Whores did not trust each other, but Lydia wouldn't know about that. "That's hard to say in a general way. Let's just say that if I need something definite from her, I make sure to hold something else in collateral."

Annie tallied all the things she knew about that went missing from behind the bar, and out of jakes' pockets. All a fine additional source of money, if you weren't on the losing end.

Lydia softened a mite. "You've been a real friend; do you know that?"

Something caught in Annie's throat. It took a moment for her to realize it was a kernel of sentiment. Damn. "Well. I'm glad that's what you think. It's good how you don't let things stand in your way."

Lydia nodded. "Pearl is pretty and brightens up a room. That will change, I suppose, as time goes on. She doesn't seem to be at ease with you."

Annie knew it. "Distrust is seldom one-sided."

"Let me tell you what I've been thinking. I'll leave it to your discretion how to handle it."

Lydia told her the plan. Annie sure as hell tried not to flinch. But it wasn't easy.

For quite some time after Lydia left the premises, Annie pondered her scheme—for a scheme was what it was. It ought to work out as planned, if everything went right. But it was a bad business altogether—especially for one that relied upon discretion and certain professional sensitivities.

Pearl would be blamed for a lot that was about to happen. It would seal the hard feelings between them once and for all. While that didn't sit well, Annie would survive it. Lydia had offered one thousand dollars.

Then there was the fact that Harrigan had to be involved. Sweet Jesus in heaven, how she wanted that man out of her hair.

Annie started pacing, thinking of how she would send Pearl

back up to Leadville while things calmed down at Ryan's. They would all get over it in time. She stopped pacing and poured a drink, toasted her reflection in the mirror. "Bottoms-up, old gal. This one is going to be a doozy!"

Stan returned to Ryan's, blowing in with a gust of hot air. He landed alongside the bar, like most everyone else. Annie sidled right on up to him. Her shoulders were damn near as wide as his. "So, you're back and looking for sport. Is that the story?"

Standing close to him on purpose, she enjoyed the way he flinched. "What of it? I would suppose that's why most people are here. Is Pearl available?"

"For thirty dollars she is. What's your name, sugar?" Annie put her hand on her hips, eyed him a bit too close for his comfort. The moron didn't seem to sense that anything was amiss, other than he seemed to object to Annie in general. No wonder Lydia was tired of him.

He pulled out his money clip and, after taking another half-step back, counted over the notes. "Stan. Do you always get this personal?"

"Only for repeat customers. Pearl is special—you're not the first to notice." Annie tried to smile in a friendly way, thinking he wouldn't be the last, either.

He shrugged and pretended to be bored. "She's all right, I suppose."

While whores seldom received glowing praises, for a man who was paying top dollar his response struck her as notably cool and distant. "Oh? Michael, bring us both a drink. What will you have . . . Stan?"

Stan warmed a bit at the prospect of a free drink. Hell, every-one did. "Whiskey. But make it the good stuff."

That rubbed her wrong. For someone who seemed hell-bent to fit in down with the dregs he sure was making it hard for Annie to warm to him. "There are other girls available if Pearl no longer suits you. May is a different type, and definitely more grateful. Nettie is probably more entertaining. Want something new?"

Stan leaned on the bar. He was staring at her again, like she was repulsive somehow. She felt like hitting him. "Sorry, darling," she said. "I'm not on the menu anymore."

He choked on his whiskey, and Annie cackled. What a prick. When he finished spluttering, he waved off her suggestion with his hand. "No need. Pearl will do. In some ways she reminds me of my wife."

It was kind of hard to stay sociable with him, when Annie felt a cold draft on a hot afternoon. Normally it would have been welcome, but it might have been a warning of sorts. Annie was sensible enough to pay attention to her hunches.

Her face must have fallen, because he seemed obliged to try to come up with something conversational. "Your place is nice, in a dirty kind of way. To hell with the consequences, I always say."

Somehow, Annie doubted he said anything of the sort. But he wouldn't be so anxious to join in, once he knew what the score was.

Annie did her best to look hospitable—although she wished like hell he would just leave. Once and for all. Leave and never come back. If he got the hell out of Denver, well, that was really all that was needed for the situation to sort itself out. It was unfortunate that people didn't always know when to fold. Especially when they were holding a losing hand of cards.

"I've always said that if wives just did what their husbands wanted, we wouldn't see so many men in here."

"Well, my wife likes to flaunt her daddy's money. Funny how that money is paying for this adventure here today." He took another sip of his drink.

Annie signaled to Michael to refill his glass. As the whiskey hit the spot, he leaned toward her conspiratorially. "She's hardly what a fellow would go running home to, if he were right in the head."

"Well, it's best to put her out of your mind, then!" Annie chimed up, like it was something to be happy about. "Be sure to come back any time at all. Say . . . you know, if you wanted to set up a time then I could make sure that Pearl was waiting for you, all nice and clean. What do you think?"

Stanley laughed. "Well, Saturday night sounds like a winner. Nine o'clock for a couple of hours."

"Make it a Wednesday night, and you've got yourself a deal." Annie said, thinking how Monday night would have been even better. The fewer witnesses, the better she liked it.

Stan gave her a quizzical look. "I suppose, but I'm not ruling Saturday out as well."

Annie lifted her glass of fake whiskey in a toast. Watered-down tea so she could keep her wits about her.

Unlike some others she knew. Mainly Pearl.

# CHAPTER 39
# THREATS AND ARRANGEMENTS
# ARE EASILY MADE

Sure as hell looking smug, Harrigan went whistling on into Ryan's. Annie slammed the till shut out of reflex to his close proximity.

"You're just the person I wanted to see." Even to her own ear, it sounded like she meant it, and she shuddered. "I'll give you a belt in my office. Whiskey, I mean."

"Watch it," he countered, noticing the shudder and all.

Once inside the office, she shut the door. "I have a business proposition I want to run by you."

He sat in a chair and she poured him a whiskey. One very full whiskey.

"Your services are needed Wednesday night, and there's an extra fifteen dollars in it for you." She handed him the glass. Intentionally keeping her tone light.

He took the whiskey and shrugged. "Fine. What is it?"

Annie smiled at him. "Just settling an old score. You're there to act as a witness, and I don't expect a whole lot of trouble to come out of it. Nine-thirty on Wednesday night."

Harrigan stretched out his legs. "That's kind of a queer night, isn't it?"

"All the better for keeping things in line." Annie peered over the rims of her glasses.

If he noticed her scrutiny, he apparently discounted it. "I'll be there."

"Of course you will." She knew she was only deterring him

from another lonely night spent in his boarding house. Come to think of it, she was probably doing the other lodgers a favor.

"Old scores can turn nasty." Harrigan stopped sprawling and leaned forward, like he was imparting something of importance.

"Oh, I'm not exactly overjoyed about this, either. It's just catching some straying husband in the act. So how wrong can it go?"

Harrigan shrugged. "Probably not too much."

His easy acceptance told her one thing. That he hadn't dealt with anything like this before. What the hell. Neither had she.

Wednesday night was running at a dull roar downstairs and the street was somewhat quiet, while Pearl was in her room getting ready for a special visit. A pre-arranged one, no less. A rare occurrence for those outside of parlor houses. The only other time such an event had happened for her was the night she became a professional.

There was no joy to be had that night, or on many others.

Even thinking about her first time drove home the notion that there were an awful lot of things she hadn't known back then. Those fancy dresses she had longed for sure came with a steep price attached to them. So many things in their world were really illusions—but it sure was a sad day when some of them fell away.

Restless, she peered out her window at the men strolling or staggering by. Everyone was always getting liquored up and ready to sow their wild oats, or to lose their hard-earned money in crooked games. What once had been exciting got old night after night, day after day.

Blowing off steam only worked if you didn't actually live there.

She moved back into the interior and took a couple of drops of laudanum. To make her eyes shine, of course.

She felt a bit close to the edge.

She sure hoped she didn't get walloped again. But if that was the price for jewelry . . . well. It just might be worth it. She toyed with the earring box Annie had pulled out of the safe. Damn good thing that hadn't gone missing, or there would have been very harsh words and some missing hair involved.

Pearl forced herself to settle down a bit. There was no need to get all jumpy like that. Stan could be nice enough, and things were looking up. A bit.

Wearing her nicest hooking clothes, she did up her hair and put on the earrings, thrilling at their creamy luster that reflected from the mottled mirror. So what if they were some other woman's earrings first? They had still cost a pretty penny.

At nine o'clock she heard footsteps coming up the stairs, but she waited for his knock. No sense in being over anxious. Of course, the footsteps stopped in front of her door. Then his rap came. Playful, almost.

She put on her brightest smile. There was no telling what he might be bringing with him this time. She thought how very nice a bracelet might be.

"Please come in," she said, as if they watched their manners at Ryan's. He entered, and she gave him the once over. There wasn't any telltale bulge in his pockets.

He winked at her, but his smile didn't seem all that friendly as he held out the customary bottle of whiskey and two glasses. Pearl poured out two measures, and gave him a look asking for permission. He seemed to approve of her restraint, and rewarded her with another smile that didn't quite reach his eyes.

"Now, take just a little sip. It's a bad habit to get into, this drinking alone. But I suppose that's what a lot of you do. Isn't it?"

She looked at him to see if it was some kind of test.

"Go on now," he said, almost daring her. "I'm waiting."

She took the tiniest of sips, never taking her eyes from him. He took the glass from her and set it on the beat-up dresser, out of reach.

She eyed the glass, wondering when she would get another sip. He caught her looking and chuckled at her longing.

Mean.

"I dressed especially for you," she told him, feeling uncertain but putting on her best act.

He pressed his tongue against his bottom lip in a lewd fashion, coming toward her. He pulled her hairpins out one by one, and her brown tresses hung down, loose and soft.

Almost clean.

He wrapped the tresses around his hands, looking at the brown hair with a strange fascination. Pearl felt herself go stiff, unable to relax. Unable to tell what he was thinking. He yanked her head back, and started kissing her on the neck. Rough. He then started pawing at her clothes, fumbling with fastenings that threatened to rip.

"Let me do a strip-tease for you," she offered, trying to twist away.

As suddenly as he'd started, he let go of her. She almost fell, pitched off balance. She struggled to catch her panting breath, her heart thudding against her ribs. He stood there cool and unmoving, hardly a hair out of place.

"Now, you sit on the bed, and I'll remove my clothes." It was one of the first things she had learned, starting out as a whore.

First the dress came off, then the petticoat, the shift, the stockings. She hadn't bothered putting bloomers on.

He seemed to like that part, but he wasn't gentle.


"Which room is it?" Lydia stood half-crouched at the landing on the stairs, eyeing the narrow, dark hallway.

"The one furthest down. The door at the end." Annie lowered her voice, but only a bit. It still carried, loud enough to give the occupants a chance.

Lydia held a finger to her lips. She was upstairs in a brothel, heaven help her.

Stanley had driven her to this.

Annie squinted at her like she was making a big deal about a small matter, which was irritating enough all on its own. Annie's heart obviously wasn't in it, but they had an agreement. *A business deal.* Lydia gave her a cross look. She couldn't have Annie backing down.

Harrigan brought up the rear, put out despite the fifteen dollars he was promised. Like climbing a set of stairs was asking an awful lot from him.

"Haven't you been upstairs in a whorehouse before?" Annie tossed the question at him over her shoulder, but it wasn't casual in the least.

Lydia gave her another warning look as she approached the door with caution. Poised, gripping the doorknob, she leaned forward and listened to the sounds on the other side of the door. It sounded a bit like wrestling, which could only mean one thing.

Annie stood beside her, eyebrows lifted in a question. Daring her.

Lydia inhaled with intent and turned the knob. Pushed on through.

Annie grabbed at her sleeve, all hysterical and false. "You can't just go barging in! What type of a house do you think this is?"

And that type of sentiment, which was words, only so many words.

Pearl and Stan were on the bed—Stan deep in the saddle.

Mid-thrust, he looked up as Lydia and the madam entered the room.

"Lydia! What in God's name are you doing?" Stan shouted, coming to a dead stop. Then he started disentangling himself.

Lydia signaled for Harrigan, who hesitated in the hallway. Annie grabbed him by the arm and pulled him into the room.

"Officer, I have found my husband in bed with a common prostitute. This, Stanley Chambers, will be the grounds for the divorce I will sue you for. It's up to you, if you want to keep it out of the papers."

The girl held the sheet up to her chest while Stanley flailed around, taken by surprise in the suddenly congested room.

"This is a set-up! A stinking, rotten set-up!" he roared, struggling with one of his pant legs. "How in the hell did you find me?"

Lydia wanted to feel detached, superior. But she didn't. She felt sick at the sight of her naked husband with a prostitute.

As she turned to leave, her eyes met Annie's.

If she had expected sympathy, she was mistaken. Annie appeared to be more concerned with Harrigan, of all people. The cop was standing in the room, looking at the girl in the bed. He just kept . . . staring at the whore.

Lydia didn't care. She wanted out of the room, and out of the saloon. Stanley tried to grab her by the arm, but the big cop grabbed him by the shoulders instead, and gave him a shake and a shove that sent Stan reeling.

Lydia rushed down the stairs. She burst through the saloon doors and into the open—which wasn't all that much of a liberating experience, considering all the men on the prowl. She stood panting on the boardwalk trying not to cry, or scream or throw up. She pressed her hands to her sides to catch her breath and calm her conflicting emotions.

That was her husband, damn him.

She looked up and down the wretched expanse of Market Street, and wondered how things had ever gotten so bad. A rhetorical question, the answer to which she knew all too well.

Neither was she entirely blameless. A lot of things in her life had become a sham of what they once had been, or should have been. Starting with her little problems that any marriage could never fix.

She gazed back at the brick brothel building—*her building*—and considered her act of defiance. Hell, it almost paled in comparison to being an owner of a brothel.

That was the silver lining she had been looking for, and she uttered a mirthless laugh.

Just maybe things were looking up, indeed.

# Chapter 40
## Losing Hands All Around

"*Lydia* is your wife?" The door to Pearl's room stood wide open.

Stan looked at Pearl like he was seeing her for the first time. "Yeah. But how do you know her?"

"From the saloon downstairs. How else?"

He ran his fingers through his hair, causing spikes. Stunned. "So you knew this was going to happen, is that it?"

"Of course not," Pearl replied, taking a half-step back.

A thought visibly crossed his face. Pearl backed up another step.

Teeth clenched and veins sticking out like ropes in his neck, he turned on her. "This is going to ruin me, you stupid whore!"

Nothing good was going to happen in that room.

Naked, Pearl started angling toward the door. Stan grabbed her, slammed the door shut. "You're not going anywhere until you tell me everything you know. And you had better make it fast."

His fingers dug into the soft flesh of her upper arms. He was going to smack her in a second. "She comes to see Annie. That's all I know!"

Wild-eyed, he shook her hard. "Damn it all to hell! This was the building Ed Chase wanted to buy!"

"I don't know anything about that." She had heard that name bandied about plenty.

"Bullshit!" he screamed, and threw her on the bed.

He pulled on his shirt, jammed his feet into his shoes. He

bolted out of the room, leaving her discarded on the bed. His heels beat a staccato on the plank flooring and the rickety stairs.

It took her a moment to realize that he'd left her door open. It was a shit way to find out she was going to be left with nothing, and had lost her best customer. She slammed the door shut knowing she wasn't special, she was stupid. A stupid whore getting older by the hour.

Her arms were going to look like hell in the morning.

She turned to the laudanum, and took a fair-sized swig before she started dressing. She would talk to Annie about what the hell had just happened.

Bitch.

Downstairs in the saloon, the miraculous part was that no one seemed to notice, or care about, the drama unfolding around them—or above them. Maybe the customers were just hardened to strange goings-on.

Michael was still pouring drinks for all comers, May was positioned on some man's lap, and the new girl was shuffling cards for a table of jakes. Card tricks, no doubt. And the men were carrying on as men tended to do in saloons and whorehouses. Which was good, and her heart slowed down a tad.

Distancing herself from the unsavory business of Stanley Chambers, Annie marched up to May and her jake to collect. Just like normal.

Just like nothing was wrong.

She gave the new girl the signal to resume hooking. The girl did something, and laughter erupted from the card table. She was a good girl, Annie thought. She considered she might want to tell her that. Sometime.

"Go get Lydia," Annie said to Harrigan, who was gazing around like he had never seen the place before.

Looking queasy, he didn't even bother to argue.

Annie surveyed her establishment, only slightly flustered. It was too quiet; things needed to liven up a bit. Hell, she might as well cut loose. So she belted out a peal of forced laughter to relieve the tension she felt. She half hoped Lydia had stuck around, not knowing what she was going to do with Harrigan otherwise. Probably try to fob him off with some booze.

A moment later Lydia and Harrigan came in through the front doors. The pair of them slinking back into the saloon, shook up and with their tails between their legs.

She *could* control some of the outcome.

"Let's go into my office," she said, drawing only passing glances from the punters who had more important matters on their minds. Thank God for that much.

Lydia didn't look any too happy. Settling old scores was rotten, but it paid to be on the winning side. Maybe Annie would tell her as much. Then again, maybe not.

"That's it, then," Annie concluded, like that was some form of consolation. Lydia shot her a cross look, which was just fine. It was a known fact that women often got high and mighty about an injustice at the hands of their men—but when confronted with the naked facts, well, they took it hard. More often than not.

Lydia took up a position next to the window, her profile hidden in shadows. Harrigan sat in a chair, uncomfortable. Business like this never ended well.

What the hell. "Whiskey all around, then," Annie said to cut through the gloom.

She poured three glasses. "Well, I for one have seen enough tonight. Never mind that it's my poor niece who's going to end up the worse of this lot."

The "poor niece" who apparently remained upstairs.

Lydia's head snapped up. "We've left her up there alone with Stanley?"

"Technically speaking," Annie said, ruffled and defensive.

Harrigan looked up at her, judging. "It's a queer family you've got, Annie."

People always judged the Ryans on the matter of family. Annie was getting pretty damn sick of it. "Well, at least I know where most of them are." As if she needed the likes of him pointing out that they would never be lace-curtain Irish.

Lace-curtain anything.

Lydia looked from Annie to Harrigan and back again, obviously expecting someone to go check on Pearl. When that wasn't forthcoming, she got on with it. "Officer Harrigan, here is the paper for you to sign. I already wrote it out for you."

Annie was pretty damn sure about what came next, and gave Harrigan a warning look. The problem with Harrigan was, he wasn't all that receptive.

"Well . . . I haven't been paid." The implication hung in the air, heavy and irritating.

Lydia, however, was faster than Annie. "Sign at the bottom. There."

Harrigan's eyes narrowed. "In a minute. *If at all.* Fifty dollars means nothing to you and your kind."

He stretched out in the chair to signal he was in no rush to sign a solitary thing. Lydia's gray eyes grew cold, with the look of a woman who wasn't going to be fucked around with. Annie emitted a faint, contemptuous laugh waiting for the second round to begin.

"Office Harrigan, the arrangement was agreed to at fifteen dollars, and I expect you to honor it." Lydia walked over to him, paper and pen in hand. "Sign it."

Harrigan shook his big head. "Why, you must think I just got here yesterday. This entire event was a set-up so you could find your husband doing something that would put him in a bad light. If you don't want to pay any more than fifteen dollars, maybe he does. It seems as if there is the distinct possibility he can pay me *not* to have seen anything."

Annie watched the two players. Harrigan's type was fairly predictable. Lydia's wasn't.

But Lydia seemed to be weakening, to her surprise. And Annie had a business to run. "No need to drag this whole shebang out any longer. I just might tell City Hall that I need a different beat cop. Not that I object to police presence, but that you sleep with the Orientals. In fact, I'll tell them I've *seen* you come out of there myself. What do they call that? Degenerate morals, or some such term."

"Now, Annie, you know that's not true . . ."

Lydia smiled, cold. "Annie might indeed know it is untrue, but how can you prove it? It will be your word against hers. And just so you know, I did have you followed. For the last week or so. I have that report describing your whereabouts and activities as they might be interpreted. Signed by the detective and deposited for safekeeping. Now, is that what you want to do? Why don't you just sign this document I have drawn up for you and be happy with your fifteen dollars."

Annie chuckled. Lydia had him, all right. That detective part was pure bluff and bluster. At least, as far as Annie knew.

Harrigan leaned forward in his chair. "Don't you actually own this building, Mrs. Chambers? I think you must, for how else would you and Annie know each other, and why would she allow a set-up to take place here? So far, Ryan's has stayed remarkably above the fray, until tonight."

Lydia, God love her, didn't flinch. "Mrs. Ryan was kind enough to come to my assistance when I needed it. That's all you need to know."

Glaring, he signed for the simple reason that everyone knew: titles for brothel buildings were never registered properly and the owners were notoriously hard to prove.

Lydia placed his fifteen dollars on the desk. "You are excused, Officer. With thanks, of course."

"This isn't the end of this," Harrigan said with a strange calm.

Annie and Lydia followed in his wake, just in time to run into Pearl, who was spluttering mad. "Just the people I wanted to see."

"Christ," Annie muttered, pointing at the office with an outstretched arm. But she remained with Lydia to watch Harrigan leave, stomping on one punter's foot and pushing another out of his way.

"Do you like him at all?" Lydia asked.

"Not a bit, but that doesn't mean he can be disregarded." Annie watched as the room readjusted and a normal night resumed.

It was clear Lydia's mind was set upon something. Flat out, Annie didn't want to know. "You don't have to stay—I can deal with Pearl," Annie told her. "You can see for yourself that she's all right. Just a bit pissed off."

"Would ten dollars help?" Lydia reached into her purse.

"It always does," Annie replied, taking the money.

★ ★ ★ ★ ★

# PART VI
# REPLACEMENTS DON'T
# MATTER TO MARKET STREET
# AUGUST 1893

★ ★ ★ ★ ★

# CHAPTER 41
# A VERY ROUGH THURSDAY
# MORNING AFTER

The next day was business as usual—boozing and screwing. Nothing about betrayal. Nothing that passed as unsavory in their part of town. But Pearl was a jumble of nerves and mixed emotions. She had started to fret, especially about Stan. Hell, he thought she was behind all of it—but she had been caught in the buff as well. Not that being caught in the act might be considered as such a big thing for a whore—but damn it, it was. She hadn't even gotten the full night off. That Annie sure was something else. And what the hell about Lydia? She didn't look so high-falutin', barging in through closed doors like that. In a brothel of all places.

It was pretty obvious what she would be walking in on, one way or another.

Although Stan complained that his wife didn't understand him, Pearl figured she probably understood him just fine. And then there was Harrigan bursting in, getting an eyeful. In one foul minute, everyone she pretty damned well knew in Denver was in her bedroom, shouting and carrying on.

It was a hell of a way to run a business.

She awoke in the morning after passing a fitful night; laudanum could only do so much, although normally it did plenty. Well before her accustomed hour to rise, Pearl got up, actually got dressed and clomped her way downstairs to talk to Annie. Again. She found her behind the bar.

"I've thought about last night some more, Annie. Ten dollars doesn't make up for it all, you know. You say this is a reputable establishment, one where things don't go missing and other such crap, but when push comes to shove, you just let everyone blow on into my room like it was a circus sideshow."

"Good morning to you, too, Sunshine." Annie stood behind the bar, arms outstretched and leaning in. Like she was drawing the line and guarding her territory. Maybe she was just holding down the bar.

Annie didn't look too bothered, all things considered, but was watching Pearl in that way of hers. "And because we are not normally in the circus business, I've decided to send you up to Leadville for a while. While all of this blows on over."

"What if I don't want to go?" Pearl snapped.

Annie shrugged. "You'll go. Care for a real drink?"

In normal circumstances on normal days, Pearl was easily bribed. Hell, they all were. But not that particular day, considering how things stood. "Stan slapped me once before, but I didn't say anything to you."

"Why not?" Annie waited for the answer.

Those words had escaped her, and she didn't have a handy lie ready to cover them up. "What else? Money. And it wasn't that hard of a slap. I've had worse. But last night, I tell you I was worried."

Annie poured without making Pearl ask for it. "I'm sorry about that part." For once, she apparently meant it. Almost mollified, Pearl took the offered drink, wanting to turn something in the mayhem to her advantage.

"Last night. How come you did it?"

Annie poured herself a glass of beer. "Several reasons. The main one is that it puts us in a better position as a going concern."

"So you got paid off, is that it?" Pearl finished her whiskey and Annie poured out another. Without asking.

Which is how Pearl knew the answer, without Annie having to say anything at all.

Harrigan made a better target than Annie anyhow. So Pearl kept an eye out for his arrival, fuming away about how he ought to be ashamed of himself on a number of scores. As far as Pearl was concerned, for him to show his face in Ryan's anytime soon would take some nerve. Maybe *he* had been in on it from the beginning.

Casey Harrigan had nerve. Either that or he was too bull-headed to care.

Eventually he came in, but he wasn't his usual cocky self as he approached the bar, pretending he didn't see her. "Hell of a night last night."

Michael shrugged. "I hadn't noticed."

"I suppose you're going to tell me you just kept your head down. Kept pulling drinks and didn't notice a damn thing was up. Is that it?"

Michael stared at Harrigan. "What the hell are you mad for— you got paid, didn't you?"

As Harrigan took a breath, ready to let loose a litany of complaints, Pearl marched up to him, bristling. "And I'd like to talk to you, Officer, on the quiet."

"I'm not exactly in a talking mood." Harrigan glanced at her from the corner of his eye. He braced himself with both hands against the bar, and stared at his drinks before picking them up, one in each hand. "Oh, what the hell."

He walked over to his usual table, Pearl yapping at his heels. "That was a low, rotten thing you did last night."

He gave her a mean look. "The way I see it, last night was pretty damn disgusting in more ways than one."

Pearl stared at him for a moment, taken by surprise. "I disgust you? Then why the hell did you want me to come to work for you?"

"Lower your goddamned voice, would you?"

He was right. There was no reason to go setting Annie off. For the moment. "I'll do what I want, thank you very much."

Harrigan's mean little pig eyes were calculating something. "As of last night, I have absolutely no interest in getting into the flesh trade. Too much damn nuisance and too many volatile emotions. I'm on to something easier, something surefire."

That set her back, and she did lower her voice. "Like what?"

Harrigan checked to make sure Annie was out of range. "Before I tell you what I'm thinking, I need to know where you stand and if you can be trusted. And if you lie to me, I'll come after you and you won't be left standing. Are we clear on that count?"

With a detached expression, he waited for her answer.

When push came to shove, it turned out she wasn't that much of a gambler. "I could take over Ryan's one day . . ."

"You probably could, knowing the way things go around here. And I'm not sure the two propositions aren't mutually exclusive. But, make no mistake. Annie won't like it because it goes against that Chambers woman."

Pearl considered the rough plank walls she had grown accustomed to. Wallpaper would make it look that much classier. "Well, give me something to go by, at least."

His look was hard. "How much money did you make off of last night? And tell the truth."

"Fifteen dollars for the arrangement, and another ten dollars from Lydia because she felt bad. Why?"

"And I got fifteen lousy dollars. Which amounts to one thing only. We have both been screwed. There's a lot more money to be had out of that deal. Interested?"

"You mean blackmail?" Pearl was almost impressed.

"So what?" Harrigan asked, leaning back.

Probably plenty, not that consequences always counted that much.

She might be on to money, if she kept her wits about her. Pure and simple.

"I'm taking the afternoon off, on account of my nerves," she told Annie, in front of some punters.

Put out, Annie shrugged as if it was of no account. "Just make sure you're in good shape to work."

Some of the men kind of chuckled. She wondered if word was getting around.

Pearl waited until Annie stepped out of the saloon. When Annie went out front, she snuck out the back.

She didn't *exactly* feel right about what she was doing, but then again, she didn't exactly feel all that bad, either. She passed through the alley and took a long, hard look at the cribs and the occupants who were stirring. She shuddered.

Darting over to Larimer, she knew that a good infusion of cash could prevent many things that befell women in her line of work, if she played her cards right. If she managed to hold on to the money that was coming her way.

She cursed the money she'd lost by giving it to Julia. She would probably never see a penny of it. Sentimentality was a mistake she didn't plan on making again. That realization propelled her forward until she stood in front of the brick edifice that housed the Sunshine. One of the seedier gaming hells, it was fancy in its own way. People usually came out worse than when they went in. It was a hell of a lot more impressive than the shack next to it, where she used to run her numbers to.

Seamy or not, Pearl went on in—into the heart of bunko games, roulette, and crooked hands of poker. Clouds of cigar smoke drifted in the streaks of sunlight that penetrated the plate glass window: some type of dicey moonshine, all bottled up and waiting to explode. The chancy atmosphere, more high-strung than Ryan's ever could be, made it exciting. Games were whirling and cards being squabbled over. Gunfire was not unknown. The Sunshine even had a couple of women dealers who glanced up at her, their expressions neutral. Almost.

Maybe they turned tricks on the side.

It took a moment to find Harrigan through the maze of punters, all anxious to lose their money. But there he sat at the back corner, with a cigar and a couple of drinks. Plotting.

"So, here I am," Pearl said, sitting down and happy to see a glass of liquor for her.

Harrigan pushed it across the table. "If Annie catches wind of any of this, she just might call in those brothers of hers. That would sure open up another can of worms we won't be needing."

"So everyone says."

Harrigan snorted with contempt. "I've got a question I want you to consider. What do you think Lydia Chambers wants more than anything else?"

"Who cares?" Pearl didn't want to talk about Lydia ever again.

Harrigan looked at her like she was slow. "You had better care. The way I see it, she wants her divorce and she's going to get it. But there's something she's overlooking. That is the fact that a fair number of people know she owns a brothel."

Pearl frowned, remembering Stanley's comment. "They know nothing of the sort. Hell, I don't even have any proof that she does. Well, other than what Annie's said, and the fact that she comes around."

Harrigan shrugged, unbothered. "The beauty of it is that those are only details. After catching her husband with you, we all went down to Annie's office to talk things over a bit. The upshot is that she threatened to get me removed from my beat by lying. Telling whoever cares that I frequent the Celestials, which just pisses me off more than I can say. So what's to stop me from going to the newspapers to say that Lydia owns a brothel? That should get splashed all over the papers nicely. *If* it needs to."

Pearl sighed, torn. Women never seemed to get ahead in the world without some man poking his nose, or something else, in. But that was the way of life, and she had to play the hand she was dealt. "Stan said the building was one that Ed Chase had wanted to buy. I don't know any more than that."

Harrigan looked startled, and more than a little pleased. "My, my. Fancy that. I told Lydia her husband would probably pay me *not* to have seen anything." Then Harrigan frowned, troubled. "But I signed a paper saying I was a witness to the two of you."

Pearl mulled that over. "That's that, then. I don't see how you could go back on a signed paper."

Harrigan chewed on the end of his cigar. "Do you know how to get hold of her husband?"

"Hell, no. And he's about the last person I want to run into. There never was any set timetable between us—just when the humor got into him."

"Well, I can manage to find him. But let me ask you this, do you think he would want to see you again?"

"What the hell for?" Pearl was starting to lose confidence.

"So you can offer to help him set up his wife, of course."

A dull throb started in her temple despite the glass full of liquor in front of her. She drained it. What he was suggesting was one sure way to set everything on fire. "That's not normally what hookers do, but I suppose so."

"Do you know how much money we are talking about here?"

"I do not." Pearl tried reading his eyes.

"I figure we could get a thousand dollars. Seven hundred and fifty for me, two hundred and fifty for you. Hell, that's more money than you've seen in your lifetime."

That ruffled her pride a bit—he was flat-out wrong. "I've seen a good deal more than that. And in the future, I'll be sure to keep more of it. What exactly do I have to do?"

"I don't know yet, other than to tell me if there are any developments I should know about. You might also act as a go-between. We'll have to see how this all pans out."

Harrigan sure looked excited at the prospect. Pearl had her doubts, but there was an easy buck to be made. Maybe. She didn't have any real loyalty to Lydia, and there was no reason why she should.

What bothered her was the effect this caper might have on Annie, and her hesitation surprised her. Annie was like a burr under a saddle. Sometimes the sensation existed long after the cause had been removed—but she was family, damn it. Annie probably felt the same.

# CHAPTER 42
## OVER-PLAYED HANDS

Lydia couldn't stand loose ends.

She felt a jumble of mixed emotions. It wasn't exactly like she had expected to see Pearl and Stanley having a cup of tea, discussing the weather. But it hurt, all the same.

Then in the next breath, she reminded herself that there was no need to waste any more time over a marriage that had not been the union of two equals. Just about as soon as she got that idea to settle, she would start getting irritated, *outright mad,* about how her husband frequented common *whores.* She had half hoped that Pearl would come down distraught, bruised and battered for all to see. But that didn't happen. Although it should have.

Not that she had anything against Pearl, but, damn it, it was *personal.*

Maybe Stanley only vented his temper on her, his lawfully wedded wife.

Her temper continued to flare and wane as many times in as many minutes. The bottom line was that she was saving money. That fundamental truth caused her pulse to moderate, her coursing blood to slow. But logic only went so far on a woman scorned. She knew that. Her temper was stirring, and that was just as well. She was going to her lawyer to file for divorce, and on to city hall to lodge a complaint. It was a Thursday, Thor's day. Which sounded auspicious, for Lydia sure felt like throwing a hammer at Stanley.

Most people might consider divorce a failing. Lydia figured she could, and would, rise up again. And it would be a hell of a lot easier to do without someone draining her money, not to mention slapping her around.

A divorce was a necessary evil. Like dragging Stanley through the mud.

He had tried to do it to her. And like so many other things he had turned his hand to, he failed.

She tended to succeed. Other than her unmentionable little habit. Solace in a bottle.

And she hated Harrigan. She felt like lashing out against someone, and he made a more than fine target.

Her anger accompanied her from her lawyer's office over to city hall, another monstrosity built in the name of progress. Gaudy, ponderous, and overblown in a manner that defied explanation, it was yet another attempt to overcome Denver's rough and ready image. Lydia wondered where the architect had studied.

She caught hold of herself. To tarry on the steps of city hall meant to be cowed by something. She pressed forward with a sense of purpose, which God knew she had.

Justice was afforded to those that could pay.

She patted one of the pillars as she passed. She would buy her way to freedom if she had to. Because she could.

Her boot heels clicked daintily on the polished marble hallway floors. She noted with interest the general comings and goings of an odd assortment of people. She went straight up to a guard and asked for directions to Captain Moorehead. The guard pointed to another corridor lined with varnished wooden doors down both of its sides. Names of the office occupants were stenciled in black letters, trimmed with gold. Lydia strode down the corridor until she came to the door marked *Police Commissioner.*

She entered the antechamber without missing a beat. "Lydia Chambers to see Captain Moorehead, if at all possible."

The clerk nodded, ducked through a doorway to an inner sanctum, and returned a moment later, accompanied by Captain Moorehead himself.

It must have been her imagination, but the commissioner didn't look as happy to see her as she had expected. "Lydia, come into my office. Can I offer you something?"

She smiled and shook her head, planning on flattery to do the trick. "That won't be necessary. I know your time is valuable."

He escorted her to his office, indicating a chair in front of his large desk. "I don't get many social calls." A confession that stood to reason, considering his lack of enthusiasm in receiving her.

Of course, she said nothing of the kind. "And I wish I could say that this strictly was a social call. But first, how are you and your wife settling into that charming house of yours?"

He smiled, but she saw something hard in his expression. "Never happier, although I've heard that perhaps we paid a bit too much."

It had been a fair price. "I don't know why you would say that."

He snickered, a bit condescending. "Your husband told me."

Lydia swallowed the temptation to scream in his face. "Well, then. I'm not all that surprised, although his interpretation of market conditions was faulty, as usual. He is part of the reason why I am here today. I have petitioned for a divorce on the grounds of cruelty, infidelity, and general low moral countenance. To put it plainly, he was frequenting Ryan's Saloon on Market Street for more than beer."

Captain Moorehead gave her a shrewd look. "Many a good man strays occasionally. He also told me you were having some trouble keeping everything straight because of some delicate matters."

"Oh, the vapors?" Damn him. But letting her temper show was not in her best interest.

Moorehead chuckled. "I didn't say I liked the man, Lydia. But he alluded to the fact that sometimes numbers escape you. He thought the house should have cost five hundred dollars less than what we paid."

Lydia waved off the implication. "He doesn't know anything of the sort, because he never gets his hands dirty with transactions or valuations. He always undervalued properties, and as a result, a lot of customers didn't get what they wanted. Eventually he left that aspect of the operations to me. So, when did this talk take place?"

"A couple of weeks ago, at the club, of course. Now, don't take it so hard."

"Well. I am sorry for the confusion, but you paid a fair price. I stake my reputation on it."

The commissioner looked a bit less doubtful. "We'll see."

It wasn't the type of reception she had expected or wanted. Best to cut her losses and get straight to the point. "The reason I am here is twofold. I need to see what type of protection can be afforded to me, as well as to tell you about a rather sordid aspect of this entire unhappy business."

He gestured for her to continue.

She took what she hoped was a feminine deep breath. "I don't know that it is safe for me to return to my home because Stanley has been known to raise his hand against me. Sometimes the bruises last for days. Then there is the matter of the prostitute named Pearl. I went to Ryan's to verify his activities in person. Of which there is no doubt. But I was counselled to hire a police officer to act as a recording witness."

He shrugged as if it were of little account. "Go on."

Lydia tried her best to look suitably mortified, as if she were compelled to disclose something truly unpleasant. "The officer was in the saloon, in uniform and on the take. I had to pay him fifteen dollars to get him to sign the document describing the events. That's not right, is it?"

Captain Moorhead's expression was stern. "Sticklers might call it grafting, but fifteen dollars wasn't such a terrible sum, was it? If the event took place after his regular hours, he's free to charge for his services."

"Is *that* how it is?" Lydia emphasized. "Well, no sense in bucking the trend, I suppose. More important is the fact that I don't want to be implicated in any of the proceedings last night."

"The police can't do much about that. That's down to the newspaper reporters, as you can imagine. Freedom of the press and all that. But Harrigan can be a pain in the . . . oh, never mind. And I'm not saying he hasn't overstepped his bounds. But I can't help thinking there's more to this story than meets the eye. Something you would like kept secret, perhaps?"

Lydia wrapped the cord of her purse around her wrist. "Perhaps I have made a mistake by coming here and disturbing you."

Captain Moorehead made a conciliatory gesture with his hands that she should stay seated. "Now, hear me out. The police are under terrible pressure right now to appear above board. Why would you care, as you seem to, about Officer Harrigan? You have already paid him what he asked, and he provided the service you requested, did he not?"

"It's corrupt," Lydia countered.

"Your husband seemed to believe that you frequent opium dens, which are corrupt, *Mrs. Chambers.* Not to mention, illegal. What do you have to say about that? For what it is worth, he seemed genuinely worried about you."

"I think I have outstayed my welcome." Lydia rose to her

feet, and decided to play the card that should tip matters in her favor. She was not above exaggerating the importance of Harrigan's comment. "Oh, and one other thing. Officer Harrigan is threatening me with blackmail. Something to do with an imaginary underworld connection, which I most vehemently deny. It has absolutely nothing to do with opium dens."

The commissioner rose to his feet as well and walked to the door. "Unless your reputation is above reproach, you are headed toward dark waters. But I suppose you know that already."

Lydia knew all about dark waters, and bade him a chilly farewell. As she retraced her steps through the corridors, she wasn't near as certain of any outcomes as she had been earlier that morning.

She grabbed a hack lurking in the hallway as she left the building. "It's all a bit sordid," she warned him. Of course, nothing could have been better.

The Denver Republic—*June 21, 1893*

*Last evening in the wicked neighborhood known as the Blue Row, the shame of Denver, equally shameful events were unfurling at Ryan's Saloon. It was at that questionable watering hole with rooms upstairs, that one high-flying society man met his match—thwarted in his lower passions by his upstanding wife. The events included the usual police witness as the room belonging to the sylph was barged into, catching the miscreants in the act. The unfortunate wife, who shall remain nameless to protect her dignity, was a witness to these terrible happenings. Without delay she engaged a lawyer and filed a petition for divorce this afternoon. What a sorry state of affairs this once happy couple has descended into—when marital bliss has been wrecked upon the rocky shorelines of the demimonde and another man falls victim to the siren's terrible lure.*

# CHAPTER 43
## SPOILING FOR A FIGHT

Harrigan found Stanley that Friday, although he never said where. It was all part of police work, he blustered to Pearl, who was already having some misgivings about her involvement. Especially right under Annie's nose. She wouldn't take kindly to any of it. More than anyone else, Annie had the ability to make Pearl's life a living hell.

"He's going to write a letter to Lydia, and send it to Ryan's," Harrigan told her in a lowered voice, annoyingly smug.

Annie was in her office, but could step out at any moment.

Pearl wrinkled her nose as if at an odor. "Why would he want to do that?"

"To help prove she owns the building." Harrigan patted his belly with satisfaction.

Pearl didn't feel anywhere near so certain. "How could he not know what she owns?"

Harrigan puffed up. "Too busy living the high life, I guess. At first, he wanted to go straight to the newspapers, but I reasoned with him. He needed a little help to see it my way. I told him how I had been paid fifteen dollars to witness the other evening. While that got under his collar, it was for all the wrong reasons. To be fair, when I found him, he had just read the newspaper article and was blistering mad. He has his own version of events. Which he is going to threaten her with. He can go to the news-papers, too. If all the dirt comes out, it would probably finish her business off, once and for all." Harrigan laughed, as if finding it all clever.

Pearl hadn't wanted to ruin anyone. "I have nothing all that much against Lydia. I just want some money."

Harrigan frowned at her like she was a slow child. "His version of the story doesn't have to get printed. He'll say he's willing to keep it quiet for a certain sum of money, and then we get that thousand we spoke about."

It really wasn't too late to change her mind, no matter what Harrigan said. But she would have to tell Annie she needed to leave for Leadville *right now,* and Annie would want to know why.

"And does he know that? Did you actually tell him you want a thousand dollars?"

Harrigan shifted. "Not exactly. I'm choosing my moment."

Pearl shrugged, not trusting the outcome all that much. "This might not be my fight, and I might not have all that much of a part to play."

"Not so fast. Stan said he wants to see you. It seems he regrets everything you got put through, and how none of it was fair. If you ask me, he looks like a man who wants to make something up to you. You're going to act as the go-between."

"I don't know." It was possible Stan might have another piece of jewelry for her. That almost changed her reluctance to cross paths with him again. It might be worth her while, just this one last time. And he did owe her, the way she saw it. She was glad Stan felt that way too.

It was only a matter of waiting things out to see what happened next. There was always the chance that Lydia wouldn't pay.

Deep down, Pearl kind of hoped that was the case. If anyone had the guts not to do the expected, it was probably Lydia.

★  ★  ★  ★  ★

Later that next afternoon, a letter sure enough came to Ryan's, addressed to Lydia. Pearl stood poised in the window, soliciting against the ordinances. No one really played by the rules, until a few fines got slapped on the house. She was giving the street a fine view of her calf and the whites above the stocking lines.

She almost lost her balance when a delivery boy delivered an envelope.

Annie took it from the boy and gave him a coin, wary. She turned the envelope over in her hands as she walked back to her office. She emerged a few moments later with her hat on.

"I'll be back in a little while," she said as she left.

Pearl shrugged as if she didn't care, and waved at a punter who rolled on in. She watched her aunt go the opposite direction to the usual. She lost sight of Annie's backside when the punter she had lured approached. "Buy you a drink?" he wheedled.

"Why not?" she replied with a sigh, thinking she sure as hell was going to need it.

Inside the hotel, Annie sat down in Lydia's suite.

"This is real nice," Annie said, appraising the surroundings that were well out of her range and reach. "But this is why I've come."

She thrust an envelope toward Lydia, who recognized the handwriting. After reading the contents without much emotion, she handed the letter to Annie. "I knew he wouldn't leave well enough alone."

Annie didn't have to ask who "he" was.

*You have pushed me to this, and you know it. How am I supposed to live this down and stay in Denver? There is plenty that I can tell the newspapers about you, too. Toward that end, I think a fair settlement price would be ten thousand dollars. If you choose not to pay, I will go to the newspapers about your business holdings and your conduct. If you pay, I will leave town and will start again elsewhere. Anywhere away from you.*

*You can meet me yourself, or use that policeman as your go-between. I want the money tomorrow night. I'll decide whether I will attend to this matter myself, or use a go-between. I will leave further instructions at the Sunshine on Larimer. Ask at the bar.*

"You're not going to go, are you?" Annie said.

Lydia shook her head. "I don't think that would be wise." From all outward indications, she was taking her husband's blackmail in stride.

"Well, you had to guess he was going to try something, I suppose. But what are *you* going to do? And don't say it involves Ryan's. I'm not even sure I can live the first round down."

Lydia gave Annie an annoyed look. "Come on now. No one noticed a thing out of the ordinary, and it is unlikely that Stanley is chomping at the bit to tell his buddies about the escapade and where it took place. They probably think he is a bad joke already."

Doubting that Lydia knew all that much about how men talked and compared stories, Annie steered the conversation back to more proven grounds. "Ten thousand dollars is a hell of a lot of money to part with. You seem to be taking it pretty well—a little too well, if you ask me. Are you planning on paying up?"

"Over my dead body. Maybe I'll offer him two, settle for four if I must, and be done with it. Unhappily. Do you think I can trust Harrigan?"

Annie snorted. "In a word, no—but it also doesn't sound like you have many other choices. But how are you going to handle the negotiations? Sounds fairly tricky to me."

Lydia sighed. "I'll send the cop with the two thousand. The instruction will be that Stanley can take it or leave it. Knowing him, he'll take it."

"Fine. But how do you deal with Harrigan in all of this? He'll have to know that something is off about the money because he has to deal with your husband during the exchange."

Lydia shrugged. "I've got no idea how I can even be assured Harrigan won't take the money himself and run away to the wilds of Wyoming, or wherever. Who knows how any of this will go when it really happens? I didn't tell you about my visit to the police commissioner. Right after I got him the house that he and his wife wanted, he said he owed me a favor and to call him in on it. Well, that tune changed because Stanley has poisoned that well. So now I don't have any strong back-pocket options. Unfortunately."

Annie understood, and she didn't like any of it.

She made it a point to stop by the telegraph office on the way back to Ryan's and sent a wire addressed to Sadie Doyle at the Fortune Club. *Urgent need to send Pearl back to Leadville in the next day or two. Send a girl in exchange if possible. No choice in matter. Agreed?*

By evening she had her answer.

Pearl was going back up to Leadville, and some girl named Polly was coming on down to Denver. Annie felt the familiar surge of optimism rise. Chances were the girl would be good looking and a good earner. Sadie was particular about the stable she kept. Heaving a sigh of relief, Annie felt that things were, once again, coming back under control.

The evening business swung into motion as it always did, even if it felt a bit flat. The greenhorns wouldn't know the difference, and the regular punters probably wouldn't, either. But Annie kept closer watch on the proceedings than usual. She wanted to make sure there was no trouble—and that shirker

Stan Chambers didn't put one toe into the saloon.

Pearl was kept well busy. Annie stood watch at the bottom of the stairs, just so no one snuck up where they weren't supposed to be.

She even thought about asking Harrigan to take up position in the saloon, just in case. But then she changed her mind. He had that strange pre-occupation with Pearl that wasn't of a coarser nature. Driven by a poke, she could understand. But since he didn't seem inclined to screwing, she decided she couldn't trust him where Pearl was concerned.

No good would come from any involvement with him.

Mulling over her prospects, Annie decided she would just bide her time until Pearl left town. Pearl would probably kick off about a return to the mountains. But it was for her own damn good, even if the girl couldn't see it.

The next day, Annie grabbed Pearl as she was about to leave the saloon dressed in street clothes. "I need to talk to you about a couple of things before you skedaddle."

A wary look came over Pearl's face.

"I'll give you a glass of nice whiskey, to smooth any bumps in the road. How about that?"

Pearl paused at the mention of whiskey. "I was going to find a new dress, but I suppose it can wait a few minutes."

"Good! And it won't even take long," Annie said. "Let's go into my office."

Pearl followed her across the saloon into the office. She sat down in the chair across from Annie's desk while her drink was poured. Annie held out the glass to her. "Sadie's agreed to take you back up in Leadville for a while."

"Leadville. I wonder who's still up there that I know."

She sounded so matter-of-fact. That set Annie back some. "Nice to hear you've decided to be reasonable." A slight affection threatened as she watched the girl drink with remnants of manners. Even better, Pearl didn't look like she had much else to say. Another good sign, Annie thought.

Annie wanted to make their bond a bit stronger. She needed the girl to come back from Leadville, and not get some fool notion in her head about running off with a miner or, worse, defecting into Sadie's operation permanently. "Now I know you've wanted some answers from me for some time. Maybe today is the day for it."

She sat back behind her desk. "This is a tough old line of business. A lot of things conspire to bring a body down. At the end of the day, survival depends on who is the toughest and most adaptable. You'd be smart to watch the booze."

Pearl rolled her eyes. "You're the one who gave it to me. I never drank before I came in here."

"Fine. But it got your mother in the end. You know that." Annie thought again how much the girl looked like Claire. "And since you are going back to the mountains, I thought we might clear up a few things about your mother. I suppose I could even answer a few questions. But I've thought about some things, so here goes.

"In the beginning I loved my sister, but I didn't love what she became at the end. No one else did, either. She started out well—not too bright in the brains department, but that didn't seem to matter much. She always had a smile in those early days. Before she started drinking and drugging. You share a lot of traits with her."

The girl shifted in her seat.

"The bottom line is that she didn't want you, Pearl. She couldn't have—or if she did, not for the right reasons. I didn't want my daughters, either. None of us choose to get pregnant, but it's a hazard of the trade. Alive and well, you're going up to Leadville on Sunday. I don't want you telling Sadie I haven't come clean with you. What is it that you're looking for?"

Pearl sat as unmoving as a stone, blinking with surprise. "Do you think she would have liked me?"

The question was like an unexpected punch to Annie's stomach. It had been a long damn time since she'd considered what or who Claire might, or might not, like. "If she was straight in the head, she would have. But that wasn't always the way it was with her, you see."

She watched Pearl swallow that information, struggling. Damn. There were tears forming in Pearl's eyes.

Pearl sniffed and looked away. "Did she really choose what she became?"

"Does anyone?" Annie replied.

The girl frowned. "I wish I could see her, a likeness or something."

Annie shook her head. "You can look in the mirror and see her. Your eyes are the same, the nose . . . the way you toss your head. That's all your mother looking back at you. As for your question, do any of us want to end up whores? It's just what happens. We are from a family of procurers and saloon keeps. This runs in our blood. There's no turning away from it."

"You should have let me be." Pearl's voice grew small and far away.

That was plain ridiculous. "An orphan alone in the world? And just how do you think that would have turned out? Laundry maid in a damp cellar or a scullery maid if fate were kind? That's what the cards held for you, my dear. Nothing more, so don't get your head turned by foolishness. A bit of a fumble and a stumble with a stable boy or ranch hand offering pretty promises—is that what you're missing? All of it likely would have been lies leading to a pregnancy and a dismissal. And we would have found you down here eventually, a few years later and a lot more beat up. Is that really what you would have preferred?"

Pearl shook the thought from her head. "This can't be all there is."

"It is—for all of us. Oh hell, Leadville will be a good change of scenery for a while. And you can visit your mother's grave, as you grew so fond of doing. But Pearl, she's not going to answer you. And if she did, it probably wouldn't be anything you would want to hear."

Pearl finished her drink and rose to her feet. "Thank you. And I mean that." Annie put on her specs. "I wish it was something better." But it never was, and never could be.

Annie started shuffling papers to make sure Pearl knew the visit had ended. There was no use in getting all sentimental. Not when she had a business to run.

# CHAPTER 44
## THINGS GO OFF

Pearl's thoughts were whirling, and time was running short. Panic was setting in, but she wanted to get what was coming to her. What she almost deserved. The timing of her departure from Denver should work out well, all things considered. She would have to explain *why* she was missing from the saloon on a Saturday evening. That alone was plenty to worry about. If she returned to the saloon by nine, she could slip in through the back alley door. If Annie caught her and asked, which was damn near inevitable, Pearl would tell her she felt a bit unwell and needed air. And the outhouse. That should work. No one usually argued with someone who couldn't leave the bog out back.

And the fact that she was leaving for Leadville without much more than a nominal tussle was proof she wasn't up to anything she shouldn't be. Annie would probably think that for once she was behaving herself.

She almost wished she were.

Her throat tightened. Whores stole when they could and what they could. Everyone knew that. And since, as Annie had so aptly explained, Pearl belonged to a family of procurers and downright whores, the occasional dodge and swindle wasn't that much of a stretch.

But Lydia might not know that. She might not understand. Lydia was sticking her nose into a world where she shouldn't. Everyone couldn't change their usual customs to accommodate

her whims when she was in their part of town. She had plenty
of money to throw around, which meant she wouldn't miss her
losses after a while. Somehow, she would just get more. All the
same, it didn't seem right undercutting Annie, not now when
she had finally come clean. But it beat the hell out of Pearl, why
Annie couldn't have just done that in the first place.

She was turning the implications of what she was involved
with—what she was truly going to do—over in her mind when
Harrigan came into Ryan's. To all outward appearances, nothing had changed. Nothing was going on.

She drifted by, but didn't break her stride. "Still this evening,
isn't it?"

He nodded. "Some of it has changed, however."

Pearl turned back around, took a couple of steps toward him.
Harrigan leaned against the bar with his back towards Annie's
office, shielding Pearl from view. "Annie's asked me to be the
go-between, and I'll deal with the Sunshine portion of the arrangements."

"What Sunshine portion?"

Harrigan shook his head in disgust. "It's getting complicated.
Stan instructed Lydia to send her go-between to the Sunshine,
where instructions will be waiting behind the bar. Of all things.
That means the barkeep is one more person who will be
involved. He'll hand over a sealed note that will specify the
place to deliver the money to Stan."

Pearl frowned. "Why the Sunshine?"

"Hell if I know. Since they see a fair share of shady dealings,
there's the chance that one more strange request will pass un-
noticed. Annie's got the money in the vault. I'll go to the
Sunshine, while you wait in the shadows out of sight. Afterwards,
I tell you where to go. Simple."

"You're not going with me?"

Harrigan shook his head. "It won't look right. There's nothing to prevent Annie from hiring someone to trail me just to make sure I don't get the notion to take the money and run. Which isn't a bad idea, all things considered. But no. At the Sunshine I'll pick up the instructions. I'm assuming the exchange will be made somewhere near Stan's house."

"I don't really like alleys." She thought about the cribs.

Harrigan didn't care. "You'll get over it. Besides, I'll be hanging back to make sure everything works out as it is supposed to. If someone is watching, I'll haul him in for potential robbery. Simple."

Pearl was getting sick of no one giving a damn about her. "But if you're hauling someone into jail, then I'm out there on my own."

Harrigan seemed to understand, but just a bit. "You're not afraid of Stan, are you?"

She tried to smile but failed. "He's already mad. And wouldn't someone trailing you see me in the shadows, when you give me the money?"

"Nah," Harrigan replied, but he sounded unsure. "It wouldn't matter so much. If someone follows me and starts after you, I'll be conking him over the head, see?"

Regardless, Pearl would be lurking in the shadows near the Sunshine at eight that evening. Hoping for the best.

"No drinking beforehand," Harrigan cautioned.

Asshole. "And how are we going to get our money? You haven't told me that part yet."

Harrigan appeared far too confident for her comfort. "We'll get it from Stan tonight, after you've given him the payoff. He gets to see your lovely face, and I'll catch up with him to collect later this evening, around ten."

And so the plan was agreed. Not that it didn't have a few holes in it.

★　★　★　★　★

At a quarter to eight, Pearl slipped out of Ryan's wearing a plain black skirt and a nondescript white blouse a little the worse for wear. She looked up and down the street, but no one was paying her any mind, other than the attention a woman normally attracted on Market Street. Which was enough, for sensitive stomachs. She struck out toward the Sunshine, and hid in the shadows across the street from it. As instructed. From the murky distance she watched Harrigan enter the gaming hell with a lump in his breast pocket. He came out with a slip of paper in his hand.

He strode over in her direction, checking the street for someone watching. Pearl glanced around, too, but only saw some drunks and a bunch of good-time jakes.

"All right, Pearl. Go to the alley that runs between Curtis and Champa between Twenty-fourth and Twenty-fifth streets. Don't tarry, but go straight there. Stan will meet you behind one of his friends' carriage houses. I'll be some ways behind you, so you have nothing to worry about."

"What friend?"

"How the hell should I know? And it's not like you would know one from the other. Jesus Christ, what are you being so difficult about?"

The entire business was making her jumpy, but she wasn't about to admit that. "If Stan gives me jewelry, that's not part of *our* deal."

"We'll see," Harrigan replied.

She gave him a nasty look as she took the money wrapped in brown paper, figuring she wouldn't bother to tell him about it. That would prove whether he was really watching out for her or not. Without saying another word to him, she headed southeast, as told.

Toward the neighborhoods where decent people lived. Those

that had money and standing. She glanced over her shoulder, checking to make sure Harrigan was still standing there. He was.

Pearl picked up her pace.

Harrigan was probably used to dealings such as these, but she wasn't. She wanted to trust him, but something prevented it. Maybe it was a sense that no one on the take was trustworthy. Whatever the case, she understood she could justify her actions all she wanted, but her stomach held a much different version.

She crossed Larimer and Lawrence streets, travelling along Twenty-second, turning down Arapahoe until she reached Twenty-fifth Street. She ducked into the alley, against her better judgement. But it was part of the plan. She had to follow the plan. If she did as agreed, she would get some money without having to do anything for it. Well, anything much.

She walked faster. Someone kicked a can down the empty backstreet, skipping it along the rutted dirt. Startled, Pearl gasped and spun about.

She didn't see Harrigan. She hoped he was keeping watch, like he promised.

Shadows deepened in the twilight. The alley behind the buildings felt chancy and remote. The money in the brown paper bag felt like a beacon that the underworld could decipher in the dark. Uneasy, she had come this far. She decided she no longer cared very much about any jewelry.

She wanted to run back to Ryan's. Instead, she peered ahead into the gloom. She could just make out the silhouette of a man leaning casually against one of the carriage houses. Hesitating, she strained to see if it was Stan.

The shadowy figure spoke. "There you are. Bet you thought you'd never see me again. Is that it?" Stan shoved away from the wall.

"I've brought the money." She held the package out to him, both hands, arms outstretching. Like an offering.

He didn't take it, but started circling her. Appraising her from all angles. "You are so very pretty, but treacherous. Why did you set me up like that?"

She turned so she could face him. "I didn't. I was caught just as much as you."

"Is that a fact," he drawled.

"Yes. Now, here's your money like you wanted. I have to get back to the saloon." Again she held out the package toward him, as far as her arms would reach. When he didn't make a move to take the money, Pearl set it down on the ground.

He lunged at her. She fell, her partial scream cut short as he clamped his hand over her mouth.

He hauled her upright, his fingers wrapped around her throat, forcing her head back.

She struggled, striking him with her hands, but no sound would come.

Kicking. Trying to peel his fingers away from her throat—fingernails gouging his flesh and her own.

But growing weaker.

Flashes of light in her vision. Stan slammed her up against a brick wall. She hit her head and went limp. Down into darkness.

Stanley continued to choke the whore until she was dead. And then some more.

Finally he stopped and dragged her body behind a tall stack of sawed lumber. He took a hunting knife from his belt and pressed it hard against her throat. Sharp as it was, it still took two hands to cut deep. He stopped when the blade struck her spine.

Then he left her.

★ ★ ★ ★ ★

Harrigan came running up to the alley, out of breath. Pearl hadn't been that far ahead of him. A minute at most, he'd have sworn. Yet he didn't see where she was. He looked up and down the alley, straining to see in the shadows. His gaze fell upon the sawed and stacked lumber.

With reluctance, he approached. He peered behind the stack of lumber and saw her body, lying in a crumpled heap. A closer look made him throw up in the alley, splashing vomit on his shoes.

He never saw Stan, although he knew the man had done this. Knowing where Stan lived, and where he might go, Harrigan went the other direction. Just as fast as his legs could carry him.

About nine o'clock that night, the saloon was livening up, and all hands were needed. Pearl still hadn't come down, so Annie went on up. Pissed off. Damn it, the girl knew the rules. That was the last time she'd do Pearl any favors. That girl needed taking down a peg or two, upset about the Lydia business or not. The night wasn't getting any younger, and neither were any of them. Punters were clamoring downstairs, and were pretty soon going to head off to other establishments if they didn't get taken care of.

Annie pounded on Pearl's door, but there was no answer.

"Pearl. Now you have work to do. I'm not paying for you to loll about!"

God help her if she was passed out from drinking. Annie pushed on in, but the girl wasn't there. She cast a quick glance around. The girl's dresses were still on hooks in the wardrobe.

Annie got a cold feeling, but there wasn't much she could do about it.

She was going to give Pearl a piece of her mind when that girl returned. She would probably even dock her some money, on account of the missed earnings. Once word got out about Ryan's not having enough girls, the loss of one evening might become a bit larger.

Her reputation was all she had to stand on.

# CHAPTER 45
## STAGNANT WATER

Annie had expected Harrigan to come into the saloon to tell her the package was delivered. But the asshole never did any such thing. Never showed up at all. That man rubbed her the wrong way, no mistaking it. He didn't have a shred of basic manners.

It took the biscuit when the world relied upon a madam to point that out.

Worse, Pearl never came home, a fact of which Annie was well aware. She kept checking the girl's room throughout the evening, finally locking up the saloon at four in the bloody morning. Annie fell asleep on the girl's bed, just in case she thought she could sneak back in like nothing happened. But the sun rose, and Annie woke up to a day already started. Without Pearl.

Annie heaved herself up from the worn mattress, with the idea that it needed replacing. She undid her tousled hair and re-arranged it in the mottled mirror, frowning as she pinned it back into place. It wasn't like Pearl to run off and leave her clothing behind. The girl probably even had money stashed somewhere. Her absence provided the perfect opportunity to find out what the girl was keeping from her. But Annie's heart wasn't in it, so she left Pearl's belongings undisturbed.

Kind of like paying penance, for any one of a myriad of sins.

She walked over to the window, hoisted the sash, and stuck her head out into the harsh morning light. The window afforded a fine view of the street, and there was the chance she might catch her niece sauntering or slinking back, as the case might be. She had warned Pearl about work-related romances.

But any girls Annie saw from that vantage point were strangers, or near-strangers.

"Son of a bitch," Annie said to the room, thinking how whores could be so damned unreliable. She headed down to the bar, hoping she might find Pearl there.

Michael had already opened up.

"Pearl hasn't come back from what I can tell," she said, heading over to the pot of coffee. He grunted something unintelligible as he kept on cleaning.

Annie poured some coffee into a cup and sat at the table nearest the window, watching the dregs wake up and shake off the night with varying degrees of success. One hard case puked in the gutter right outside the window.

"Lovely," she commented, sipping her coffee.

Punters started coming in for the hair-of-the-dog that bit them. A wonderful practice to get into, as far as the saloon was concerned. But none of the traffic was Pearl, drunk or sober.

At eleven, Harrigan came in, not stopping at the bar, but heading straight for Annie.

"It's about Pearl," he said, looking uncomfortable. "There's a problem."

Annie didn't say a damn thing. One look at his face told her all she needed to know. She anticipated the worst.

"She's dead," he said, met by her silence.

Annie didn't even get to her feet. A coldness gripped her stomach and spine. *She hadn't managed to keep the girl alive.* "What happened?"

"She got her throat slit, and she's at the morgue," he replied, looking a helpless kind of bothered that spoke volumes of guilt.

"It probably happened last night."

"Then what the hell took you so long to come tell me?" Annie snapped.

"It's really bad," he replied. "I just found her this morning."

Michael came out from around the bar and stood at her side.

"You found her? You found her where?" Annie didn't trust anything about the story that was unfolding.

"In the alley at Champa and Twenty-fifth. Don't you want to go into your office to discuss this?" Harrigan took off his cap, sweating.

Annie thought she was going to burst into tears. It had been a hell of a long time since that happened. She just sat at the table staring at Harrigan, trying to make sense of what he was telling her. Smothering any feelings she had on the matter.

"We're closed," she said to Michael. "Get these people out of here." She looked back over at Harrigan. "Champa and Twenty-fifth. She had no reason to be out in that neighborhood. What the hell happened last night?"

"I can't talk to you about it," he said, fidgeting.

"Why the hell not?" Screaming might make some headway.

"I'm a witness," he replied, shuffling his feet and shifting his bulk.

"Witness to what, her murder? The deal was to happen last night, you found her body this morning, and you're a witness to boot. How does that all work out, exactly?"

Harrigan didn't answer her questions. "Like I said, I can't tell you. But I can take you to the morgue so you can collect Pearl's body. That is, if you want to."

Annie wanted to spit in his face. There was more he wasn't saying. A lot more. "I'm hardly about to leave her there, surrounded by *the law*." She turned to face the room at large. "Everyone clear out now," she bellowed, for any stragglers' benefit. "This saloon is closed!"

Michael pushed the remnants of the clientele out of the saloon and bolted the door behind them. He scrawled out a note and stuck it in the window. *Business open as usual Monday.*

He looked at Annie, crossed out Monday, and wrote *Tuesday* over it.

Together the three of them left the saloon by the back door, Annie leading the way, walking fast. The principal morgue was located in city hall, a clearing station of sorts for the violent aftermaths before interment could take place. When the three of them entered the massive building, newspaper hacks were huddled together, as were some of the police. Annie looked at them all and sneered.

*And Harrigan was some sort of god-damned witness that couldn't tell her a thing about it.*

"Where's the morgue?" she snapped at the guard on duty.

"Annie, I said I would take you there," Harrigan chided her. She turned to face him head on. He looked worried.

"Then do it," she said, "and quit fucking around."

The guard seemed to enjoy that exchange as they turned away, heading toward the back of the building and the dark, subterranean stairs there.

Upon arrival down below, Annie did her best to ignore the smell of the place. Sweetish, sickly, all chemicals and decay. "We're here for Pearl Kelly," she told the coroner.

She threw annoyed looks at Michael and Harrigan, and wondered why the hell she had bothered to bring them with her if all they were going to do was trail along on her heels. Men were often next to useless when things got hard. That included the coroner, who looked unhappy as he pulled back the sheet to reveal the body.

Annie looked at her broken niece, Pearl's face distorted and brutalized, her slender throat slashed to the bone.

She met Harrigan's eyes. "I never want to see you again. I mean it. Test me if you don't believe me, and you'll sure as hell find out."

Denver Republic—*Obituary June 23, 1893*

### *A Sad Ending to a Dissolute Life*

*The end of Pearl Ryan's wayward life was as sad as the last few years of it had been—found, as she was, in the alley in the 2500 block of Curtis Street, lying among the trash, nearly decapitated. After the crime scene was investigated, her body was deposited at the city morgue with the coroner. The next day, she was collected by another demimondaine, Annie Ryan— reputedly her aunt and the keeper of the house of ill-fame where Pearl was an inmate. The familial association begs the question, from what type of family did these ladies originate, and why should Denver tolerate them?*

*Pearl was described as a lively, good-looking girl—a beauty, even. She started life with the Sisters at the Home of the Good Shepherd, but abandoned the convent for the gin mill. By the time of her death at the tender age of eighteen, she had fallen so low that depravity was her only future. Still, no one deserves such an ignominious end.*

*The brutality of this murder is sure to be a topic from sermons to street corners, all of which demand an answer and a culprit. Without a doubt, there is a madman loose in Denver.*

*Pearl Ryan was fitted with a coffin in the morgue at the expense of the city of Denver due to the state of her corpse. Her mutilated remains were loaded on a hearse, her procession a multitude of Cyprians that accompanied the body to the undertaker's parlor. A charwoman, faded, bent, and worn, stood silently beside the coffin in the dim light of the undertaker's chapel. Had that simple woman once been a member of the sporting life? Brief services were held as the members of the half-world shed copious tears. One could not help but wonder who those tears were shed for: the poor, murdered girl, or for themselves and the infamous lives that they have chosen?*

*Pearl Ryan was interred in the Riverside Cemetery without benefit of clergy, her final sad, resting place marked with a plain headstone paid for by collection.*

*What a terrible, queer story this has been, but, alas, not unique except for the manner of demise. None of the citizens of Denver shall be afforded a good night's rest until the murderer has been found. City Hall has declared resolve in bringing this unfortunate matter to a swift close.*

# CHAPTER 46
## CRIME PAYS HANDSOMELY WHEN IT COMES RIGHT DOWN TO IT

There were plenty of accusations to go around. A lot of them among the remaining members of the Ryan family. After the burial, Annie and her brothers adjourned to Ryan's Saloon, a morbid business meeting if ever there was one.

"It might help matters along if you tell us exactly what happened," John said when the second round of drinks were poured.

Annie stared into the amber liquid. "I thought I had made my position clear."

Jim cleared his throat. "Listen, darling. We don't mean anything by any of it—we're just trying to figure out what we should do, and what kind of response there needs to be to all of this. Don't you want justice for Pearl?"

"Justice." Annie spat the word out with a dry laugh. "I would be surprised if there truly is justice in this world. Or the next."

"That's blasphemy," John muttered, having found a modicum of religion with his second wife. A distinction that the other two found almost funny, prompted along by strained nerves and booze.

"What the hell kind of reverse wake is this we're holding?" Annie grumbled, caught between laughter and anger, tears welling. "Damn this all to hell."

"Now, from the beginning, Annie," Jim coaxed, as the three Ryans regained their sense of propriety.

"I don't exactly know the beginning. Bloody hell! Lydia got beaten up by her husband. I agreed to assist in finding him with a whore in a compromising situation—and that whore was Pearl. That was supposed to be the end of it."

"Why would you do a thing like that in the first place?" Jim poured out some more booze.

Annie took a stiff drink, wiped her mouth with the back of her hand. "The way I saw it, there wasn't all that much of a choice. Something had to be done, and she offered me a month of free rent. That's nothing to sneeze at, for the record. And before you two ask, no, I'm not telling you the amount."

The boys exchanged glances and shrugged. John motioned for Annie to continue.

"Harrigan and Pearl were getting kind of chummy as of late, and I never did figure out what they were up to. Probably he said he loved her, or some other damn fool thing she would want to hear. At any rate, Lydia's husband took a shine to Pearl as well, even to the point of giving her a pair of Lydia's earrings. Stan was trying to blackmail Lydia for ten thousand dollars, threatening to go to the newspapers with how she owned a brothel. Lydia, being Lydia, only sent two thousand dollars. Harrigan was the go-between. And the rest doesn't add up."

"So Harrigan killed her?"

"He must have. But I don't know why. Other than Pearl seemed to take a fancy to Lydia's husband somewhere along the line, although she did say he hit her once. Whatever it was, she could be cagey when she wanted to be."

All three of them shrugged. There was nothing terribly rare in any of it. Other than the decapitation.

John leaned back in his chair, his look shrewd. "So Harrigan got promoted to inspector out of all this. How do you explain that?"

Annie threw her hands up in the air. "So, now you're expecting me to explain City Hall to you. Is that it?"

Jim slid a finger under his shirt collar, pulled it away from his neck. "He sure is coming across well in the newspaper accounts. Taking a stand against the prevailing corruption or some other load of shit."

"So he is. Where is this husband—does anyone know?" John sounded tired.

"No one cares. Like Lydia said, he took the two thousand dollars and ran. I doubt we'll ever see him in Denver again." Annie rubbed her face.

"So—in a way, Lydia is responsible for all of this. At least that's how I see it. Don't you agree, Jim?"

"I do, indeed."

Annie looked from one brother to the other. "Look, boys, I'll handle Lydia. But I don't know how to handle Harrigan, and I'm not too keen on dealing with another cop that I have to pay. I was thinking maybe we could combine forces a bit more than we have in the past. Maybe one of you could help me run Ryan's in the evening hours, just so the law knows there's a bit more backbone than they've seen previously. What do you say?"

"For a cut, we're always willing. And we've got a couple of new girls we could run by you. Along with some more booze that needs off-loading. But," John looked at Jim, "I'm still mighty unhappy about what has happened here."

Jim shrugged. "We can't have accidents happen to inspectors. City Hall would be all over us like a ton of bricks if anything happens to a hair on Harrigan's head."

"For now," John said. "That don't mean he can't get drunk and fall in the Platte, hitting his head on a rock on the way down. At some later, unspecified date. Probably during spring run-off. Sometimes the bodies go pretty far downstream where no one would even know him. Or care."

"He's getting away with murder, boys. Murder of our niece." Annie leaned forward, searching their eyes to see if her point was taken.

And it was.

"But there's no use in any of us ending up in the state pen over this. We'll bide our time, although it does chap my butt that he got a promotion out of the deal. And, Annie, that doesn't leave your friend Lydia off the hook."

"I know it," she said, knowing just as well that she never should have gotten involved in the first place.

It never, ever paid to make friends with women, and especially not drug fiends to boot. Annie had known better all along, and was at a loss to explain how and why she had let her guard down. Maybe she was just getting soft in her old age. Everything had started out as a business deal, and a business deal it would return to.

If Lydia didn't come to her, she would go to Lydia. The boys were waiting, and they weren't the most patient of sorts.

Tuesday, Ryan's was back up and running although few hearts were in it—the punters that hadn't known Pearl didn't care and seemed not to notice the pall one whore's death cast over the proceedings. Lydia, however, came in wearing mourning.

"So you've heard," Annie said, coming out from behind the bar.

"All of Denver has heard. I'm so sorry," Lydia said. It sounded sincere.

Together the women walked back to the office. "Pearl was the heart and soul of the place," Annie remarked, while Lydia looked doubtful.

Annie poured out the customary drinks, didn't even bother to offer sherry. "So, you haven't heard from your husband again, have you?"

"No, and I don't expect to." Lydia looked sharp and alert.

"That's good news, I suppose." The way Annie said it left

room for doubt.

"You sound tired, Annie. This has been a terrible ordeal for you."

Annie felt herself weaken. For a split second. "I can't help but think Pearl would still be alive if I hadn't gotten her involved in all of this."

Lydia stiffened. "No. I suppose you are right. Do you have any idea how this all transpired?"

Annie wasn't sure if she should fall for that or not, noticing a wall come down in Lydia's expression that reached into her eyes. It was the look of a woman guarding her territory. Under normal circumstances, Annie would have approved. "Hard to say, considering Harrigan doesn't have to talk because he is a witness, or so he says."

"What?" That seemed to snap Lydia out of any assumptions she might have held on the matter.

"He says he can't talk about it. And he's been promoted to inspector. So something tells me he's going to get away with it."

"Get away with what?" Lydia's eyes narrowed in apparent confusion.

If it was an act, it was a good one. "Pearl's murder, of course. What did you think I was talking about?"

Lydia spread her hands wide, still looking unconvinced. "Well, I sure don't know why you think Harrigan did it, for starters."

"She was in the neighborhoods. Her body was found in an alley by Champa and Twenty-fifth. And Harrigan admitted he was a witness. He must be referring to himself in some sort of odd way. Besides, those two were acting thick as thieves. But none of this would have come to this pass if I hadn't gotten involved in that damn setup."

"So, her body was found in an alley near my house."

"So it seems. What of it?" Something in Lydia's tone made

Annie sharpen up.

Lydia emitted a low sigh. "It's strange that it's near my house. That's all."

Annie snorted. "Harrigan always did have aspirations. So did Pearl. Maybe she followed him for some reason. Then he killed her because he could, or she said she was going to turn him in or something equally stupid."

Preoccupied, Lydia sat quietly, and offered no further comment. Either that, or she was making Annie work for it.

To think Annie had stuck her neck out for this woman. "I'm not quite clear how you figure your husband is out of the picture. He's going to think you double-crossed him not once, but twice."

Lydia frowned. "He's a coward, already long gone. He was always the kind to take the money and run—he has a history of that kind of thing. That he's been shortchanged—frankly, I think he's been overpaid for far too long. It might be worth it to drag him into court to prove my point."

Annie didn't believe the court business for a second. That had been what Lydia was trying to avoid. "None of which means he can't write a letter to the newspapers. Nor does it mean he isn't holed up somewhere local. You are his monetary bloodline, darling. I spoke with my brothers, and umm . . . they think you might be in danger."

Lydia's head snapped up. "I thought you all weren't close."

Annie tried to look contrite. "We have to be, now of all times especially. It's tired but it is true; family is what counts in the end. Well, more or less. It is a known fact that families pull together at times of tragedy. Either that or everything blows sky high. Thankfully, we've decided to combine forces."

Lydia frowned. "Well. I'm just a bit surprised, that's all."

"And I'm surprised to learn you are back at your house. Aren't you just a bit worried?" Annie never took Lydia for being foolish, but perhaps she was wrong on that count as well.

"I'm having the locks changed." Lydia sounded less certain.

"Bully for you," Annie replied, lifting her glass in a mock toast.

Lydia looked a fair bit exasperated. "Okay, Annie. I know you're trying to tell me something, so why don't you just come out with it."

"I don't think it's good for you to be around Denver or Ryan's, for the time being. Stan could easily come back, splash your name all over the papers, and then you'll be the laughing stock of your fine social circles. Owning a brothel, publicly, would be a hard thing for the likes of you to live down."

"I don't frequent those circles."

"Oh, you don't sell houses to them? I could have sworn you did." Annie could see she was getting under Lydia's skin. "Tell you what. Sell me the building, and get out from under this mess free and clear. The way I see it, you owe me. Pearl is dead because of getting involved with providing evidence for your benefit. She was the mainstay of the operation, and I think that deserves some form of payment."

Lydia looked at her, cold and level. "Annie, somehow part of that sounds a bit close to a threat."

"It might," she agreed. "Owning a brothel is threatening business when you have a reputation to maintain. I do think there is something you are not telling me, and I find it hard to believe you are just going to stay put in that damn house like a sitting duck. I think it would be fair if you sold the building to me at cost. It's turned out a fine investment over time, there's no use in getting killed over it."

"And who's going to do the killing?" Lydia's blue eyes were icy, her voice expressionless.

"Does it matter? *Dead is dead.*"

Lydia sighed. "Ten thousand dollars and you have yourself a

deal. And I think I'm going to go up to Georgetown for a while. This conversation has pretty much settled me on that fact."

Annie started feeling a bit softer toward her. "Good," she said. "I think it's all for the best. You'll have the papers drawn up?"

Lydia nodded. "Yes. And I mean it, Annie. I am sorry about what happened to Pearl. Are you going to pursue the matter further, getting Harrigan arrested or something?"

Annie rubbed her forehead. "I sure would like to. But cops don't kill whores, even if they did. If you know what I mean."

Lydia nodded. City Hall did not care about the death of one whore.

It was comforting to realize that the business transaction worked better than Annie had expected.


After Lydia left, Annie went over to her brothers at the Monte Carlo, knowing they could get the money one way or another. "I need to borrow twelve thousand dollars," she told them. "Lydia is selling me the Market Street building at cost."

Everyone was happy with the development. It just proved good deals were still to be had in Denver, and things worked out fine in the end. The Ryans were once again coming up in the world, adding another property to their list.

And life in Denver rolled along, and Market Street still belted out a good time for those prone to adventure and vice.

And the sun would rise on another morning, hangover or not. Until the day came when it didn't, one way or another. Everyone would die when their number came up. It was all just a matter of how, when, and where.

Sometimes the kicker was in the why.

# ABOUT THE AUTHOR

**Randi Samuelson-Brown** is a Colorado native who lives in Denver with her husband and two evil (yet adorable) cats. Originally from Golden, she enjoys roaming around old mining towns and seeking out anything to do with history. Having spent a fair amount of time in Ireland both for university and holidays, coupled with a stint working in the UK for three years has resulted in many stories rattling around inside her head. She has a B.A. in history, with postgraduate research in Irish history at Trinity College, University of Dublin, Ireland.

She is a member of the Lighthouse Writers Studio in Denver, Women Writing the West, and the Historical Novel Society. Randi has also participated extensively in the UCLA Writers Program. *The Beaten Territory* is her first published novel. You can visit her online at www.randisamuelsonbrown.com.

The employees of Five Star Publishing hope you have enjoyed this book.

Our Five Star novels explore little-known chapters from America's history, stories told from unique perspectives that will entertain a broad range of readers.

Other Five Star books are available at your local library, bookstore, all major book distributors, and directly from Five Star/Gale.

Connect with Five Star Publishing

Visit us on Facebook:
    https://www.facebook.com/FiveStarCengage

Email:
    FiveStar@cengage.com

For information about titles and placing orders:
    (800) 223-1244
    gale.orders@cengage.com

To share your comments, write to us:
    Five Star Publishing
    Attn: Publisher
    10 Water St., Suite 310
    Waterville, ME 04901